RED

MEASHA STONE

Copyright © 2019 by Measha Stone
All rights reserved.

No part of this book may be reproduced in any form or by any electronic or mechanical means, including information storage and retrieval systems, without written permission from the author, except for the use of brief quotations in a book review.

This book is a work of fiction. Any resemblance to persons, living or dead, or places, actual events or locales is purely coincidental. The characters and names are products of the author's imagination and used factitiously.

The publisher and author acknowledge the trademark status and trademark ownership of all trademarks, service marks and word marks, mentioned in this book.

Editing and Proofreading by Wizards in Publishing
Cover Design by Simply Defined Art

CHAPTER 1

*C*affeine really was a girl's best friend. Whoever made up that lie about it being diamonds obviously hadn't been introduced to the right cup of coffee.

Melinda entered Into the Woods coffee house, taking a deep breath to enjoy the brewing beans. It had been a long day, and she needed the pick-me-up before heading home for dinner with her grandmother.

Melinda stepped to the end of the line and grabbed her phone from her jeans back pocket. Swiping the screen to life, she dove into her emails—having been too lost in her writing to check them earlier.

She deleted the garbage cluttering her inbox until her eyes landed on a possible life changer. An email that could either break her heart or make her day. Taking a deep breath, her insides shaking, she opened the email. This could be it.

Two sentences in, the shaking stopped, and the nagging twist of despair surfaced.

Her heart sank into her thick wool socks.

Another rejection.

She knew it was bound to happen. Over and over again,

she'd be rejected before a literary agent picked her up. And then it would be another few rounds of rejection before a publishing house picked up the book. A lot of agony to get to the big payoff at the end—a publishing deal.

It was what she'd worked her ass off for the last two years. With her MFA degree in one hand and her dreams in the other, she'd jumped out into the world. Each new rejection chipped away at the newfound confidence, but she'd get there.

She had to.

It was all she really had left.

"Excuse me, can you move up?" A woman behind her tapped her shoulder. Melinda looked up, noting the large gap in front of her. While her career had taken a step back, the rest of the line had taken a step forward.

"Oh. Sorry." Melinda hurried forward, tripped on her own boot, and stumbled smack into the next customer's broad back.

"Oomph! Sorry!" She retreated a small step.

He twisted halfway around, but it was enough for her to see his rugged features. Clear blue eyes peered down at her. Full lips curled into a joyless grin. She couldn't see his chin beneath his thick dirty-blond beard, but, judging from the muscular mass of the rest of him, she easily assumed it was tense.

"Are you okay?" he asked in a low tenor.

"Yes. Thanks. Sorry about that." She pulled the lapels of her coat together, needing to feel more guarded with him.

"Maybe you should put the phone away. It seems to be distracting you." His pointed gaze moved to her hand gripping the device.

Her cheeks heated at the obvious reprimand.

"Yeah. Maybe." Her lips tightened, but she kept smiling.

She had bumped into him, after all. But he didn't need to be such an ass about it.

"Well?" He raised his brows at her, like he was waiting for something.

"Oh. Uh." She blinked a few times, not really sure what was happening.

"Put it away," he said in that same deep voice. Quiet enough the rest of the coffee shop couldn't hear their exchange, but she heard it. The authority in his tone, the steely resolve in his eyes, all of it sent a familiar tingle through her body.

A tingle she didn't have time for, she reminded herself. No distractions. Just work. The thick air of authority hanging around him made it more difficult, but she would have to power through.

With a huff, she slid the phone back into her pocket. If it would get him to turn around, she'd put her phone away. He just needed to focus his attention elsewhere.

"What can I get for you, sir?" The young girl behind the counter rescued Melinda.

He stepped up and gave his order. A black coffee. Simple. It seemed to fit him.

She shook her head. Fit him. What the hell was she thinking? Deciding to tune out his presence, she focused her eyes on the menu. She already knew her order. Medium Caramel Latte. Same as always. Always knowing what was coming. That was safety.

After he paid, he moved to the left to wait for his drink. Melinda stepped up, doing her best to ignore his hulking presence.

The cafe was nestled in the heart of downtown, near the university. Most of the patrons were students or people who worked in the nearby shops. He didn't fit there. Though with his bulk and those rugged features, she wondered if he would fit anywhere that didn't involve tearing down trees.

He'd make a good lumberjack.

"That will be five fifty-three."

"What? Oh, right." Melinda snapped out of her head and handed over her credit card, sensing his glare still focused on her. After she got the card back and slid it in her wallet, she glanced up. His stare pinned her. She cast him another smile and moved around him to wait for her drink.

"Erik," the barista called from behind the counter, his arm outstretched with drink in hand.

The rude lumberjack stepped forward and took the small cup. Melinda's gaze flicked between the barista and Erik.

As he stepped away from the counter, she caught a glimpse of a silver medallion hanging around his neck. He didn't wear a tie, and the top three buttons of his shirt were undone, exposing the piece. A wolf. A cold shiver ran down her back. She'd seen the medallion before. His shirt shifted, covering it before she could get a closer look to jog her memory. Where had she seen it?

"Excuse me," he muttered, walking around her. He brushed up against her as he made his way through the small crowd.

He paused at the door, glancing at his watch. Such strong hands.

"Melinda." The barista drew her attention from him.

"Melinda, isn't that you, hon?" The woman from the line was beside her, nudging her again.

"What? Oh, yeah. Thanks." Melinda took the drink and checked the door again. He was gone.

She definitely needed to take a break from *all* men, not only the dark broody sort who made her heart leap into her throat. Just looking at him made her all weak in the knees, and that wouldn't get her very far in her new endeavor.

With college in the rear view, she had an uncharted road ahead of her, and she was going to make the most of it.

She zipped her coat clear up to her chin when she stepped back out into the blustering wind. Only the promise of one of Grams' home-cooked meals could have driven Melinda out in the cold night.

Nothing compared to Grams' home-cooking. The microwave mac 'n cheese dinners she'd been eating weren't exactly the comfort foods of her youth.

Melinda's coffee sat nestled in the cup holder of her sedan while she drove up the winding road to her grandparents' subdivision. She owned an old house in the middle of a cul-de-sac, but it had always felt like home.

The soft-yellow glow of Grams' porch light acted as a signal, calling Melinda home. She'd been living in her own apartment for the past two years, but it never felt truly like home. Nowhere felt as safe and warm as Grams' house.

Melinda parked in the driveway. She grabbed her coffee and purse and climbed out of the car.

Two identical black sedans with dark-tinted windows were parked in front, sending an eerie shiver over her neck. Obviously, she'd gotten deeper into the first draft of her horror novel than she'd thought.

An easy night with her grandmother would settle her comfortably into reality. Monsters weren't real.

Melinda slipped her key into the lock only to find it wasn't needed. She opened the door and stepped inside. Grams must have heard her pull in and unlocked the door for her. Although the neighborhood was safe, Grams had been living on her own since Melinda went off to college in the city. She didn't leave her doors unlocked at night.

"Grams?" she called when her grandmother wasn't in the front room. Melinda dropped her purse on the table in the foyer and headed to the kitchen. She couldn't smell

Grams' usual chicken pot pie baking; maybe she wanted to order in.

"Grams? I'm here." Melinda took a sip of her coffee, making a face at the chilled beverage. She left it behind with her purse and walked down the hall.

"In the family room." Grams' voice shook. She sounded forced, scared.

Melinda hurried to the rear of the house. The family room was right off the kitchen, overlooking the backyard.

Her grandmother was there. Sitting on the love seat, her knees pressed together, her hands folded neatly in her lap. But it wasn't her that had Melinda's heart climbing up her throat. It was the hulk of a man standing beside her, staring at Melinda.

"Grams?" Melinda's gaze roamed over him, until it settled on the silver wolf head hanging around his neck.

The man from the coffee shop.

"Melinda." Grams sniffed back a sob. "I'm so sorry. I didn't know. I swear I didn't know."

Melinda stepped down from the kitchen into the family room. Keeping her eyes focused on the wolf, she made her way to her grandmother.

"Grams, it's okay. Whatever it is, it's okay," she assured her, sinking beside her grandmother on the couch. Wrapping an arm around her shoulder, Melinda regarded Erik.

"What are you doing here?"

"Collecting what's mine," he said coolly, as if that told her anything.

"Are you hurt, Grams?" She pulled back to examine her grandmother.

With red, swollen eyes, her grandmother peered back at her. The woman who'd taken her in after her parents' death, the woman who'd kissed every skinned knee, hugged away every nightmare had regret weighing down her expression.

"No. He didn't hurt me. He's not—" Grams took in a long shaky breath. "Your grandfather…" She closed her eyes for a brief moment. "Your grandfather did something horrible. Terrible. Beyond forgiveness."

Her grandfather had had his issues, but Grams always forgave him, and they'd kept a happy home.

"What are you talking about?"

"When you were in high school, he had a problem with his card games. He loved playing them, but he was no good at them."

Melinda remembered easily beating her grandfather at poker whenever they played a friendly game. He didn't have a knack for knowing when to fold and when to hold.

"Yeah?" Melinda scooted closer to her grandmother on the couch.

"He almost lost the house one year. You don't remember because you were so young. But it was worse when you were in high school."

Melinda tried to keep up with her ramblings, but Erik's narrowed gaze made her uncomfortable.

"Grams, what did he do that you can't forgive? Why is"—she cast a quick glance at Erik—"he here?"

"Your grandfather gambled away everything he had and even more he didn't," Erik interjected with annoyance.

"Funny"—Melinda turned a hot glare on him—"you don't look like my grandmother. I'm talking to her, not you."

"No, don't fight with him." Her grandmother gripped Melinda's knee.

"Can you go away for a minute? You're scaring my grandmother, and I want to talk to her."

"No," Erik said with finality.

"No?"

"Melinda—" Her grandmother grabbed her arm when Melinda stood up from the couch.

"That's right, no." He set a firm stance, planting himself right there in her grandmother's family room. The room she'd played board games and video games with her grandparents. This man acted like he owned the room.

"Melinda, please." Grams stood up with her and yanked on her coat until Melinda was facing her again. "He's telling you the truth. Your grandfather lost everything, and he kept playing, kept going back, taking more loans, selling more things, until the only thing he had left to sell"—tears ran down Grams' cheeks—"was you."

Heat drained from Melinda's face. Her hands dropped to her sides, and she blinked. Her grandfather had died a year before her high school graduation. He'd never mentioned... never talked about his gambling. He'd promised he'd stopped.

"No." She shook her head. "You can't sell people!"

Grams gripped her coat harder. "He did, and I didn't know. Maybe he thought he could get the money before the man came to get you. But he never told me, Melinda. I swear, he never told me."

Melinda sank onto the couch. "Gramps has been gone for years," she whispered.

"The terms of the sale were to allow you to finish school. College wasn't discussed, but there was a delay due to some restructuring," he began.

"Shut up." Melinda rubbed her temples.

"Excuse me?"

"Melinda." Grams sat beside her. "Don't—"

"I said shut up. Stop talking. Give me a minute to process this insanity." Melinda didn't look at him. She recalled the way her insides melted during their encounter at Into the Woods; seeing his possessive glare now would send her into a full fit.

Into the Woods.

He'd stopped for coffee on the way to collect her.

Like some bag of coins?

"So, Gramps got in huge debt, and he sold me...to you?" She pointed at Erik.

"No. Not me, my uncle, but like I said, there's been some restructuring."

She closed her eyes and took a cleansing breath before reopening them to face the mess at hand. "Okay, so your uncle. And you're here now to collect me?"

"Yes." Erik's eyebrows rose a fraction. His impatience for her confusion showed.

"Okay." She leaned back and unzipped her coat. Stripping it off, she tossed it over the arm of the couch. "No."

"No?" Erik's brow wrinkled.

"No. You can't buy people."

The same joyless grin twisted up his lips. "There's a lot about the world you don't know."

Raw fear shone through Grams' tears. "I can't stop him."

"I'm not going."

Erik gestured, and two men stepped out of the shadows.

"If you don't come with us like a good girl, Nico and Ian will escort you to the car. Though, I'll warn you—and I rarely give warnings—if they have to escort you to the car, you won't be riding in the back seat."

She huffed a laugh. "What? Are you going to throw me into the trunk?"

Erik's lips twisted into a wide grin. "They won't throw you, but yes."

The empty humor fell from her voice. "Grams, there has to be something we can do."

"Yes, you can get up, put your coat on, and walk out with me now." Erik made a grand gesture of checking his watch. "I have more business to do this evening, and we have to get to the other side of town."

"Why, Grams, what a deep voice you have. I hope you aren't getting ill," Melinda snapped as panic and fear brought out her temper.

"The better to command naughty little girls with. Now, get your coat."

"I'm talking—"

"You're stalling."

The other two men shuffled their feet while keeping their glances between them in a sort of silent communication. Was her abduction boring them?

"You can't just buy people!" How could something like this be happening? How could her grandfather have done something so horrifying?

"You said that already." Erik turned his attention to Grams. "The house will be paid off, along with any other lingering debts you may have. It was part of the deal. Upon collecting, the rest of the money would be paid out."

"I don't want your money," Grams said, shoving up from the couch. "I want my granddaughter."

"Regrettable. She's the one thing you can't have. Say your goodbyes." Erik turned to his men. "Give them two minutes. If Melinda refuses to walk on her own, then do what you have to."

He breezed out of the family room and through the kitchen, boots tapping against the hardwood flooring along the hallway until he got to the front door. The creak of the hinges and the echo of the door slamming woke her from her stupor.

Melinda eyed the hired help. She wouldn't be able to fight them off, and Grams could get hurt in any attempt.

"Grams. I will figure out something, okay? Don't worry." Melinda snatched her coat and shoved her arms into the sleeves.

"Don't fight him. He's not the sort of man to take to your temper."

"I'll be fine. I'll get this straightened out, okay?" She zipped her coat. This could be the last time she saw her grandmother.

Melinda hugged her tightly, memorizing the moment—just in case.

"I'm so sorry, Melinda."

"No worries." Melinda pushed her lips into a wide grin. "It's going to be fine."

"Let's go." The darker-haired lackey gestured for her to get moving.

She wouldn't allow her grandmother to witness her being dragged off and stuffed into a trunk. No. She would walk on her own feet into the fire, and, with any luck, come running right back out.

Once she had a plan.

CHAPTER 2

The girl had told him no. And meant it. Erik smirked over the memory. She'd been a bit more than surprised to see him standing in her grandmother's family room, and shocked into brief silence when she grasped the full situation.

And then she'd told him no.

He couldn't remember the last time a woman, or anyone, denied him anything. He didn't make requests, and his demands were never optional.

But she didn't know that. Yet.

Melinda Manaforte had grown up in a quiet subdivision on the outskirts of the city. She hadn't been raised with the cruel reality of the world as he had, so, of course, she believed she had options.

"Okay, she's settled." Nico entered Erik's office with a loud exhale.

"She gave you that much trouble?" Erik shut down his laptop. He had all the information he could handle for one night. His research would resume in the morning.

"She gave me that much lip." Nico shook his head. "She

wouldn't stop asking questions, and when I wouldn't tell her anything, she threw a few choice insults my way. Next time, Ian can handle the girl when we get back from the collection."

"There won't be a next time." Erik let the statement fall. "She's the last one on the list." A grueling, stomach-churning list holding the names of three unsuspecting, innocent girls.

Nico stopped short of the wet bar in the corner of the room. "We're done? Good." Nico continued toward the bar, seeking his drink.

None of them enjoyed the task dealt to Erik, but they were too wise to complain. "Uncle Kristoff left a fucking mess."

His youngest brother poured himself two fingers of whiskey.

"He left more than a mess." Erik pointed at the glass. "You going to offer me one, or just drink all my liquor?"

Nico stopped mid sip and poured him one.

"Where's Ian?" Erik asked, noticing his younger brother hadn't made an appearance since their return from the Manaforte house.

"He went out. Said he'd be home by morning." Nico lounged in the dark-brown leather armchair near the bar. "I need one of these for my place." He patted the overstuffed arm.

"Yeah? When's that going to happen? You having your own place." Erik made his way to the bar and poured himself a second drink.

"Soon as we finish this last sale, and we get that casino built." Nico played with the ice cube in his glass. "We have the last girl. We can get this over with, right?"

Erik left his empty glass on the wet bar and shook off his suit jacket.

"There's still the little matter of the inheritance. We need that to get the ball rolling. I can't get the permits, the real estate, or any of the million things we need to get the casino started without the money Uncle Kristoff left you." Nico continued listing all the blocks still in the way of Erik's plans.

Erik cast a wary glance at his little brother. "'Yes, I'm aware."

"And you're aware you can't collect that money until you fulfill all of Uncle Kristoff's requirements," Nico pushed. Being younger rarely stopped him from trying to climb over Erik.

"I know what my duty is." Erik turned a hard stare on Nico. Brother or not, he would plant his fist between his teeth if he didn't stop badgering him. "I don't need you to explain it to me, little brother."

"So, let's unload this girl and then you can pick out your wife."

"Pick out my wife?" Erik laughed. "Is there a store I can shop at? Maybe she's simply sitting on a shelf waiting to be plucked up and given a good home?"

"You know what I mean." Nico grimaced.

Erik did know. Get a girl. Marry her, collect the money, and put the family back on track. Kristoff Komisky and his fucking son, Marcus, had derailed the entire family with their conniving stupidity. It was up to Erik to pull it all together again.

First, the girl.

The other two had been easy to deal with, but they had been aware of their futures. One of them had seen it as an opportunity to get out of an even worse situation. The other had come to terms and left with a long trail of financial debt —but she had her freedom. Her debt was now owed to a brick-and-mortar loan shark and not to the Rawling family. Melinda's grandfather had wiped away any hope of her being able to pay off his debt when he requested the house and any other debts he owed be paid off as well. He put a steep price on his granddaughter's head, making it impossible for her to find a way out of Komisky's clutches.

But Melinda had something different from those girls. She had a fire in her, and she wasn't going to take this situation lying down. Even now, she probably paced the bedroom she'd been locked away in, trying to figure a way out. Of the house. Of the transaction.

He almost looked forward to thwarting her attempts.

Almost.

He, like Nico, wanted the whole business over with. The sooner they had all the money, they could move to the next step and get out from under the shameful shadows their uncle had cast over them.

"Mr. Rawling?" A soft knock came on the door.

"Come in." Nico winked at Erik. He liked pissing his big brother off too much. It was probably time to knock him down a peg or two.

Marianne, a woman who played both housekeeper and motherly roles in the house, stepped into the office, wringing her hands.

"I'm sorry to disturb you, but I was putting away the towels upstairs, and I heard glass breaking in the bedroom adjoining the master suite." Marianne pointed behind her. "I knocked, but no one answered."

Erik was on his feet and out the door before Marianne could register his movements and get out of his way. He nearly barreled over the old woman to get to the stairs.

He'd known Melinda would be trouble.

She had the air about her.

But he'd figured she'd wait at least until sunrise before starting a fight.

"Do you need help?" Nico called.

"No," Erik yelled down the stairs. He would handle her.

She needed to understand her place and what was happening. And he would be happy to help.

He shoved the key into the lock and pushed the door open to the bedroom adjoining his. A cold breeze hit him from the window; drapery flapped in the wind. He stepped in farther, but she wasn't to be seen.

Broken glass crunched beneath his boots.

"Melinda," he called.

He peeked out the window, in case his gut was wrong. If she had jumped from that distance, she would have broken her neck.

Other than some shards of glass littering the grass, there was nothing below the window.

"Melinda. Come out. Now." He firmed up his voice. He wouldn't be running all over the room searching for her. She was either hiding in the closet or the bathroom, but she would come out to him.

The bathroom door opened, and she stepped out with a towel wrapped around her hand.

"What are you doing in here?" Melinda asked, as though he was the one out of place.

"You could have broken your neck." He pointed a finger at the glass covering the floor beneath his feet.

She tilted her head with a furrowed brow. "By slamming a window shut? Doubtful, but I'll be more careful."

"You slammed it shut?" Erik glanced back at the window. "Why was it open to begin with?"

"I wanted some fresh air." She kept her head down as she uttered her lie. "Did you really think I'd try to climb out that window?" she asked. After she'd peeked her head out, she would have noticed how high up she actually was. With nothing but the flat surface from the window to the ground, she didn't have a chance at climbing down.

He grasped her hand and unwound the towel to find a

small wound across her palm. Her slender hand was soft against his rough fingers. His thumb caressed along the edge of the wound. Blood trickled from the gash.

"How'd you cut yourself?"

"When I went to pick up the glass, there was a piece sticking up from the carpet I didn't see, so when I reached down, it cut me." She pulled her hand out of his grasp and snatched the towel. "I'll live. Don't worry." She wound the cloth around the wound again. Her snark did very little to appease his growing agitation.

"Why did you slam the window?" he demanded. She would have to admit to her childish behavior.

"Are you serious?" she deadpanned. "I was angry. But I didn't mean to break the window."

"Do you always act so childish when you're angry?" He moved the large shards into a pile with his foot.

"Do you always abduct innocent women from their homes?" She held her hand to her chest.

"It wasn't your home," he said. "You have an apartment in the city, near campus."

Her emerald eyes widened. "You really do your homework, I suppose." She unwound the towel and flexed her hand, wincing at the pain.

He pulled his phone out of his pocket and dialed Nico, who was no doubt working his way through more of his whiskey.

"Ask Marianne bring up the vacuum. And we need the glass replaced in the window." He kept her in his sights as she returned to the bathroom.

"She tried to jump out of that room?" Nico asked.

"No." Erik followed her to the bathroom and took another peek at her palm. "And call Dr. Abbante. She might need stitches."

Erik hung up before Nico's next question came through.

"I don't need stitches. I just need to clean it again." She yanked free from his grip.

He leaned a hip against the bathroom counter and folded his arms over his chest. For a woman who should be cowering in fear at her bleak future, she had an overabundance of fortitude.

"The doctor will be here soon. You will let him examine your palm. You won't fight him, or question him, or ask him to help you in any other way than checking your wound."

She turned off the water and peered at his reflection in the mirror. "What exactly are your plans for me?"

A typical question, though the other girls had asked with more quiver in their voice. But not Melinda. She shot straight for the truth. He could give her that.

"I don't know yet."

"You don't know?" she repeated. "Then why take me if you have no plan? Am I to be your—" She blushed, a dark red flame bursting across her cheeks. "Your whore?"

He grinned. "Do you have any experience in that area?"

She turned away. "Are you going to sell me to someone else, then?" There was a hint of hope in the question.

"Hmm…do you want me to sell you to someone else? Am I so frightening to you?"

Fire blazed in her eyes when she turned them on him.

"You can huff and puff all you want, but I'm not afraid of you. Whatever you do, I'll be fine." She thrust up her chin and rolled her shoulders back. She wasn't trying to convince him; she was giving herself a pep talk.

He picked up a lock of her red hair and rolled it between his fingers.

"I think you have the wrong story in your head, Red." He dropped her hair and ran his thumb over her jawline. So tight and tense, ready to fight him, and she didn't even know what she was fighting for.

"Red?" She jerked away from him. "How original. I've never been called that before."

Her insubordination teetered on the line of unacceptable. She was still unaccepting of her fate, still unsure of what was coming. It was only natural she be scared, a little fired-up, but he couldn't let it go on for too long.

"You can't stay in this room with the broken window, and you've shown me you can't behave on your own, so you'll have to be moved into my room."

The initial flash of fear in her eyes wrapped around him like a warm blanket.

"Mr. Rawling?" Dr. Abbante's voice carried from the bedroom.

"Remember what I said." He tapped her lips. "Don't try to involve him."

"Oh, there you are," Dr. Abbante said from the doorway.

"Yes. Here we are. Let's do this in my room. Then Melinda can go right to bed once you're done caring for her wound."

Erik cupped Melinda's elbow and led her from the bathroom.

A shiver ran through her body at his touch, making him grin.

This might be more fun than he'd thought.

CHAPTER 3

Melinda was going to vomit. Her stomach rolled with every step she took across the bedroom, through the adjoining door, and then into another bedroom. She didn't have time to look around, too busy trying to keep her stomach inside her body.

"Okay, let's have a look." Dr. Abbante, a short, older appearing man, pulled a chair out from a small writing desk and offered it to her. She sank onto it, lifting her hand for the doctor when he gestured for it.

He unwrapped the towel and dropped it on the desk. After pushing up his glasses, he held her palm closer to his face.

"Hmm, not very deep. Looks like you got lucky. I don't think stitches are needed, but you'll have to keep the area clean, which will be hard to do with where you cut yourself." Dr. Abbante let go of her and opened his medical kit.

Erik's phone rang, and he stepped away. Melinda watched him slide one hand into his pocket while the other held the phone, and he paced across the room while he talked.

"Does it hurt a lot?" the doctor asked.

"What?" She refocused on the doctor. He smeared an oily ointment across the cut. "No, it's better now."

"Good. I'll wrap a clean bandage around your hand, but you'll need to change it in the morning. Keep it wrapped for a day then you can leave it off, so long as the cut has started to heal."

"Dr. Abbante," she said in a hushed and hurried manner. "You have to help me. Please."

He blinked a few times at her; his graying bushy eyebrows rose. "I am helping." He held up the gauze and medical tape.

"No." She shook her head. "I mean, you have to get me out of here. Erik abducted me." She cast a quick glance to be sure Erik was still wrapped up in his conversation.

"You're saying he brought you here against your will?"

"Yes!" She urged and touched his arm. "Please, help me get out of here. Please."

He frowned in the way a father did when one of his children disappointed him. But she didn't get the feeling Erik was the disappointment.

"So, you clean the wound in the morning and rebandage it the way I'm going to show you."

"Wait. No." She pulled her hand back. "We need to go. I'll get this bandaged later." She cast another glance, but Erik wasn't where he had been.

"Couldn't help yourself, could you?" His deep voice came from behind her like an ax chopping her only lifeline.

She cast a pleading stare at Dr. Abbante, but he simply grinned at her and went about bandaging her wound.

"He already knew," she said to herself while the doctor tore off the excess tape.

"Of course, I did." Dr. Abbante patted her knee. "Now, take care of this the way I told you. I'll offer you more advice, too. I wouldn't rattle his cage too much." He winked. "But a little poke here and there will keep him on his toes."

"Thank you, Dr. Abbante. Nico will see to your payment downstairs." Erik gestured toward the door, escorting the doctor halfway.

"You were testing me." She raised her gaze to him as he stalked over to her.

"Yes. And you failed." He picked up her hand and inspected the bandage. "Does it hurt?"

"No." She lowered her eyes. She'd been stupid. Too hurried. She needed to get more information before acting so rashly.

"Good." He retreated a step. "Get ready for bed."

She peeked over at the king-sized, four-poster bed. Thick iron rings hung from the top and bottom of each post. What the hell were those for?

"I'm not— I can't sleep here."

"Why not? It's a damn comfortable bed." He put his hands on his hips, one finger slipped beneath a belt loop.

"This isn't my home. I don't want to be here." She should have fought harder. She should have run from Grams' house. Anything but walk to his damn car and let his goons drive her away.

Now, she was stuck in his house. In his room!

"Get ready for bed, Melinda. I'm not going to repeat myself. You've been shown all the generosity you're going to get from me."

That caught her attention.

"Generosity?"

"Yes. I'm not punishing you for your childish fit that resulted in a broken window. And I'm not going to punish you too hard for disobeying me just now with Dr. Abbante. I've been plenty generous, but I'm about done. Get ready for bed."

"What do you mean, punish me too hard?" She stood from the chair, pulling it around her and placing it between them.

"Did you think it would go unpunished?"

She blinked. Her stomach rolled again.

"How...I mean...what are you going to do?"

His gaze wandered over her face. "Take off your clothes, Melinda."

Her stomach dropped. "What?" Bravery was all fine and good until the brave one had to strip.

He let out a hard sigh. His patience was thinning; what would happen when it was gone?

"Remove your clothing, fold it, and put it on the dresser."

Her hands flittered at the hem of her shirt. His stare made the awkward moment stretch unbearably long. Undressing in front of a man wasn't an issue for her, but this man in particular made it painful. Hadn't he already taken enough from her for one day? If he was going for humiliation, he could choke on his dreams. Fear turned into anger as the moments ticked by with his irritated glare heating her up.

"If I have to repeat myself one more time..." His warning faded away as she gripped the cotton material and jerked it over her head.

She dropped the shirt to the floor and leveled a scowl on him while hooking her thumbs into her jeans. He seemed unmoved over her aggravation. His reaction remained blank, completely stoic.

Melinda snagged her shirt and jeans, neatly folding them and placing the short pile on the dresser as instructed. Then she put her fists on her hips and locked eyes with him. She would not cower. No matter how much everything inside of her shook.

"Bra and panties, too." He wiggled a businesslike finger at her.

Some of her bravado slipped. With less jerky movements, she undid the clasp of her bra and let the straps slide down her arms. The satin cups dropped from her breasts, exposing them to his eyes, his scrutiny. She tossed the item onto the dresser, rolled her panties down her legs, and stepped out one foot at a time. Balling up the panties, she dropped them on the pile.

"Good. Now, stand over there." He pointed a spot in the middle of the room.

Stinging retorts brewed in her muddled mind, but they were lost somewhere between her brain and her mouth. She took the few steps to the designated spot, wanting to wrap her arms around herself, to shield her vulnerability from his darkness.

He stepped toward her, stalking her as he moved around her naked form. Her jaw set, she slowed her breathing. If he wanted to degrade her, it would take more than an inspection of her physical flaws. And fuck him for trying.

"Hmm...it seems the best way to keep you from all your brattiness is to take away your clothes." If he was joking, she wasn't laughing.

He stopped in front of her, nudging her chin with a knuckle until she peered up at him. Those clear blue eyes of his peered straight through her.

"No comment?" He schooled his features, creating a mask.

"None for you, no," she said, doing her best to ignore the nagging sensation she was pushing too hard, too fast. It was her way. The more scared she got, the angrier she became. She'd given up on being ruled by fear after her parents died.

She'd been scared to get in a car for almost a year after their accident. More fearful of her grandparents driving anywhere. If something happened to them, after all, she would have no one left. But she'd given that up, stopped being afraid. And if fear started to creep up, she battled it.

The tendons in his neck scrunched up, matching the fierceness in his eyes.

"Do you have any idea what I can do to you, where I can put you, what sort of life I could give you if I wanted to?" His menacing tone shot a shiver through her. She didn't know the details, but she had a pretty good idea of a man like him was capable of.

"Let me go." She tried to jerk away, but he gripped her chin. To make matters worse, he grabbed hold of her hair, fisting it at the base of her neck. Now, she was trapped, and in his control. He could turn her this way and that, like his own personal marionette.

"I can sell you to the most ruthless men in the world. The things they would do to you would give you nightmares. Even on nights they don't touch you, you'll feel their skin on yours, their cocks shoving into your pussy, your ass, your mouth."

Tears burned her eyes and slipped down her cheek. She'd heard plenty of horror stories of women sold into sexual slavery. He didn't need to go into detail for her to get a bright image in her mind.

"I can keep you, lock you away, and give you to my brothers. You can be their own personal fuck toy. Or maybe I'll stick you on the corner, let you pay for your freedom by sucking off the gentlemen who pay for this pretty mouth of yours." He released her chin and ran his fingertips over her lips.

"Do you understand the situation now, Melinda?"

The urgency in his tone stunned her into deeper silence. As though he hated what he threatened, that merely saying it made him as sick to his stomach as she was.

He tightened his grip on her hair, shaking her a little.

"Answer when you're asked a question." Frustration broke out in his eyes.

"Yes!" She blinked, sending tears rolling down her cheeks. She'd been an idiot trying to get Dr. Abbante's help. Of course, only people within Erik's circle would be allowed access to her.

"Good." He released her.

She dragged in a heavy breath, rubbing the tears from her eyes. Lesson learned.

"Now, get into the bed and go to sleep. You will not leave this room until I allow it. Do you understand?" He bent over at the waist, leveling his gaze with hers like a parent who wanted to be sure their disobedient child was listening.

She nodded, not sure if she could trust her voice yet. Her insides shook with rage and cowered in fear at the same time. This man could break her.

Melinda climbed into the bed, pulling the quilt up to her chin. Finally, covered from his eyes, she settled into the pillows.

"Sleep," he commanded as though she were some robot, and he could flip her on off switch. The lights flicked off and the door slammed, signaling she was alone.

Blissful silence flooded the room. With his overpowering presence gone, she could find peace for the moment.

But what would come in the morning?

CHAPTER 4

"Where's the girl?" Ian jogged down the steps into the workout room where Erik had finished his run and was getting ready to go a few rounds with the heavy bag. After the night he'd had, he needed the outlet.

"She's in my room." Erik finished wrapping his hand.

"Abbante was here last night. What happened?" Ian demanded, stepping in front of the heavy bag.

Erik dropped his hands to his sides and glared down his younger brother. Ian's jaw set, he wasn't backing off.

"She broke a window and cut herself. That's what happened. Now move." Erik jerked his head.

Ian stepped aside but continued his interrogation. "Why isn't she in her own room? Why is she in yours?"

Erik connected with the bag. "Because she broke the fucking window in hers." He swung again, hooking it with his left hand.

"What did you do to her?"

Erik stepped away from the bag, ready to use his brother's face instead. "Nothing. I put her to bed." After making it clear who held the power.

Forcing her to strip had been meant to put her in her place, embarrass her. She'd been anything but humiliated. She covered her fear with anger, the emotion ruled her. He could see it in her eyes, the ship fighting the storm. But she would sink if she didn't start using her head.

She'd pushed and pushed him until he had to unleash all of the possible horrors that could be awaiting her. It had made his insides knot to spew such disgusting options, but he needed her to get under control.

"This is the last one, Erik." Ian demanded.

Erik set his jaw. "One, you don't fucking give me orders. Two, she *is* the last one. After her, we're done with the fucking list."

"You still have to—"

"I know what I have to do. I'll get to that once I have Melinda settled."

"I want to check on her." Ian squared off with him.

"No." Erik turned back to the punching bag. He hadn't given her any clothing yet, and no fucking way his brother or anyone else was putting their eyes on her.

"Why not?"

"When I'm done here, I'll bring her down. You can see for yourself she's unharmed." Erik hit the bag. "I should fucking flatten you for even suggesting it."

"What about her grandmother?"

Erik continued his routine despite his brother's interference. "What about her?"

"She thinks her granddaughter is going to be sold off into slavery or something."

"Ian." Erik grabbed the bag, stopping it from swinging. "Go away. If you say one more fucking word, I'm using you instead of this." He tapped the heavy bag.

Ian's eyes narrowed into aggravated slits. "I fucking hate this."

"I'm not enjoying myself, either, little brother, now go find something productive to do. Maybe start exploring some real estate options for once this is finished." Erik turned away from Ian and returned to his workout, ending the conversation.

He worked out his aggression. His annoyance at being questioned. His frustration of having slept next to a naked woman who clung to the edge of the bed like he was going to pounce on her any second.

The image of her stripping out of her clothes, standing with fire burning in her eyes, played on a loop in his mind as he continued his routine. She'd been all spit and fire, but when he'd stripped away her clothes, it was like he'd taken away a bit of her armor. Was she vulnerable because of her nudity, or because she'd been obeying him?

Covered in sweat, his frustrations mostly worked out, Erik unwrapped his hands and moved into the shower.

Melinda would be easier to deal with when he brought her up some clothes. She'd be in a softer mindset. Nico was still working on a few viable solutions, and, once they were ironed out, Erik would present them to her. Until then, he needed her to behave.

Showered and dressed, Erik left the workout room and headed up to his bedroom.

Stopping at his office, he grabbed the bag of clothes he'd ordered for her. Ian shook his head as he passed him in the hall, but at least he was smart enough to keep his lips zipped. Erik had had enough of him for one day. If they could avoid each other until this was finished that would make everything easier.

"Erik!" Nico stopped him at the foot of the staircase. "I got Melinda an interview at the Annex."

"When?"

"Tomorrow night. There's also a catalogue party. You've been invited. Melinda can attend with you," Nico explained. "But you know with them, she has to be completely free of any obligation to you. You can't force her. If Titon thinks for a second she's being sold against her will, he won't even consider it."

"I'm aware. The relationship with the Titons is thin already. She'll be on board. This will be her decision." Erik nodded. He'd lay out her options, and she'd pick. The only option not available was to walk away.

His fucking uncle was a prick, even from the grave. All debts due had to be accounted for before his estate would be turned over to Erik, his next of kin. The old man had taken his son down with him, leaving Erik, his oldest nephew, next in line.

"How are you going to get her to agree to this?" Nico asked.

"I'm going to lay it out for her. The annex is the safest place for her if she chooses that route. Otherwise..." Erik shook his head. They were out of options, really. He would not sell her to any of those men he'd threatened her with, but if she didn't cooperate at the Annex, he might not be able to find a good man for her. She'd be able to get the money up front from Ash Titon if she signed a long-term contract with him. It was her best bet. The safest option.

Selling women was not how he'd seen his future when he was growing up. He wanted to own a business. In particular, he wanted to build casinos, hotels, resorts. He wanted an entire fucking empire. Once he got his hands on his uncle's fortune, he could make all the dreams come true.

"Go find Ian and knock some sense into him. He's brooding again." Erik patted Nico's shoulder and made his way up to his bedroom.

Erik removed the key from his jeans pocket and slipped it into the doorknob. Turning it, he wondered if she'd still be in bed. When he'd gotten up before the sun rose, she was asleep. Still curled in the far corner of the bed, but she was peaceful.

He eased the door open and slipped inside, not wanting to disturb her if she still slept. She'd had a rough time so far. A little sleep could make all the difference.

As he shut the door, he noticed a flash of metal. Melinda lunged from his right, a knife aimed at him. He easily maneuvered out of her range and grabbed hold of her wrist, twisting it until she dropped the blade. Screaming in outrage.

"What the fuck do you think you're doing?" he demanded, dropping the bag of clothing and picking up the knife.

"Let me go! Let me go!" She yanked on her wrist, but he twisted her arm behind her, pinning her wrist to the small of her back.

He found the knife on the floor and picked it up. A steak knife. Another sweep of the room revealed a breakfast tray sitting on the nightstand. Untouched scrambled eggs and a thick piece of ham.

Apparently, the docile woman he'd put to bed the night before had awoken a mountain lion with her claws outstretched this morning.

"Did you think you'd kill me and then what...walk out of the house naked?" He shook her, eliciting another cry. She swung her free arm uselessly at him.

"It's better than just sitting here waiting for you to destroy me!" she shouted.

"We'll see if you think so in a minute."

CHAPTER 5

*H*er idiocy had no bounds, apparently! Every move she made with him turned out to be the wrong one. Each attempt to improve her situation failed on an epic level.

The knife clanked onto the dresser as he forced her toward the bed. He sat on the bed and, with a quick fluid motion, flipped her over his lap. Her stomach lurched at the impact, her mind swirled—trying to catch up to the movements.

Her body acted on autopilot, scrambling to get off his lap, to get away from him, but he anticipated her panic. His heavy leg shifted from beneath her to over both of her legs, trapping her to him.

"No!" She bucked, but it did no good. Her arm was still pinned behind her, her free hand useless in doing anything other than grabbing hold of the bedding.

His palm connected with her ass. The hard, stinging slap silenced her for a moment. Her struggle renewed, but still he held her firm.

The sound of his palm spanking her naked ass over and

over again echoed in the room, masked only by her cries for him to stop. The burning ensued; the sharp sting renewed with each blow of his hand. Each smack intensified the next, and there seemed to be no end.

A series of hard spanks concentrated on her thighs before he broke the cycle to speak. His words were controlled, much like his voice.

"If you ever raise so much as your voice to me again, you'll be worse off than you are right now." His hand cupped her ass cheek; the intimate sensation cut through the pulsing throb.

She clenched her eyes, not willing to see him, not willing to face what was happening to her. Spanked like a child throwing a fit.

"I had to do something," she whispered when he kept quiet.

"You were doing something. You were waiting for me to come get you." He didn't let her continue but, instead, fell into another round of spanks, covering every inch of her ass and her thighs.

She grabbed for a pillow and buried her face into it, hiding her sobs and her humiliation as best she could.

Five more hard smacks to her right cheek then he stopped again, trailing his fingertips down the crack of her ass. She clenched, sucking in a breath. How much humiliation could he dole out in such a short span of time?

"Do you want to say something to me?" he asked softly. She'd expected anger, rage at her show of aggression, but she received only more control, more authority in response.

"I hate you," she whispered.

He chuckled.

Her face heated. The lump in her throat kept her from saying anything more. Her attempt to hurt him had been thwarted with a flick of his hand, and when she spewed hatred, he laughed it off. More proof of his strength compared to her weakness.

She'd never seen herself as weak.

Not until she'd met him.

His fingers sank between her ass cheeks, touching her clenched asshole for a brief moment before sliding lower. She squeezed her eyes shut and bit down on the pillow.

He loosened his grip on her legs and shoved her right leg away, opening her body to him. His fingers continued their exploration, and he hummed when he brushed her sex.

Her wet, wanting sex.

"You may hate me, but your body doesn't." He glided his finger through her folds, gathering her own betrayal and rubbing it onto her thighs. "I bet, if I play with this little clit of yours, you'll come for me."

"No!" She shook her head. Not like this. She wouldn't let him take her self-control like this.

The pad of one finger pressed down on her clit, and she clenched her teeth. They would break before she let out a satisfied moan.

He began to rub the sensitive bundle of nerves in a circle. Round and around, with more pressure, then less, then more. She tugged on her hand, but he held her arm firm against her back.

"You're close," he said softly. His fingers continued to dance, to work an orgasm from her body. No matter how much she tried to shut out what he was doing, her body continued to be played. He knew this song well and kept strumming to his own beat.

An orgasm loomed. She bit down on the pillow again, hoping for her body to explode and dreading the outcome at the same time.

"Such a sweet little pussy. I can see your thighs tightening; your cheeks are clenched. You want to come. You want to burst all over my finger, don't you?"

"No!" She shook her head, but fuck she wanted to, needed to.

"If I do this…" His thumb slipped into her pussy, giving her enough sensation, her body began to shake, the dam was going to explode. Just one more little touch, a little flick, and she'd be flying.

"But bad girls don't get to come." He yanked his hand away from her sex, and, in the next second, he peppered her thighs and ass with another onslaught of spanks.

She screamed out, for the loss of the orgasm, for the pain he ignited, for the humiliation of being played so easily.

Finally giving over, she stopped fighting, stopped struggling. The spanks slowed to a stop.

"So red." He brushed his fingers across her ass. She imagined how horrible she must have appeared. She'd be bruised for days.

In a graceful motion she hadn't been prepared for, he swung her up to straddle his lap, her legs wrapped around his hips, her ass pressed uncomfortably against his legs. She didn't miss the erection in his pants, or the aroma of her own arousal.

He wiped the tears from her cheeks. "You cry beautifully, Melinda," he said so quietly she wasn't sure she'd heard him right. "Do you know what happens if you actually get away? Not fulfill the deal my uncle made with your grandfather?"

She shook her head, words beyond her. Her ass throbbed, and his gentleness muddled things even more.

"Your grandmother's house becomes mine. Her car, her bank accounts. Everything gets taken to fulfill the debt. It won't cover everything, though, so she'll have to cash in her life insurance, her retirement funds, everything. And it still won't be enough. Everything you have will be stripped away, too. You both will be destitute."

She blinked a few times, letting everything sink in.

"I can take care of her," she whispered, finding a bit of strength.

"You won't have anything to take care of her with. You'll be homeless and penniless. Completely ruined."

"You can't just take everything. A judge would never allow it," she said, knowing even an attorney was outside her financial abilities.

His eyes narrowed a fraction, creating a gentle wrinkle around his eyes. "Do you think any of this would even present in court?"

She felt foolish. Of course, there was no real legal course for her to take. None of this was legal.

"What happens to me if I stay?" Tired from lack of sleep and the tension of being touched and spanked and wrung out like a wet rag, she didn't fight what he said. She would never let her grandmother lose everything. Not if she could help it.

He stared at her a moment. "There are options. I'll go over them with you later."

She turned her head. "And forgetting about the debt, about what my grandfather did, isn't one of them."

"No, it's not," he said, voice heavy with finality.

Taking her face in one large, calloused hand, still warm from the spanking he'd dished out, he forced her to look at him. "Your obedience is not optional, either, Melinda. You will give it to me."

His eyes searched hers, but she wasn't sure what he was searching for. More fight? More fear? Her world was collapsing in front of her, and he spoke of obedience. She met his gaze, a bubble of anger rolling around her insides.

"Or you'll simply take it." She stated the plain truth. He'd taken her clothes, spanked her ass until it pulsed with pain... What would be gained by hiding the obvious?

He tilted his head, studying her in silence. "You're a smart girl, Melinda. Don't let your pride get in the way of finding the right solution here."

He let go of her chin and pushed her off his lap. She staggered to her feet. "I have clothes for you." He retrieved the bag he'd dropped during her pathetic assassination attempt and tossed it on the bed.

He pulled out shirts, skirts, pants, and a few sweaters.

"There's no underwear here," she pointed out.

He grinned. "That's right."

"I can't wear jeans without underwear." She curtailed some of the snark, but she could still hear her annoyance.

"Then wear the skirt." He shrugged. "Makes no difference to me."

A knock on the door made her stiffen. Erik's narrowed gaze traveled to the door. He frowned.

With a flick of his wrist, he dismissed her. "Go stand in that corner."

Whoever was at the door would get a clear view of her naked punished backside.

"Melinda." His voice held enough warning to push her into action. Not wanting to push him into another spanking, she obeyed, grabbing a T-shirt from the bed on her way. The garment wasn't long enough; the bottom of her ass still peeked out, but it was better than being on full display.

The door opened. A deep voice, intense and annoyed, started talking, but she couldn't make out what they were saying. Erik responded in curt sentences, and, a moment later, the door slammed behind the intruder.

His heavy steps carried through the room to the bathroom. The faucet turned on then off. A towel jerked from the towel rack.

"Come here." His order was brash. She met him in the center of the room. "I have business to take care of. I will leave the door unlocked. My brother, Nico, is downstairs. If you give him any trouble, so much as a curse word, he will punish you—and then it will be doubled when I get back. Am I clear?"

"I can leave the room?" Was he testing her again?

"You didn't touch your breakfast. Take the tray downstairs to the kitchen. They'll make you something warm."

"I'm not really hungry," she said. "But I would like to go for a walk."

He stared at her for a long moment then shook his head. "Sorry, no walk. Eat something." He pressed a kiss to her forehead and headed for the door, pausing after the second step before pushing forward and leaving her alone again.

She touched her forehead, the spot where his lips had met her skin.

What the hell was that?

CHAPTER 6

He'd kissed her.
Fuck.

It had only been a peck, a quick brush of his lips across her forehead, but it had happened so naturally, so easily. He hadn't thought about it, merely acted. And he didn't do that.

As he made his way downstairs, his cock pressed against the zipper of his jeans, reminding him of the spanking. How beautifully her ass bounced beneath his hand. How sweet her cries were, and how gorgeous she appeared with her puffy eyes and tearstained cheeks. He'd meant to punish, to teach her her place, but ended up waking something in himself he'd promised would lie dormant through this ordeal.

Nico met him at the bottom of the stairs.

"He's in the office, helping himself to your brandy." Nico pointed to the closed door.

"Did he say what he wanted?"

Mr. Bertucci, a previous associate of their uncle's, didn't visit for personal reasons. There was no relationship between the Rawling and Bertucci families. And Erik would keep it that way. The business practices of his uncle and some of the old families turned his stomach. He would not lead his brothers into that world.

"Of course not." Nico eyeballed the stairwell. "Everything okay up there?"

Erik ran his fingers through his hair and nodded. "She's fine, getting dressed. She can go anywhere in the house, but she may not go outside." Erik pointed a finger at him. "I'm not fucking around, Nico. Don't let her go out."

"Got it. I'll babysit her while you're in your meeting." Nico grinned.

Erik stepped closer. "You don't touch her, understand? If she needs something, you get it for her, but that's it. And make sure she stays inside and away from my office. I don't want Bertucci getting any ideas."

Nico dropped his smile, finally getting the picture about Melinda. "You'd better go."

Erik glanced up the stairs. He didn't like this. Having Bertucci in the house while she was roaming free was a risk.

"I'll watch for her," Nico promised.

There were few people in the world in whom Erik would place all of his trust. His brothers were high on the short list.

Erik gave a curt nod and went into his office.

Bertucci stood at the front window, staring out into the street. After their uncle passed away some of the inheritance was released to Erik, mostly because it put him in a better position to carry through with the rest of the requirements. Living in the house had been allowed while he was actively working on collecting the unpaid debts. If he refused, or was unsuccessful, he and his brothers would be turned out.

"Mr. Bertucci." Erik extended his hand.

The crotchety old man turned from the window. He glanced at Erik's hand and frowned. "Erik Rawling." His name was given in two short bursts of air, like he dropped them into the room. Bertucci shook Erik's hand. "I'm used to your uncle coming through that door when I visit. I was sorry to hear of his passing."

Erik tensed. Although nothing was ever confirmed and would never be fully investigated, Erik knew well enough Bertucci's hand in his uncle and cousin's death. Loyalty to family kept him from outright condoning the actions of the members of the old families, but they'd done the right thing. His uncle had been a canker sore on society.

He'd betrayed an oath given to the other families. And in their circles, the sin of a broken word often came with fatal consequences. From what Erik could gather, his uncle had not only gone against the heads of the other families, he'd outright attacked a protected man.

"Thank you." Erik gestured to the chair on the other side of his desk and took his seat. As a child, he'd played in this office with his cousin when his mother would permit a visit. Now, he sat in the chair he'd once climbed as though it were a mountain, staring down one of the most powerful men in town.

"What can I do for you?" Erik rested his fingertips on the edge of the desk.

"Well, I heard a rumor, and I've come to see if there's any truth to it."

Straight to it, then, good. Beating around the bush only resulted in fatigue. And after dealing with Melinda, he could bet the rest of his inheritance he'd need every ounce of strength to combat her.

Erik tilted his head. "What rumor?"

Bertucci sucked in his cheeks as though he were chewing on them, making a smacking sound when he finally began to speak. "I heard you were rounding up the girls your uncle was supposed to be collecting as payments."

"My uncle left very specific requirements in his will that force me to collect some debts before his estate is fully turned over to my family." Erik tapped his middle finger on the desk.

"That's what I heard." Bertucci cleared his throat and gripped the rounded edges of his chair. "I also heard Melinda Manaforte was one of those debts."

Erik's ears twitched. Her name on Bertucci's lips was a sacrilege.

"How does this concern you?" Erik moved to the offense. Melinda came from an average family in a normal suburb. She had no ties to anything more than a gambling-addicted grandfather.

"I'll make this easy. I want her. I'll pay off whatever the debt is outright and 10 percent for your trouble." Bertucci's knuckles whitened.

Erik stared at him for a long moment, processing the offer.

"Why?"

"Why what?" Bertucci asked with forced casualness, like a man wanting to hide his excitement over the prize coming his way.

"Why would you want to buy Melinda? Have you met her?" Erik moved his fingers from the desk to his knee.

"I don't see how that matters," Bertucci said.

"What will you be doing with her if I agree?"

Hints of pink blossomed on Bertucci's cheeks.

"Do you want specific details, or will general descriptions be enough for you?" Bertucci put a hand in the air. "My intentions aren't any more sinister than yours. I know you have a distaste for your uncle's business practices. Hell, most of us did. I can help you with this. I'll take her off your hands."

"And make a larger profit on her resale." Erik took a deep breath. Did Bertucci understand they were talking about a person, or were these women simply product to him? Try as his uncle had, he'd never succeeded in training Erik to see women as less than human. To Kristoff, they'd been product, playthings—fun to screw around with until they were broken and then tossed aside.

Bertucci's lips spread into a wide grin. "Exactly."

"It's a generous offer, and I do want to get all of this over with as quickly as I can." Erik stood from his desk. "But I can't accept just yet. I've had other offers, and I need to weigh them all."

Bertucci's grin faltered. "How much are the other offers?

"The amount isn't the only issue."

Bertucci's cheeks wobbled. "Okay, then." He stood. "I'll go 25 percent over the debt amount and offer you a 5 percent return on the selling price once it's done. A finder's fee of sorts."

Erik slid his hands into his pockets and shrugged.

"An even better deal, but again, I need to weigh all the offers and options."

Bertucci's ears wiggled, his composure lessening. He wanted Melinda badly enough to pour money out of his checking account to have her.

"When?" Bertucci asked in a hard tone, the time for pleasantries apparently past.

"Day after tomorrow," Erik stated.

"Fine, then. I can wait that long. Not like she's going anywhere." Bertucci forced a laugh. "I'll expect to hear from you no matter your answer."

"Of course."

"You know, I remember you as a little kid, running around here with Marcus." Bertucci buttoned his coat. "I remember your mother, too. Sweet woman. I understand why she kept you and your brothers away from Kristoff and Marcus. They weren't honorable men."

"That was a long time ago." Erik opened the door.

"Yes." He paused. "It was. Your uncle has the last laugh here, though, doesn't he? Making you do the work his sister was so repulsed by."

"I'm sure he had his reasons." Kristoff Komisky was a disgusting parasite who preyed on the fear of women—his sister was no exception.

"Yes. I'm sure." Bertucci grabbed his hat from the desk and walked to the door. "Make this easy on yourself. Get it done fast and with the most profit for you and your brothers. Take my offer."

"I'll consider it." It would have to be enough for the moment. Erik wasn't going to simply hand Melinda over to him. Not without fully understanding why he wanted her. Erik had dealt with two women before her, and Bertucci hadn't darkened his doorstep until she arrived.

"I look forward to hearing from you then." Bertucci nodded his goodbye and made his way out.

After the front door closed, Nico appeared, always eager to be the first to know something. "So?"

"Where is she?" Eric asked, nerves rattling.

"The girl? She's in the kitchen eating." Nico's brow furrowed. "What did he want?"

"To make a deal." He started toward the kitchen.

"He wants her? That's good, right? Makes it easier."

"No." Erik turned on his brother. "This makes it more complicated. Melinda is the third girl we've dealt with, but this is the first time Bertucci has shown any interest. Why do you think that is?"

Nico blew out his lips. "Yeah, that doesn't sound right."

"He knew her name. Not only that we had a girl, but exactly which girl. He wants her specifically."

"But why? What's so special about Melinda?" Nico asked. "I mean, aside from the obvious."

Erik's lips pressed together while heat rose through his

body. Knocking out his brother for alluding to Melinda's attractiveness would derail him from his task, the only reason he didn't pull back his fist and let it fly into Nico's nose.

"That's what we need to find out. I'm going to talk to Melinda. You are going over to her grandmother's house. See if you can find out anything from her. Promise her a visit with Melinda if she hesitates."

"Don't bother." Ian walked up to them, sporting his usual annoyed expression. "Her grandmother's gone."

"What do you mean gone?" Erik demanded.

"Gone. As in, not there anymore, packed up and left town. She's gone." Ian's jaw set firm.

"My grandmother's missing?" Melinda asked, appearing in the hallway.

Erik took a deep breath. He knew nothing and couldn't offer any information.

"Melinda, go back up to our room. I'll be there in a few minutes—"

"You said she was safe. If I stayed, she'd be safe. Where is she?" Melinda took a demanding step toward them.

"I will find out. Go upstairs." He squared off with her, blocking his brothers' interference. When she hesitated, he patted the buckle on his belt, drawing her attention to it. Her cheeks flushed. "Go upstairs."

Her throat convulsed as she swallowed. She wanted to fight him, to yell at him, but when he fingered the end of his belt, she pinched her lips together and shoved her way through them. Ian and Nico were saved by stepping out of her way, but she made a concentrated effort to shove her shoulder into Erik's arm as she passed.

He'd let her have her moment of victory, but she would pay.

After she answered some questions.

"At least she has some grit. I suppose she'll need that when you sell her off." Ian's accusatory tone hit his last nerve like a sledgehammer.

"Exactly how do you know her grandmother is gone?" Erik demanded.

"I went to talk to her," Ian said, rolling his shoulders and setting his jaw.

"Why?"

"Because I wanted her to know Melinda was okay. She deserved that much from us." Ian raised his chin.

"I know you don't like what we have to do, but that doesn't change anything." Erik narrowed his gaze. "You need to decide which side you're on."

"I didn't realize there were sides here, other than yours."

"You don't like the decisions I make for this family?" Erik challenged.

Nico pressed himself farther into the background.

Ian ground his teeth together, an old habit from an anxious childhood. "Melinda isn't guilty of anything, but she's been given a life fucking sentence. I don't like that decision. No."

"That wasn't my call."

"We can walk away from this. At least we could have. But two girls have already been sent away, haven't they? We don't need Kristoff's money. We have Dad's."

"It's not enough to get the land and the building contracts. You know that."

"So? We invest what we have, or we find another way. Are those girls' lives really less important than your fucking dream of being a big casino boss?"

"Ian," Nico warned from behind him.

"I'm not fighting with you about this. If you want out, there's the fucking door. I won't stop you." Erik's breath came fast. He'd never shown his brother the door; it wasn't something he thought he could do.

But since his uncle's death, he'd been doing a lot of things he'd never thought he'd be able to stomach.

"Ian. We should find her grandmother. We'll figure out what happened and then move on from there." Nico placed a hand on Ian's shoulder, pulling him away from Erik.

Ian's nostrils flared. "Yeah. I'll take care of that." With a shove at his younger brother, Ian stalked off down the hall.

"I'll talk to him." Nico turned to go, but Erik stopped him.

"Leave him be. Just get to the bottom of her grandmother's disappearance."

CHAPTER 7

Melinda paced the bedroom, nibbling on her fingernails. Her grandmother had lived in the same house for fifty years. She wouldn't simply abandon it now.

Not when she could still be so close to Melinda.

The door opened, and Erik stepped inside, the tension palpable the moment he closed the door.

"What did you find out?" she asked, hurrying to him.

"Nothing yet. Ian and Nico are looking into it," Erik said with a bland expression. Maybe he couldn't grasp the situation. Or he didn't care. Why would he? After all, her grandmother served no purpose for him.

"Looking into it?" Melinda stopped short, and her shoulders dropped. "Right."

"My brothers will find out what happened, and if she's in any sort of trouble they will help her." Erik's tone hardened. Had she offended him by not throwing herself at his feet in gratitude?

"She wouldn't up and leave."

Erik shrugged. "Maybe she thought since you were…well,

here, she could go."

"Go? Where? On a cruise? A vacation?" She shook her head. "No. Grams wouldn't do that."

"Did you ever think she'd stand by and watch you be escorted off as payment for her husband's gambling debts?" Erik's question was cold, callous. And valid.

Melinda pressed her heels into the floor. Flying at him wouldn't find her grandmother. It would give him reason to hurt her again.

"She didn't just stand by—"

Erik's eyebrows rose. "When you arrived at *Grams'* house, my brothers and I were already there." His sarcastic use of the moniker sent her stomach into an angry boil.

"So?"

"You don't live with her anymore, Melinda. She invited you to dinner that night. Told you what time to be there." Erik moved toward her, slipping pieces into the puzzle she didn't want to see yet.

"I saw you at the coffee shop," she said.

"Right. I had to hurry, but I did beat you to your grandmother's house."

She closed her eyes and pulled in a calming breath. "She was expecting you." She opened her eyes to find him watching her intently.

"Yes. She was." Erik let the statement drop between them.

Her grandmother had known. She'd invited her over in order for Erik to collect her. Grams had served her up on a silver platter.

"Dinner wasn't cooking." Melinda retreated to the bed and sank down onto the mattress.

"What?"

"When I got there, when I walked in, I noticed. Usually, the house smells like dinner. But she hadn't even started cooking yet." She looked up at him, tears threatening. "There's no way out of this, is there?"

"No, Melinda. There isn't. But I have questions for you."

She blinked and flicked the tears from her cheek. "Why would Grams send me to college? Why let me finish school if I was to be sold off? She could have used the money maybe to offset what Gramps owed."

Erik's brow wrinkled in confused for a brief moment. "She wasn't lying to you. She didn't know about what your grandfather had done until I showed her the letters he'd signed. That was only the day before."

"She could have told me, warned me. I could have left." Melinda's mind spun.

"If you had, we would have found you," Erik said.

Of course, they would have. She was to make him a lot of money when he sold her into hell.

"So, it's possible your grandmother simply left town," he continued when Melinda remained silent.

If Grams had served her up so easily to these men, it wasn't a far stretch to imagine her running away afterward. Melinda rubbed the heels of her hands against her eyes. The burst of pain ricocheting in her chest stole her breath away. She truly had no way out of the situation.

Shoving the impending meltdown to the side, she took a long cleansing breath and peered up at him. "Can you go, now? I just want to be by myself for a little while." She gestured to the door.

"I have to ask you some questions."

She clenched her teeth. "What questions? You seem to know more about my grandparents than I ever did."

"What about your parents?"

"My mom and dad? They died when I was in middle school. A car crash on the bridge. I've lived with my grandparents since then. Gramps died last year of lung cancer, but I'm sure you knew that already."

"What did your parents do for a living?"

Melinda sighed. "What does that have to do with anything?"

"Melinda, I know this is hard for you, but—"

"Hard for me?" She bounded off the bed. The last straw snapped into a thousand pieces. "Hard? No. Losing my parents was heartbreaking." She choked on a sob. "Watching my grandfather slowly decline into a bag of bones before he died was horrifying. Learning he sold me like a piece of furniture and my Grams did nothing to protect me…" She sucked in a breath, willing herself not to cry, not to let another tear drop. "Hard doesn't describe it."

Erik took a step toward her; his hand extended as though he would cradle her in his arms if he got close enough.

"Dammit, just leave me alone!" She hurried into the bathroom and slammed the door, flicking the lock on the handle in case he got any ideas of joining her.

Melinda sat on the edge of the tub and pinned her hands between her knees. Her grandmother had abandoned her. Her grandfather had sold her. The truth played in a continuous loop.

How had she grown up not really knowing them, not knowing how easily they could discard her?

A click sounded, and the door opened. Of course, he had a key.

"Don't lock doors against me." His heavy voice filled the space between them. Leaving the door open, he walked away. She heard the bedroom door open and shut from where she sat on the cold porcelain tub.

A tear rolled down her cheek and dropped silently to the floor.

CHAPTER 8

*E*rik pinched the bridge of his nose and rolled his chair away from the desk. His eyes burned, and his back ached. He stood up and stretched.

"Get anywhere?" Nico entered the office, carrying a bowl. A spoon stuck out of a perfectly rolled scoop of vanilla ice cream.

"You hate ice cream." Erik eyed the sweet dessert.

"It's for Melinda." Nico shrugged. "She didn't come down for dinner."

The tray he'd had sent up came down untouched. Could she be trying to starve herself?

Erik scratched his chin beneath his beard. "I'll take it to her. I'm going to head up there anyway." He held his hand out.

"What makes this one different?" Nico asked, handing the bowl over.

"How do you mean?"

"I mean she's the third girl we've had to do this with, but she's the first who stays in your room. The first to have even seen your room."

RED

Erik laughed. "I think you're making too much out of nothing." He slapped Nico on the shoulder. "I'm going up. I'll see you in the morning."

He'd given Melinda enough time to sort through what he'd told her. He needed more answers about her parents. His gut told him there was a connection between her family and the Bertucci family. Small as it might be, there had to be something.

Melinda sat on the bed with her legs crossed, her laptop perched in her lap. She looked up from her screen and frowned.

"I brought you something." He put the chilled bowl of ice-cream on the nightstand beside her and peeked at her screen. "What are you doing?"

"Writing. Your brother brought up my things from my car." She closed the laptop and held it to her chest. After Ian came home with her car, Erik had given permission for her laptop to be brought to her. All Internet connections were on lockdown. She could work on her writing, but that would be it.

"You didn't come down for dinner." He put space between them.

"I wasn't hungry."

"Yes, you were," he countered. "You just didn't want to see me."

Her gaze met his for a brief moment before flicking to the ice cream. "I don't really want to see you now, either."

He smiled. "Not much of a choice, though, seeing as you're in my bedroom."

"I could go back to the other room." She exchanged her laptop for the bowl of ice cream and scooped up a bite. "I heard people working on the window. I'm sure it's been replaced."

He watched the soft vanilla ice cream disappear into her

mouth. Her full lips pulled the sweet concoction from the spoon, and her tongue lightly touched her lip.

"I want you in here," he said.

"Why?" she asked before shoveling in another spoonful.

"Because I do." Why did everyone feel so damn determined to figure out the reasons behind every one of his fucking orders?

She put the bowl down and slid from the bed. "That's not much of an answer. Did you think you'd get to sample the goods before selling me off?" Her hands rested on her hips as she confronted him.

Her long red curls were all bundled up in a messy bun, showcasing her long neck. Creamy skin he could sink his teeth into, suck and lick—much like the ice cream melting on the nightstand.

"You're tired. If you don't want the ice cream, go to bed."

"No." She dropped her hands and straightened out her body, a human steel beam.

His gaze narrowed; heat built on the back of his neck. "What did you say?"

"I said no." She took a deep breath, rounded her shoulders, and pushed on a fierce scowl. He wasn't entirely sure which of them she was trying to convince with her show of false bravado.

"You said no." Anyone who knew him would recognize it was time to back off. But she didn't have the same history with him—yet.

"That's right. No. I haven't had a fucking say in any of this, but I can decide when and if I go to fucking bed!" Her arms pumped at her sides throughout her little tirade. If the situation had been different, he would have found it adorable. Even the freckles on her nose seemed to dance with her irritation.

"You are getting a choice in this—"

"Choice? You told me you have to sell me to honor my grandfather's debt. You said that. So, my choices are what? Who gets to buy me? Who I get to be a slave to for the rest of my life?" Her cheeks reddened. "You are a monster. A disgusting monster."

Erik's heart clenched. "You think so?" He took a menacing step toward her.

Her eyes darted to the door, but she'd never make it. "You— I—"

"What's wrong, Melinda? Run out of bravery?" he mocked her. She'd had all afternoon to gather up her anger and spew it at him when he walked in, but she would learn to keep her venom fanged from now on.

"Why can't you leave me alone?" she asked in a more placating tone. But it was too late. The claws had been unsheathed.

"Oh, I will," he promised. She tried to dart around him, but he caught her.

In a fluid motion, he spun and hoisted her over his shoulder.

"No! What are you doing?" Her fists banged against his shoulder blades, but he wouldn't be stopped. She wanted to see what a monster truly was, and he was going to give her the lesson she needed.

The door bounced off the wall when he flung it open. Marching down the hall and down the stairs, taking little care to be sure she wasn't bouncing too hard, he headed for the stairs leading down to the basement.

Nico popped up from the couch in the living room when Erik passed by with Melinda screaming and kicking over his shoulder.

"Stay the fuck there," Erik barked at him as he rounded the corner and went for the room he needed.

"What are you doing! Put me down!" She pounded

harder, and her legs kicked. He readjusted his grip around her knees and smacked her ass hard enough to knock some sense into her.

"Stop wiggling like that!" He smacked her once more then threw open the door to the basement.

"I don't want to go down there!" she cried when his boots clattered down the wooden staircase.

"Sure you do. You want to see the monster." He flicked on the lights.

His uncle had a special basement. At first glance, it appeared to be an ordinary man-cave with a large screen television set. A dartboard hung on the wall. A minibar and fridge nestled in the corner. Really cozy.

Erik put her on her feet but held onto her upper arm. Most of her hair had tumbled out of the elastic band and rained down around her shoulders. Her face was red from dangling upside down, but her eyes held his interest. Wide and curious.

She had no idea what a real monster was. But he'd show her.

He pulled her forward, past the leather couch to the wall beside the television. Pressing against the paneling, he popped open the secret door. To the casual observer it would be missed. The crease of the edge fit nicely into the pattern of the panels.

"What— Erik, wait—" She dug her heels in, her voice remorseful and soft.

"Too late." He yanked her forward and pulled the door shut. She wouldn't get out now. She didn't know where the lock was or how to disarm it.

Melinda turned away from him, shoulders moving up and down in a drunk cadence as she tried to find her breath. The room took up the rest of the square footage of the basement.

Four times the size of the little man cave they'd walked through.

"What is this?" she asked, curling her arms around her stomach. If she was trying to ward off the chill, it wouldn't work. The temperature here never climbed over fifty-five degrees, and the cement flooring and walls didn't do much to keep the space heated.

He watched her take in the cages, the whipping post, the numerous implements hanging from the walls. Memories of the screams of the women his uncle had kept here still haunted him. Uncle Kristoff often brought the boys down to watch a movie in the man cave while he went into his twisted playroom. Erik had only once tried to intervene, tried to get in to save the girls. A hard backhand across his face for his effort and the threat of more to come to him and his brothers if he ever set foot in Uncle Kristoff's playroom kept him compliant.

He hadn't been big enough or old enough to do something about the horrors then, but he wasn't a little boy anymore. Erik released Melinda's arm and set his jaw. He was not his fucking uncle.

"Erik." Her soft voice, full of fear, of uncertainty, blanketed him. He lifted his gaze and caught sight of her apprehension.

"This is where my uncle kept his girls." He walked past her to one of the three cages. "Not all of them; he couldn't house them all here. Most were kept in worse places. This is where he kept his favorites. The ones he wanted to play with before he sold them." He wrapped his hand around the thick, black bars. The cage was not big enough for a person to lie down in, barely wide enough for someone to sit cross-legged.

"He played with them until they were broken. Then he sold them to anyone who would have them. Made a lot of money on the broken ones from what I remember." He walked over to the whipping post and ran his fingertips along the wooden beam.

"The men who bought them liked them broken. They didn't have to fight to get the girls to do what they wanted. They could fuck them in the ass, the mouth, the pussy, anywhere, and the girl would obey, mindlessly, because not to do so..." Erik walked over to the wall and picked up a studded flogger, running his fingers over the metal rivets.

"Erik." She withdrew from him, backpedaling until she hit the door. Flipping herself around, she fumbled her hands along the wall, searching for the lock, for an escape.

"Come here, Melinda," he commanded in an even tone. She wasn't getting out, and she wouldn't get away. She hadn't learned yet.

"No!" she yelled.

"You haven't learned what a monster truly is yet," he said and hung the flogger on its hook.

"I know. I know." Her fingers flittered along the door's edge, but she wouldn't find the mechanism. Even if she did, it was far beyond her reach.

"No, you don't see." He unlatched one of the cages and opened the door, the creak of the metal echoing. "Sometimes, he had six to seven women down here."

Melinda stared over her shoulder, at the cages. Understanding bloomed across her face. Three cages, six women, sometimes seven? Her eyes widened.

"He didn't really care if they were comfortable or not," he explained and slammed the door. "He fed them dog food. Made them use the drain over there for their toilet. And if one of them had an accident. Couldn't hold it until someone came down to let them out of the cage to go—they were forced to lick it up." His cousin Marcus had enjoyed sharing stories of the horrors his father had trained him to inflict.

Eric's mother had been able to protect her three sons from having to see it, but she couldn't stop them from learning about it.

The color ran from Melinda's face as he went on.

"None of *them* slept in a warm bed. Not one of them was given ice cream for dinner. They were kept nude and cold—no brand-new clothes for them." He took soft steps in her direction, holding her captive with his words.

Her lips trembled.

"They cried, begged, screamed for mercy, but none ever came." He grabbed the neckline of her blouse and ripped it clean down the center. "It's time you answer some questions."

She screamed, but he wrapped his hand around her throat, choking off the sound. He turned them and pushed her backward until she hit the whipping post.

"Put your arms over your head," he ordered, his stare fixed on her eyes. Everything he needed to know was displayed there. Every emotion played out like a personal note to him in the depths of her emerald orbs.

Her shaking hands joined together over her head. He kept her pinned to the post with his hand firmly around her throat, giving her enough air but no wiggle room. The cuffs were easy to maneuver one handed to get her locked up, something his uncle would have requested.

Erik shook off the demons of the past. The haunting atrocities would never take place again.

Once she was secured, he stepped away from her, inspecting her beauty and admiring her curves. Even with, or maybe because of, the fear dancing in her eyes, making her body tremble as she stood before him, he found her more exquisite than any other woman he'd touched. Even with the uncertainty that must have been plaguing her every thought, she maintained her strength. Scared as she was, she would not crumple before him—and it was beautiful.

"Erik. Please." She tugged on the cuffs, but she wouldn't be going anywhere. The height of the restraints pulled her to her toes, elongating her body even more for him.

He plucked a knife off the wall, admiring the craftmanship of the blade. Nothing but the best for the worst men.

At least it was clean.

Erik quietly went to work, cutting through the fabric of her pants and tearing the jeans away from her. She stopped her wiggles when the blade brushed her thigh. If she got cut, it would be her own doing.

The thin blouse tore easily from her arms. He gathered the ruined materials and tossed them to the corner, leaving her naked before him.

"Please. I'm sorry. I didn't mean what I said." Her words tumbled out. All the fire, all the anger from upstairs was gone, leaving her heaving for breath and begging. Making the fire in her burn brighter, and his desire for her reach white-hot levels.

"What did your parents do for a living?" he asked, returning to stand in front of her, the knife still in his right hand. He needed to remain focused. Get through to her for once and for all that he wasn't the monster she thought, and she needed him more than she knew.

She looked up at her hands then at the knife. "My father was a carpenter. My mom stayed home with me." She took a breath between each sentence.

Erik mulled the information over. "Did your father work on his own or for a company? A union?"

She blinked. "I don't know. For a company, I think." She twisted her hands, trying to squeeze through the binds. Wouldn't happen. He was no stranger to bondage, though typically his women writhed with pleasure not fear.

"What company?"

"I don't know!" she screamed out, panic filling her words. "I was a kid! I didn't pay attention to stuff like that."

His jaw set. He'd never been hidden from his family's business. His mother tried to keep him and his brothers from Kristoff, but he knew. He'd been introduced to it, and even her shelter didn't keep him from knowing. She had little power over her older brother.

"Do you know anyone in the Bertucci family?" He gripped the knife harder.

Her brow furrowed; her lips trembled. "I don't know!" She turned her face up to the ceiling, dragging in shallow breaths. "I know the name. I've heard it before, but I don't remember from where."

She could easily have seen it in the papers, on the news. Bertucci had too much influence with the law to need to hide anymore.

"Think, Melinda. Do you know anyone related to Bertucci, did your grandfather bring home any of his associates?" Erik pressed harder.

"I don't remember. I don't think so." She blinked, sending fat tears rolling down her cheeks and dripping onto her exposed breasts.

The knife clanked onto the cement flooring. Erik stepped up to Melinda, the heat of her body washing over him. He captured her face with his hands, forcing her to look at him.

"Bertucci wants you. Why?" He turned her face to the right then the left, as though he were inspecting every inch of her face for a resemblance. No, if she was related, he wouldn't have come with a checkbook; he would have come with guns.

"I really don't know," she whispered—the sound more ragged than before. Her eyes locked with his. "I'm sorry for what I said. I'm just so scared." Her body trembled.

"I know," he said softly, bringing his mouth to hers.

He shouldn't kiss her. She wasn't his, and it wasn't a moment of passion, a moment of reverence shared between two lovers. Yet, once his lips brushed hers, he couldn't stop himself.

He pressed his body against hers, taking the kiss deeper and sweeping his tongue past her lips. Emotion rolled through him when her tongue touched his. She wasn't fighting him; she wasn't trying to kick him away.

Greedy, he slipped his hands from her face and down her shoulders. His fingertips traced her shoulders, eliciting another tremor, a soft moan from her lips.

He broke the kiss, stung by the passion evolving too quickly from their touch. She blinked up at him; shock flittered across her expression.

"You were good and answered my questions." He ran his hands down her chest, over her breasts, softly kneading them. "No more tears." He wiped the stains from her cheeks with his thumb. "The things that happened down here. They will never happen to you." He didn't speak the words to make her feel better; he said them to solidify his decision

She tensed beneath his touch. "How do you know?"

He dragged in a long breath, taking in her scent. "I won't allow it," he promised. "Now, take your reward like a good girl. Spread your legs."

CHAPTER 9

Melinda's body tightened. The cuffs hurt her wrists, but the pain paled in comparison to the confusion of the moment. He'd kissed her. Not merely brushed a peck on her cheek, but really, truly kissed her.

His promise shook her with the need to believe him.

"Open for me, Melinda," he said again shoving his knee between her legs.

She took a small step out with her left foot. Being lifted to her toes made it impossible to go any farther with it, but Erik didn't care about impossible. He only cared about what he'd told her to do.

"I…this is as far as I can go," she said.

His hands, large and worn from work she couldn't define, roamed over her skin. Rough sensations mingled with gentle touches as he made his way down her body, pressing kisses to her torso and belly as he sank to his knees.

He picked up her left leg and ran his tongue from her knee to her thigh. Internal shockwaves ran through her, each new spark ignited by his next touch. She fisted her hands, ignoring the burn of her shoulders, and focused on the sweet torture of his tongue.

Erik draped her leg over his shoulder and leaned closer to her sex, inhaling deeply.

"So sweet," he muttered. A finger trailed up through her folds. "And wet. So fucking drenched." He kicked up a smile. Her cheeks heated. "Do you like being tied up and helpless for me?"

Now that the danger had dissipated, now that she knew he hadn't dragged her to this horror room in order to hurt her, she wasn't sure how she felt. Only that there was an ache where his fingers had left her.

"Melinda," he warned, "if you can't answer me, maybe I should take you down from there and use your mouth for something better. A hard face fucking might get your words to come back to you."

A tingle shot straight from her ears to her clit; the alarm sounded.

His chuckle reverberated along her skin. "You like that, don't you, my sweet girl?"

She closed her eyes and tilted her face toward the ceiling. Fuck, she really did. Her responses were all backward. But what else did she expect when her entire world had been turned upside down?

"Don't worry, you'll get everything you like." He nipped her thigh. "When you're a good girl."

His tongue swept across her skin, right above her clit. "Tell me what happens to bad girls, Melinda." His teeth sank into her flesh, giving her a jolt.

He wanted an answer, but her mind had already elevated. Another bite, harder this time, dragging her out of her aroused haze.

She opened her eyes, seeking him out. "You'll spank me again." The words climbed into each other, and she spat them out quickly when he bared his teeth, as if ready to take another bite.

"Hmm, that's right. But it won't be a little hand spanking like before." His fingers spread her pussy lips open, displaying her clit to him.

"I think you liked it too much. No, next time you'll have worse than a spanking." The tip of his tongue flicked over her clit, knocking the breath from every inch of her lungs.

"Maybe I'll keep you on the edge of orgasm all night." A long swipe up through her lips, stopping short of her clit. Her hands fisted; she needed tension in her body.

"Or maybe, I'll overdose you on orgasms. Five, six, maybe more?" His mouth closed over her clit, and he suckled while his tongue lapped and dance over the sweet treacherous bundle of nerves.

She moaned, sinking her body lower, needing to get closer to him.

"All of this appeals to you. Me playing with you while you remain helpless to stop me. You're under my control now, Melinda. And I think you fucking love it," he muttered while tracing her entrance with his fingertip. "I think you want a solid fucking. I should leave you dangling for an orgasm that will never come. Why should I do that?"

His hot, wet tongue lavished pleasure over her clit, flicking and prodding it until she was near crying with pleasure. She arched her hips toward his mouth.

"Tell me, Melinda, why wouldn't you get to come?" He thrust his fingers into her pussy while increasing the pressure on her clit.

She cried out. Air stuck in her throat, and another sound, guttural and animal bolted from her mouth.

"Bad girls don't get to come!" The words burst from her, matching the intensity of his pumping in and out of her.

"Very good, sweet girl. Very good." His fingers picked up

speed, curling slightly, catapulting her into a downward spiral.

Standing on only one foot, on her toes, made her leg shake. Or maybe it was the practiced way he strummed her body. He slipped another finger in, stretching her, filling her.

"Oh fuck! Erik! Erik! Erik!" she chanted until her mind blanked and all the stars in the Universe danced before her. Firecrackers went off inside her, exploding and sizzling.

"Shhhh, sweet girl," he cooed when she finally fell from the heavens down into her own body. All of her muscles shook. Tremors ran from her head to her toes and back again, but she was no longer cold.

"So good for me." He kissed her pussy once more then gently returned her foot to the floor and rose to his feet. He quickly undid the wrist cuffs and caught her as she started to slip to the floor.

He swept her up into his arms, and she wrapped herself around him, gathering his heat, his protection as he unlatched the hidden door and carried her from the room that, at first, terrified her and then had brought her to a plane of pleasure she never would have guessed existed.

He silently carried her through the rest of the basement and up the stairs. She noticed the warmth once they were on the first floor of the house, but she remained snuggled in his arms.

"Erik." An accusatory voice boomed from behind them. He tensed but didn't stop walking.

"Not now, Ian." Erik's chest rumbled when he spoke, his low voice reminding her of a parent keeping the sound down to let their child sleep.

"What's going on?" Another voice, not as harsh, but more concerned. Melinda tucked her face into Erik's neck. Looking up would break the spell, the peace he'd brought to her, and a few more minutes wouldn't hurt.

"I want Simpson here first thing tomorrow," Erik commanded as he started up the steps to the second floor.

"Why?" the hard voice demanded.

Erik paused briefly, tightened his arms around her. "Because there's been a change in plans."

She searched his face for answers, but true to Erik's form —there were none. He carried her up the stairs and to their bedroom then laid her on the bed.

She wiggled beneath the covers and pressed her head into the pillow.

"Sleep." His rugged and raw voice countered the light press of his lips against her cheek. The room darkened, and the bathroom door opened and closed, leaving her in resounding silence.

Sleep tugged heavily on her eyelids. All of her energy depleted, she gave up the fight.

CHAPTER 10

"But it is possible." Erik pressured Walter Simpson for a straight answer. His uncle's attorney had been rambling on about the requirements of the will, completely avoiding a real response.

The old man flipped through papers, appearing flustered.

"There's nothing here prohibiting it. It's a bit of a loophole. I suppose it's up for interpretation." Walter dropped the last piece of paper to the desk and pushed his thin-rimmed glasses up his nose.

"Whose interpretation? Yours or a judge's?" Either could be bought with enough capital. He only needed to know where to deliver the cash.

"Only my signature is needed to turn over the estate in full, or that of one of my associates."

"So, you could have ignored all of this bullshit and simply signed it over?" Nico's question boomed from where he sat in the corner.

Erik waved him down. Getting emotional wouldn't help the situation.

"Technically, no." Walter let out a long breath. "I would be accountable to my partners as well. As you know, a portion of the debts collected by these sales are turned over to my firm for payment on services rendered. If I were to sign over the estate without the debts all being cleared as specified in the will, I would have to come up with that money on my own."

"Kristoff was a fucking prick," Ian muttered from his corner of the room.

Erik had been unsure whether to include his brothers in the conversation with Walter at first, but this affected them as well. What he decided was for the betterment of all three of them.

Walter cleared his throat. "That he was."

"I thought you held him in great esteem. Wasn't that what you told me when we met?" Erik walked over to the desk, surprised to hear the attorney changing his views.

"Yes, well, I had not met you prior to then, and, well...I wasn't sure of your temperament. If you were like—"

"Our uncle." Erik finished for him. "As you've seen, we are not."

"No." Walter shook his head slightly. "You are not."

"So, you're on board, then," Nico piped up again. "If one of us marries her, and we pay off the debt with our own cash, we're done with this whole thing, and the estate gets turned over in full?"

"Not one of us. Me." Erik's snapped his teeth, and he narrowed his gaze on his little brother.

"It would have to be Erik," Walter explained, turning in his seat toward Nico. "The will stated Erik take a bride."

"No judge would hold that up," Nico pushed.

"A judge also wouldn't have made us collect Kristoff's debts, but here we are, Nico." Erik leveled his brother with a glare. "It doesn't matter that it's not the letter of the law. This isn't about law, it's about what bullshit our uncle conjured up in order to fuck over our family. Going to court over the legality of any of this would've opened up an entire can of shit we don't need."

"Unfortunately, Erik is correct. If you were to bring all this to court, there could be other issues brought up. Other interested parties might become involved." Walter hinted at what they all knew. Any disruption in the easy flow of their uncle's death and disappearance could upset the other families. The matter needed to be resolved quickly and quietly.

Ian made a huffing sound from his corner but kept relatively silent.

"Okay, so, Erik marries her," Nico agreed, his cheeks flushed.

"Don't you think she should be the one to decide?" Ian's question burst from him as though it had been pushing against his seams the entire afternoon.

"Ian." Erik put a hand up. "We're just exploring the options here."

"Options." He stood from his chair. "Like any of this has been an option. What options does she really have, anyway? If you're willing to use what's left of our inheritance to pay her debt, then why not simply do that and let her be?"

Erik's aggravation peaked. Let her be? As in go? As in let her leave him?

"Because I still have to marry in order to get the estate and return the money we'll be using to pay off the debt." When had life gotten so damn complicated?

"So find someone else." Ian waved a hand through the air.

"Do you not like her?" Erik asked with a tilt of his head. "Or is it you like her too much? Maybe you want her for yourself?"

Ian's jaw clenched, and his hands fisted at his sides.

"Ian, it will be her choice." Nico got up from his chair and placed himself in the middle of his brothers. Erik wouldn't move from his desk, but if Ian charged at him, he wouldn't allow the attack.

"Isn't that right, Erik?" Nico gave him a pleading look.

"Yes. It will be her choice," Erik agreed. And he would be sure she chose correctly.

Ian opened his mouth but snapped it shut.

"Would you rather Bertucci get his hands on her?" Erik asked, squaring off with his brother. "Because he wants her."

"Why?" Ian asked in a hard tone.

"I don't know yet. I'm working on it, but he offered more money than was reasonable for some girl he doesn't know."

"If she marries Erik, she stays protected," Nico pointed out.

Ian's lips pressed into a thin line. "Fine," he muttered and stormed off, slamming the door behind him.

Nico's shoulders lowered, and he blew out a breath. "Okay, then. So." He turned to Walter.

Walter turned fearful eyes on Erik. "Yes. If you marry her, pay the debt with your own cash, it's all legitimate."

"And how long will it take for the estate to be turned over?" Erik asked. If he was going to bankrupt them, he needed to know how long they'd be out of money before the till was refilled.

"The bank accounts would be transferred to your name the next business day. The holdings would turn over to you immediately. It's all ready for completion once you've met all of the…requirements your uncle put in place."

"Good. I expect to see you tomorrow, then. We'll finish this once and for all and be done with it." Erik glanced at the door. The meeting was over.

MEASHA STONE

"Tomorrow?" Nico stepped closer. "So soon? You haven't even spoken with her yet."

Walter packed up his briefcase then gave Erik a wary grin. "Tomorrow, then." He inclined his head and made his way out of the room.

"Walk him out, Nico," Erik said.

Nico's jaw tensed.

"Nico. Go." Erik had let his brothers sit in on the meeting because the inheritance, although in his name only, affected them as well. But it changed nothing about who ran the family.

Nico stalked out, following the attorney who would finally put an end to the mess his uncle had put them in.

Erik picked up his phone and dialed.

"Hello?"

"Daniel. Hey, it's Erik Rawling." He leaned into his chair.

"Erik. Hey," Daniel responded.

"My brother set up an interview for a girl, Melinda Manaforte, for tonight, before the catalogue party."

"Yeah. I talked with him a few days ago."

"I need to cancel the interview and respond to my invitation with a plus one." Erik drummed his fingers on his desk. His eyes caught Nico's when he walked back into the office.

"Plus one. No problem. What's the name for the list?"

"The same. Melinda Manaforte."

Silence broke out over the phone.

"The girl? You're bringing her as a guest?"

Erik kept his gaze fixed on Nico's. "Yes. My guest. Is that a problem?"

"Of course not. I'll get the names on the list. When you get here, enter through the rear of the house. You'll walk through the gardens—"

"I remember." It had been a while, but this wouldn't be his first catalogue party at the Annex.

"Good. I'll look for you. Be good to see you again."

"Yes. I'm looking forward to it." Erik stilled his fingers on the desk. "Tonight, then."

"See you then." Daniel ended the call. Erik's uncle had disgraced their family, keeping Erik from attending any parties at the Annex or conducting business with its owners. But the time had come for that to end.

With the estate finally coming to him, he could start working on the building of his casino. And he would need the Titon family to do it.

"You're taking her to the party?" Nico's tone held a forced casualness.

Erik rose and tucked his phone into his pocket. "Yes. You wanted her to have the choice, right? She's going to need to see all of her options."

"You're so sure she'll chose marriage to you?" Nico asked. He'd appeared more than a little on edge after seeing Erik carrying Melinda to bed the night before, but Erik didn't make a habit of explaining himself to anyone. And he wasn't starting today.

"I am. Has she come down yet?" He'd left her sleeping. For the first time in as long as he could remember, he hadn't wanted to leave the comfort of his bed. She'd slept deeply beside him, snuggled up to his body. He'd felt every breath, every sigh, and held her tight when she shivered from the slightest chill.

Nico sighed. "I think she's in the kitchen." He paused a beat. "She's not going to go along with this, Erik. She wants her freedom, not a marriage proposal."

"Have you found her grandmother yet?" Erik asked.

The tension in Nico's stare softened. "No."

"Keep looking." Erik nodded and left Nico stewing in the office.

* * *

Melinda had her hip pressed against the counter, a steaming cup of tea cradled in her hands while she talked quietly with Marianne.

"Let me make lunch." Melinda grinned. Her genuine, happy smile forced a deep-rooted twist in Erik's gut. What would it feel like to have that smile aimed at him?

"Absolutely not." Marianne waved Melinda away from her prep station. "I do the cooking; you do the eating."

Erik paused in the doorway, not wanting to interrupt yet. This was the most relaxed he'd seen her.

"I can cook, you know. I lived on my own for two years, and when I was living with my grandparents, I cooked for them all the time." A brief shadow crossed Melinda's features, but she tried to hide it with a sip of her tea.

"I don't doubt your skills, but if you do the cooking, where does that leave me?" Marianne turned a stern frown on Melinda. "Out of a job, that's where."

"He'd fired you for letting me cook one meal?" Melinda asked with wide eyes.

Marianne was the only member of his parents' staff who had stayed on after his parents passed away. It had only been natural for her to move into the new house when his brothers made the move.

"Of course, I would," Erik boasted, making his presence known.

Marianne put her hands on her hips. He'd become immune to her annoyed glares when he was in high school. She was no more dangerous than a house fly.

"You would not," Marianne announced. "Who would do the laundry and the bed making? Not you and your brothers, for sure." She wagged a finger at him.

Erik raised an eyebrow and shrugged. "Melinda would do it."

Marianne looked over her shoulder at Melinda then back at him. "No." She shook her head.

"No?" Erik had to stifle his laughter, lest Melinda got the impression he could be persuaded by a little objection.

"No."

"Well, I am pretty good with laundry. I never mix up the dark colors with the whites." A playful smile tugged at Melinda's lips, bringing a lightness to his chest.

"You two are trying to get me riled." Marianne tsked. "If you want to help with lunch, Melinda, you can prepare the salad."

"Actually, I need her for a few minutes." Erik placed his fingertips on the marble countertop of the kitchen island. "Then she's all yours to boss around as much as you'd like."

He caught Melinda's gaze.

Marianne, always the most observant person in a room, clapped her hands once. "I have to switch the loads in the machines. I'll handle that, and you two can talk."

Marianna breezed past him, out of the kitchen.

"She's very comfortable with you," Melinda said once they were alone.

"She should be. She practically raised me." Erik shrugged. "She worked for my parents when I was younger."

"She doesn't seem that old." Melinda's brow furrowed

"She's not." Marianne's age wasn't the topic he wanted to discuss. He made his way around the island and collected her hands in his. He shoved the long sleeves of her shirt up.

A pale red line wrapped around both wrists. The cuffs on the post had marked her.

"I'm fine," she whispered, trying to pull away. He intensified his grip, bringing her wrists to his mouth and pressing a soft kiss to each of them.

"There won't be any more anger between us, Melinda," he promised.

"How can you say that?" She slipped free when he loosened his hold. The carefree air hanging in the room when he'd arrived started to turn cold and stale.

"Because anger gets us nowhere. You end up with a hot ass, and time that could be used finding pleasure is wasted." He rested his hand on her hip, keeping her close enough for him to sense her. She might be able to control her words, but she hadn't learned yet to restrain her body from reacting. Right now, beneath his touch, she was soft, but, at any moment, she could tense up.

"You could not spank me every time you got angry with me," she proposed with a sarcastic smile.

He leaned in closer to her ear. "But you love it when I spank you—even when you hate it. Hell, I think you love it more when you do."

She stiffened beneath his touch but didn't move away from him, as though merely his words could freeze her for a moment.

Perfect.

After the silence stretched out, she blinked and turned away. "Is there something you want me for?"

His cock twitched in his pants, answering for him.

"Yes." He stepped away. Letting her feel his erection wouldn't sway her to accept the new life he was proposing.

"Okay." She hopped up on the counter, crossed her ankles, and folded her hands in her lap.

"I spoke with the attorney this morning, and I think I've found a way to help both of our situations." He put the island between them again and rested his fingertips on the counter.

"Yeah? Like I can go home?" Hope tiptoed into her voice, making his throat thicken.

"No." He shook his head. "But you don't have to go anywhere else, either."

"What does that mean?" she asked hesitantly.

"It means, you stay here." He paused a beat. "As my wife."

She tensed a fraction of a second before a laugh burst out. "You're kidding, right? Marry you?"

He'd known she'd be less than thrilled, but laughter didn't exactly register as a promising response.

"I'm not kidding. You can fulfill the deal by becoming my wife."

She slid off the counter. "How does that fulfill the debt?"

"One of the requirements my uncle left in order for me to collect the estate is for me to marry. So, I will pay your debt to the estate, fulfilling the debt, and then, once we're married, the estate gets turned over to me in full, which will reimburse the money I paid out."

She blinked. "And then I can go home? We can divorce and end this?" There was that hope again.

He curled his fingers into his palms. "No. There wouldn't be a divorce." Another of his uncle's little *fuck yous* to Erik and his family. If the marriage dissolved within a year, all monies and properties would revert into a fund until he married again.

His uncle had enjoyed harassing his little sister, and when she made it clear she wanted her sons to have nothing to do with his business—he found a way for them to have no other future without getting their hands dirty in his work. If Erik wanted to use the Komisky estates and funds, he would have to play by the rules set forth by his twisted uncle.

"No." She shook her head. "I won't marry you."

"You understand the alternative?" He pushed, trying to keep the sting of rejection from touching his tone.

"You'll sell me?" Her gaze flicked away from him. Could that really be a better alternative to marrying him?

"Yes. That's one of the options. Another would be for you to sell yourself. Work off the debt." Selling her off couldn't become an option she chose. He'd find another way, but she would not be sold to anyone who would use her as a plaything and toss her aside.

"Can I think about it?"

"You hate me so much?" he asked, surprised.

She wrapped her arm around her middle, cupping her elbows. "I hate this whole situation."

He checked his impulse to go to her and hug her. She had that ability with him, to force empathy and engage his protectiveness.

"Okay, some time to think." He switched the topic. "We're going out tonight. I'm taking you to the Annex for a party they're holding. It's a catalogue party."

She wrinkled her nose. "I've heard of those. It's a sex party."

"Yes and no."

"And you're taking me." She gave him a pointed look. "It's one of my options?"

"It can be, yes, but tonight you'll go as my fiancée—even if you decline my offer—and you can see the alternative. If you haven't already made your decision."

"And if I don't want to go?"

"There will be times when you have a choice and times when you don't. This is one of the times you don't. I'll have a dress brought up to the bedroom for you. Be ready by nine o'clock." He tapped his knuckle on the counter.

The discussion was closed.

"I've decided to let you make lunch," Marianne breezed into the kitchen with a smile. "I'll supervise, of course."

Erik used Melinda's distraction to slip out of the kitchen. She needed to think about his proposal. Not that it was much of a marriage proposal, but it was better than the other options.

He'd already made his decision.

She wasn't going anywhere.

Married to him or not, she was staying right where she was.

CHAPTER 11

The yellow glow of the streetlights flashed over Melinda's lap as the car made its way through the city. She twirled a strand of her hair around her finger and tried to convince her stomach to stop dancing around.

She'd managed to stay clear of Erik since their conversation in the kitchen, but there was no hiding from him in the back seat of the car. He didn't push her for an answer to his proposal, just let her keep to her own thoughts.

Which was turning out to be worse than talking with him. She'd conjured up all sorts of horrifying scenarios she could find herself in. What if one of the men at the party offered to buy her from him right there?

Her stomach turned again. She'd already wallowed in all of the *why mes* she could handle. This was the situation, and she wasn't getting out of it unscathed. But she could be the one to decide how she became tainted. And by whom.

"While we are here, you are not to walk off by yourself. Stay by my side at all times. Do not talk with anyone unless I introduce you." Erik straightened his collar as the car pulled to a stop.

"Why not just put a leash on me?" she muttered. Watching him do typical things, normal things like fix the errant bend of a shirt collar sent the butterflies into full attack mode. In the normal moments, he didn't seem so scary.

His lips spread into a wide grin, exposing perfect white teeth. "It's not a bad idea. Behave and maybe you'll get your wish when we get home." And then he winked, setting the butterflies on fire.

Before she could gather up all the words flying around her muddled mind to form a sharp comeback, his door swung open, and he climbed out. His hand reappeared, and she grabbed on to it.

His hand was warm and rough, and she wondered what work he was in before he'd been called up the ranks by his uncle. It occurred to her she didn't know much of anything about him. Other than he was arrogant and overpowering, and his grin could send her heart into a fluttering mess.

"Don't be nervous. You're my fiancée. No one will say or do anything against you." His grip tightened.

She nodded, assuming he wanted some sort of reaction. She was busy watching the other people walking through the gates into a garden area. The winter had taken all the beautiful blossoms away. She took in the marble statues positioned throughout the garden walkway. She'd learned about similar styles in the mandatory art class she'd taken during her undergrad degree program.

"You like these." Erik slowed his walk, giving her more time to enjoy the work.

"I have no real eye for art, but yes, I do." She shivered in a cold breeze that ran up her skirt. "I like heat, too. Can we go in?" She tried to release his hand, but he wouldn't have it.

He chuckled and tugged her along.

"There aren't any other women here," she remarked. Men

in suits overwhelmed the room, but she still hadn't seen another woman.

The door to the mansion opened, and Erik gestured for her to pass through ahead of him. He stopped them at a coat check area and removed her coat for her and then handed it over along with his.

"Erik?"

"There will be plenty of women inside." He picked up her hand again and pulled her down a long hallway, keeping up with the crowd.

They were stopped at the entrance of what appeared to be a ballroom.

"Erik Rawling and my fiancée, Melinda Manaforte," Erik announced.

The stuffy man holding an iPad searched a list of names and tapped his screen.

"Welcome, Mr. Rawling. The announcements will begin in five minutes," the man stated in a flat tone.

Erik began to walk past, but he was stopped.

"I'm sorry, I didn't see this. There's a note. Mr. Titon would like to meet with you and your fiancée after the announcements have been made. You can wait in his office or follow him once he's finished."

Erik's ears twitched. "We'll meet him in his office after he's spoken. Thank you." His hand tightened around hers.

Erik pulled her into the buzzing room that was brimming with more men dressed in suits, but there were women, too. The dark carpeting soaked up any sound of the high heels the women all seemed to be wearing.

Melinda had grown up with little to no fashion sense. Grams wasn't into the fancy stuff, and Melinda's friends, what few she had, didn't care about clothes or makeup. But these women milling around, they cared—a lot. Not an eyelash was out of place.

Melinda tugged at the neckline of the dress Erik had given her to wear. A simple black dress with a scooped back and a deep neckline.

"You look beautiful," he whispered in her ear. The man had a knack for hearing her thoughts.

She touched her neck.

"I think the words you're searching for are thank you." He winked again and grinned.

"These women. Are they all here to be sold?" Her throat dried. This would be her future soon if she didn't take the offer Erik was making.

Erik pulled her into his side. "Most of them. A few, like you, are here with a guest, and even fewer are here to make a purchase themselves."

"And this is where I'll go if—"

"This is one option you have, yes." His fingers tightened around her hand. "Not my favorite option."

She could agree with that.

"None of these women are forced to be here, Melinda," Erik began. "This is a safe place for them. They have complete control over who they work with and if they take a contract. Nothing here is as unsavory as you're making out in your head."

She noticed the confidence with which the women walked through the room. She detected no fear or trepidation from any of them. Men gave them appreciative stares, but none of them touched or made derogatory comments. These women owned the room.

"Why did you bring me here?" she asked.

"Because you seem torn with your decision."

"If these women are so well cared for, why would I not prefer this to marriage?" She tried to add snark, but her heart wasn't in it.

Erik stiffened beside her. She glanced up at him, sure to

find a scowl. But his attention wasn't on her, it was focused on the entrance. She followed his gaze to see a man, same height as Erik, but much older, walk into the room.

"Do you know that man?" Erik asked her forcefully.

"I don't think so. Should I?" she asked, searching Eric's expression. His face had transformed into the blank shield again. She'd get no answers from him now.

"Erik. Good to see you." The stranger encroached into their space and held out his hand. Erik had to drop Melinda's in order to reciprocate.

"And you."

The man's dark pencil-point eyes swept over her, and she stepped closer to Erik. If the stranger continued to stare at her that way, she'd need to shower off the sleaze when they got home.

"And this is?" His head inclined toward Melinda. A warning shot up through her spine.

"This is Melinda Manaforte," Erik stated with his hand possessively pressed against her back. "I would think you'd recognize her."

"I do." He turned his attention away from Melinda, and focused on Erik. "And she'll be worth every penny I offered. I'm sure. What brings her here? I didn't see her on the menu. Is she a late addition?"

The hair on Melinda's neck stood at attention. This man had offered money for her. Erik could hand her over and collect the debt and be on his way. But he hadn't. He'd offered her marriage instead.

"About the offer…" Erik began.

"Welcome, everyone, to this evening's catalogue party!" a deep voice rang through the room, cutting off Erik's conversation.

"We can continue negotiations later. I'm getting a drink." The man slunk away toward the bar.

Questions burned Melinda's tongue, but the man standing on the stage continued talking, capturing everyone's attention. She stared at Erik while the rules and regulations of the party were listed at length. He could have been done with her already, so why hadn't he handed her over? What game was he playing?

Why did she want to kill him one minute and sink into his strength the next?

"You're not listening to the rules," he muttered without casting her a glance.

"Are you going to be contracting one of these women? Is that why we're here?"

He shook his head with a laugh. "You're all the woman I can handle tonight." He slid his fingers through hers, capturing her hand once again. His was so much larger than hers. It made her feel small and cradled. How could one little touch, something as innocent as hand holding, be so intense?

Finally, the announcements wrapped up, and the room came to life again. "I have to speak with someone." Erik said.

"Do you want me to stay here?" she asked, suddenly aware if she were left alone, the men who'd been circling them for the past moments would easily swoop in like the vultures they appeared to be.

"No. You're coming with me." He caught the eye of the speaker and tugged her into moving. "His name is Ashland Titon. This is his house—his business." Erik led her through the people and to the door.

She recognized the name from the greeter. This was his party.

Erik paused outside a door and ran his thumb over hers. "Behave in here, Melinda." It was all the warning he could give before the door opened, and he escorted her inside. She didn't need him to give much more information—she remembered what happened when she disobeyed. Her ass still had a mark across one cheek, but the pain had faded away.

"Erik." The man who'd been talking on stage shook his hand.

"Ash," Erik responded in kind, moving his palm to her back. "My fiancée, Melinda."

Ash, a man who mirrored Erik's stature, a warm greeting sort of smile probably meant to put her at ease. It didn't. She pressed closer to Erik.

"Melinda. It's nice to meet you." He inclined his head, not making any move to touch her or shake her hand. How loud was Erik's possessiveness, exactly?

"Maybe you'd be more comfortable waiting in one of my guest rooms."

Erik's fingers curled into her flesh. "No."

Ash's gaze shot back to him.

"Would you allow your wife to be parted from you in this situation?" Erik challenged.

Melinda noticed the stern set of Ash's jaw through his thick beard.

"Fair enough." Ash nodded and gestured to a love seat pushed against the wall. "Melinda, I'm sure you'll be comfortable here. Can I get you something to drink?"

The pleasantries made the room stuffy. She'd never cared for forced civility.

"No. Thank you, I'm fine." She glanced at Erik as she made her way to the love seat. The leather was soft and supple, and creaked when she moved on it.

"I heard about your uncle's requirements." Ash raised his eyebrows as he started.

"Seems the whole town is aware." Erik's tone was unreadable. He was in business mode now. He wouldn't give away his thoughts for free.

"Well, those who have interest in that sort of thing. Yes."

Ash leaned back in his chair and steepled his fingers. "Melinda is the last one?"

Erik's shoulders tensed. Even through the fabric of his suit jacket, Melinda could make out his muscles constricting.

"Yes."

"You say she's your fiancée, but she had an appointment scheduled to meet with Daniel and Peter for a possible position here," Ash said.

Melinda's fingers dug into her palm; he'd planned to throw her into sexual slavery before giving her any of her real options.

"The options of either gaining an advance from the Annex to repay her grandfather's debt or simply signing over a portion of her pay to my family was on the table at first," Erik agreed. "It's not anymore."

Melinda's chest lightened. He wasn't set on throwing her to the wolves.

"I understand you managed to acquire buyers for the other women," Ash continued.

Melinda forced herself to remain calm. She didn't know Ash. If she appeared confused or upset, he could see that as a disloyalty to Erik. In their world, she didn't fully understand what the implications of that would be. And she wasn't willing to find out.

"For one, yes. The other was able to obtain the funds to repay the debt," Erik said.

"And your fiancée is unable to do so?" Ash continued.

Irritation at Ash's questioning started to build in Melinda.

"Her ability to repay or not, isn't your concern," Erik said, lowering his voice. She understood that tone. Ash was edging close to triggering his temper.

Ash eyed him silently, his jaw tensing and relaxing as the moments ticked by. Erik didn't offer any more information. He actually relaxed beneath Ash's scrutiny.

"No. What you do with her is your business. But you brought her here to find prospective buyers. And that's my business." Ash's tone turned hard.

"She's not for sale." Erik matched him, stone for stone.

"You're sure?" Ash's eyebrows raised.

"Why the interest?" Erik asked, flicking a piece of fuzz from his knee. Was he bored? She could chew off every fingernail from the nerves bouncing around her body, but he seemed only mildly curious.

"Bertucci has an interest, and that makes me want to know details."

"His offer is being rejected."

What exactly was the offer? Melinda was ready to scream. Maybe she should have sat in another room. She wasn't getting any more information by being so close to the conversation anyway.

"Because you're marrying her." Ash pointed a long finger in Melinda's direction.

"That's right. I thought we'd already established that."

"Your uncle—"

"My uncle aimed his attentions on your wife and moved against you, going against the agreement with the other families. Maybe, whatever happened was justified. I have no ill will toward you or the others," Erik stated, rolling his shoulders. "None of this has anything to do with you or your businesses. Melinda is merely a spectator tonight."

"Right. Because if she doesn't marry you…this will be her fate?" Ash startled her with his heated stare. "Melinda, are you free to leave at any time you wish?"

Melinda swallowed down the whimper dancing around her throat. Erik didn't turn in his chair to look at her; he expected her to answer correctly. But she no longer knew what the correct answer was.

If she told the truth, that no, Erik would find her and drag her home if she left, she'd be putting herself in danger. If she lied, she could be putting herself in danger with Ash. And that man out in the party room seemed to have some big interests where she was concerned.

"Melinda. Answer honestly," Erik said in a softer tone. He wanted her to tell the truth, or was this another trick?

She licked her lips. "No. My grandfather sold me to Kristoff Komisky when I was younger in order to pay off a large debt. They agreed I would be able to finish school, and now that I have, Erik—Mr. Rawling—collected me."

Ash tapped his fingers on the desk. "So, you are being held against your will?"

"No." She sank into the couch. "My grandmother will lose everything if I don't honor the sale my grandfather made." She swallowed again, her throat was so damn dry. "I'm not being forced." Not completely, but she didn't add to her answer. Keeping the conversation simple felt the best course of action.

There. The whole fucking sordid truth. She could walk out and let her grandmother suffer the consequences, but she wouldn't.

Ash tapped his fingers along the edge of his desk. "Erik is a smart man. He wouldn't have brought you here if you were completely without options. He's aware I won't work with unwilling women, and if you were to mention to my men that you needed assistance in that area, you would be safe. So, I'm sure you're telling me the complete truth."

Melinda's breath caught in her throat. He'd beat around the bush a bit, but in the end, he was offering her a safety net —if she went against Erik. Wouldn't Erik see that as an insult, or had she watched too many late-night movies?

"Bertucci's interest concerns me." Ash turned back to Erik, apparently satisfied with her testimony.

"He won't have her." Erik shrugged, seemingly indifferent

to the quick change in focus. "Do you have any idea why he made the offer?"

Ash scratched his temple. "The other girls. Have you kept tabs on them?"

"No, but I vetted the man who made the purchase." Erik's hand flexed. A tiny movement, but she noticed. "You think he's connected to them as well?"

"I think when Bertucci makes an offer like he did, there's reason."

"I agree." Erik nodded. "I'm looking into it, but you have more resources than I do. My uncle's disgrace has left me outside the loop."

Watching the exchange was like being a spectator at a tennis match. Melinda couldn't keep up with everything they talked about, but she got a clear image that Bertucci wasn't a good man. And his interest in her was a danger sign.

"I would suggest you keep the engagement short. The sooner you have her legally under your protection, the better." Ash's words shot through Melinda.

Protection?

"Do you have any ideas why Bertucci is so interested?" Erik pressed.

"He's been slowly taking over since your uncle's death. He's already gained much of his territory. He had some loose ties with Bellatrix Gothel before she left the scene; I assume he wants to start trade back up."

"And these requirements with my uncle's will have given him easy pickings?"

"That's the concern." Ash nodded, his eyes shifting over to Melinda. If he was looking for her to react, he could keep waiting. Bertucci sounded like a new breed of evil. Erik would protect her from him. She didn't need Ash or anyone else.

"You'll let me know if you find anything out," Erik stated.

The two men reminded her of two pack leaders circling each other, trying to sniff out the danger of the other one. Part of her wanted to throw a ruler on the desk and tell them to get it over with.

"I will. And this evening—"

"Last night of freedom." Erik glanced over his shoulder, giving Melinda a knowing grin. "For both of us."

CHAPTER 12

*A*sh Titon wasn't a man Erik wanted on the opposing side of any argument. Loyalty to his family should have made him the enemy, but Erik wouldn't blame a man for protecting what was his. And everything Ash had done against Kristoff Komisky was to protect his wife. Erik wouldn't lay hate on him for that.

When Erik led Melinda back into the main ballroom where couples were already being paired off and negotiations for contracts were taking place, he sensed her apprehension. She'd been silent in the office, kept her confusion to herself, and he'd reward her once they got home. But he could feel the questions bubbling up inside her.

"You were a very good girl for me," he complimented and kissed the inside of one wrist.

"What did he mean other girls?" Her green eyes searched him.

"We can talk about that when we get home," he said softly. And they would. If he was going to get her to cooperate with the judge, to say her vows, and go through with the marriage, he would have to come clean. If it meant keeping her safe, and getting the rest of the inheritance, he'd tell her everything.

"Then let's go home," she said.

He straightened to his full height and dragged in a breath. "It wouldn't look right to meet the host and then leave. We need to stay for a bit more," he explained.

"You aren't afraid I'll do like he suggested?" She pointed to one of the men standing guard at an entry point. "I could just walk right over there and be free of you. Or you'd be free of me, as it were."

"Yes, you could."

"You weren't mad at him for suggesting it?" Her head tilted slightly. Her ignorance of the disgusting world his uncle had forced him to play in shone a light into the darkness for him. Reminding him there was another side to all of this, there was an ending.

"He was right. I already knew he would give you an option of staying back without me. Ash is a good man—well, mostly good."

"So, working here really would be a safe alternative to marrying you?" She surveyed the room again.

"I didn't say that." His voice dipped at the idea of her walking around the room, trying to attach herself to a man for the night.

She sighed. She was learning his tones and his mannerisms. He'd never let her work at the Annex. And from the unsettled way she watched the conversation between him and Ash, Erik had plenty of confidence that she wouldn't be walking over to any of the guards.

"If you aren't here to get a girl, then why bother coming? It seems my future is pretty well laid out for me now. All those choices you said I'd have. They're off the table, aren't they?" she pressed.

His phone buzzed in his inside jacket. pocket, and he

plucked it out. The distraction came at the perfect time.

Found an airline ticket in Melinda's grandmother's name

Erik tapped a response to Ian. *Where to? When? Alone?*

The answer came quick. *Not used. She wasn't on the passenger list. She didn't board.*

Erik glanced up from the phone at Melinda. Her attention had been caught by a woman bent over a table in the far corner of the room. Not every man was a gentleman at the Annex. Some of them liked to test drive the women in public before making an offer for a longer contract.

He stepped closer to her, pressing his chest against her back. "Is that the road you want to choose?"

Her body went rigid.

His phone buzzed again, but he slipped it into his pocket without checking it. There'd be time for investigating in the morning.

"You need to make your decision." He trailed his fingertips down her neck. She'd piled her hair on top of her head, and curls cascaded from where she bound them, but her neck, her creamy, sensual neck was bare to his touch.

She turned around, tilting her head back to glare up at him. "I want my questions answered first."

He scanned the crowd for Bertucci. Rejecting the offer in a public setting might keep him from blowing his top, but Erik couldn't count on it. Nor did he want Melinda anywhere near the man.

Erik cupped her elbow. "Let's head to the car. You can ask your questions on the way home."

"But the host—" She threw a sarcastic hand toward the room.

"We've stayed long enough. It won't be noticed." And even if it was, Erik couldn't give a fuck. The Titons might rule their portion of the underworld with their own set of moralities, but Erik didn't dance to their drummer. He had his own damn rhythm.

"You just wanted me to see what I face if I don't take your offer." The accusation lingered between them as Erik escorted her to the coat room.

He helped her into her coat, zipping it to her chin—and enjoying the flash of annoyance in her eyes when he did it— then put on his own. "In part," he said, grabbing her hand again. Feeling her fingers twitch inside his palm settled him. She was safe; she was with him; she was right where he wanted her to be. The whys of all of that could wait.

"In part what?" she asked as she stepped into the garden. She checked out the statues as they walked down the path to the exit, and he made a mental note to find similar pieces for the house. He'd noticed her admiring them earlier when they arrived as well.

"My reasons for bringing you tonight." He smiled down at her. His car pulled up, and he opened the back door, waving off the driver. "I did want you to see this as an option." He also wanted to question Ash about Bertucci's offer, but he didn't bring that up yet.

He shut the door to the car and reached over to her hair, plucking out some of the pins.

"What are you doing?" she asked, trying to smack his hands away.

"Why do you twist it all up like this?" He continued on his mission until all of her red spirals were fanned around her shoulders.

"If you wanted it down, you could have just asked. You don't have to paw at me like some"—she blinked—"wolf."

He laughed and dropped the pins into her hand. "Fair enough. I'll ask next time, though I would rather you never put it up. I like having it down, ready for me to touch." He picked up a curl and ran it between his fingers.

"I'll try to remember that," she said, twisting in her seat and smoothing the skirt beneath her legs.

He silently observed her as the car maneuvered through the city traffic. The streetlights lit up her face as they passed, accentuating her high cheekbones and the subtle slope of her nose.

"That guy, the one who came up to us at the party. He wants to buy me?" she asked. "Fuck, what an absurd notion, buying a person. And me, it's me we're talking about." She laughed a little with no humor but chock-full of anxiety.

He palmed her knee. Even through the fabric of her dress, he felt the tremor.

"No one's buying you, Melinda. That's off the table." How could it ever have been on the table? One look at her at her grandmother's house, and he'd known she was different. Somewhere inside him, a spark had lit, and no matter how much he'd been trying to stamp it out, it only grew brighter with each encounter with her.

"Oh, really?" She added a quirked eyebrow to her frown. "I thought I got to choose."

He inhaled a long breath. "I changed my mind," he said. "I told you about my uncle's requirements. Us getting married fixes things. So, tomorrow, we'll get married."

"Just like that?" she asked, but she didn't move his hand from her knee. Progress.

"Just like that." He nodded.

"How does it fix things for me exactly?" she asked, unleashing more accusations with her tone.

"Because men like Bertucci don't just give up. He's expressed interest in you, and if we aren't married, you aren't protected from him."

She looked away, the light catching the unshed tears

clinging to her lids. He recognized the helplessness of her situation. She had no actual recourse. He understood. His future had been mapped out for him since childhood.

His mother had thought she'd escaped the horrors of being Kristoff Komisky's little sister when she married Travis Rawling, but she had been wrong. Erik grew up being groomed with two separate ideals. His parents who wanted him to follow the path of the Rawling name into business and financial trade, while his uncle exposed him to the underworld and taught him the realities of his bloodline.

He hadn't been taken by force the way Melinda had been, but he'd been given no choices. His future was laid out for him, and when his parents died, followed shortly by his uncle, his destiny had been cemented in place. The only way for him to get out from beneath the heavy shroud of sin attached his to his family because of his uncle's betrayal of his partners was to continue forward. To remove the choice from Melinda's hands.

He played with the hem of her dress, running his fingers along her silky skin beneath. "I know it's not what you want, but it's what is going to happen."

She took a shaky breath and sniffled. "And the rest of my life? How does that look when I'm your wife?"

He detected a strong undertone of sarcasm, but there was something else, too. Something hinting at curiosity. He wouldn't go so far as to think she was caving. She wasn't that simple. She would fight him every inch of the way, but she wanted to end up exactly where he'd put her. She wanted it and hated wanting it at the same time.

Erik brushed his fingers across her thigh. "Similar to the past few days, but with more freedom." He smiled. "You wouldn't be caged in the house, but I would expect to know where you are." He crooked his neck. "For safety of course."

"Safety? I thought once I was your wife, I would be safe?"

He turned in his seat, moving his free hand to her shoulder.

"You will be. But, like you mentioned, Bertucci has some interest in you, and he's not going to like having his toy snapped out from under him."

The muscle in her neck softened beneath his touch.

"I can pursue my writing?" she asked softly, looking down at her lap.

He outlined her earlobe. "Of course. I never took your computer away from you, and I won't." As his wife, she would never have need of a job, but he wouldn't tamp down her passion.

"My grandmother."

"Ian is looking into it. I promise you, we'll find out what happened." He pinched her earlobe. "There is nothing for you to decide anymore, Melinda. You're going to be mine. Completely." He leaned into her, taking away the space blocking him from her sultry skin. He nipped at the soft spot behind her ear, and his eyes nearly crossed when she hissed.

But she didn't shove him away.

"I want to hate you so much," she shocked him by saying.

He pulled back. His hand left her leg and cradled her face, drawing her attention to him. A tear rolled down her cheek.

"It would be safer if you did," he confirmed.

"Then why do I want to agree to this insanity?"

He lightly touched her lip with his thumb. "Because you're cornered, and you're a smart girl. You can't win here."

Her green eyes shone beneath unshed tears, and the streetlights cast her into a golden shadow. He recognized the buildings they passed in the car. Home was only a few minutes away.

"You said there would be no more anger between us, but that's not true. People get angry, couples fight—even ones who don't love each other." She was rambling. It was cute.

"True. We will probably get angry with each other, but I will never hurt you."

"So, what you did…in the bedroom…?"

"When I spanked you?" He laughed and pulled away from her. "I'll do that a lot. Sometimes you'll love it, and sometimes—when you do something outrageous like try to kill me—you won't."

"I'm sorry about that," she said softly, tugging the hem of her dress down. The car pulled into the alley leading to the house.

He picked up her hand, pressing a kiss to her wrist. "After we see the judge tomorrow, I'll arrange for your apartment to be packed up."

"You didn't answer my questions."

They pulled into the garage.

"You didn't ask any." He shrugged. "Now. It's time for bed." He climbed out of the of the car and gestured for her to follow.

"You said—"

"Erik!" Nico called from the kitchen as soon as they stepped into the hallway.

"Go on upstairs. I'll be there in a few minutes." Erik pressed his hand against Melinda's back to aim her toward the stairs.

She ignored him and went to Nico. "What's wrong? Is it my grandmother?"

"Melinda."

"No. I'm sorry, it's not." Nico gave her a small smile.

"Melinda, go upstairs." Erik said again with more force. She'd been so pliable, so sweet on the ride home, but now her steely resolve had returned.

"Is this also how it will be? You sending me to my room whenever you feel like it? Like I'm some annoying child always underfoot?"

He studied her features quickly, having started to learn her mannerisms. All bluster. Her hackles were raised because she'd given him a few moments of surrender. Small as the victory was, she hadn't fought him off, hadn't hurled insults and refused him. She'd been soft and reasonable. And now, standing in front of his brother, she would put on a show.

"If you're going to act like a child, I'm more than happy to treat you like one." He positioned himself between her and Nico. Maybe if she didn't have the audience, she would back down slowly and go up the stairs.

Her jaw worked into a tight knot.

"Big bad wolf now that your brother is here to witness?"

"Nico, I'll find you in a few minutes."

"You got it." Nico disappeared from behind him. He didn't need to turn around to see him go. When he gave an order, it was followed. Except by Melinda.

"I think you forget what happens to little Red when she confronts the big bad wolf." He lowered his head, bringing his eyes level with hers. "He ate her up."

"Erik—"

"It was a simple thing—go upstairs."

Her eyes widened, her lips parted, but no sound escaped. She froze beneath his glare.

"I'm—" She bent forward, lowering her gaze from his.

"Go upstairs, Melinda. I'm not saying it again." His hand went to the buckle of his belt.

Her gaze flicked to the threat—no, the promise, of punishment if she decided to keep fighting him.

"Good night, then." She backed her way to the stairs, only turning around once her foot hit the first step. He watched her climb to the second floor, her coat and dress flapping around her legs.

"Well, that was a quite a show," Ian muttered from the office doorway.

"Glad you enjoyed it." Erik shook out of his coat. "Too bad you won't get to see the encore." Erik tossed the coat onto an empty chair and stalked up the stairs.

CHAPTER 13

Melinda washed the last traces of cosmetics from her face. Erik had sent out for all fresh makeup for her to use for their evening out.

She grunted. Evening out. Like it had been a date or something as ridiculous. She couldn't even picture Erik on an actual date. Opening doors, paying the check—sure, but giving a woman the option of telling him no? Making small talk without giving orders? It didn't fit him.

The door to the bedroom opened and closed. Her muscles clenched as she waited for the booming demand for her to present herself.

Erik popped up in the bathroom door, his inquisitive stare settled on her. She glanced at him in the mirror and grabbed the towel, wiping the last of the water from her chin.

"You don't need all that paint." He pointed to the pile of mascara and eyeliner mixed in with eyeshadows—most of which she wouldn't use with or without his comment.

"Did you rush up here to make good on your threat?" she asked, too tired to keep up the anger she'd let out downstairs.

He had been right; it was an easy request. He wanted a moment to talk to his brother, and she'd acted like a brat.

"Do you want me to?" he asked, tucking his hands into his pants pockets. His posture rounded out when he stood so casual, making him look less menacing. Which was dangerous. Taking her eye off what he really was could break her.

"What?" She leaned a hip against the counter.

"Do you want me to take you over my knee and spank you?" If he hadn't said it with so much damn silk in his tone, she may have played it off with a laugh.

But he worsened it by stepping into the bathroom. The dark glare she'd grown accustomed to washed away beneath the bright lights.

"Melinda. I won't repeat myself." A warning lingered between them. Did she want him to?

Her fingers fluttered at her sides, and she twisted around to accommodate his presence. Her ass pressed against the edge of the counter.

"I was out of line down there, and I'm sorry." She raised her chin. It was the best she could do with him looking down at her with such expectation. Did he want her to beg him not to spank her, or did he want her to plead for him to touch her? If he got much closer, she'd probably do both.

"You were." He brushed her hair over her shoulder. "You've had a rough week."

"Week?" She huffed. "It hasn't even been that long." Her world had been turned upside down and spun around so much she wasn't sure exactly what day it was.

"No, it hasn't. Once we're married, it will get easier." He touched her chin. "Between us, too."

"So, there's no chance of a quick divorce after you get your inheritance?"

He pushed her chin up, lining her mouth up with his. "Now, why would I want to let you go?" He brushed his lips across hers. Her heart fluttered with the brief touch, trying to fly off with the butterflies living in her stomach no doubt.

"Because it's the right thing to do," she whispered, tilting her head and giving him access to her throat. He kissed her jaw, the little spot behind her earlobe, and continued down her neck. If this was her punishment for being a brat, she'd consider doing it more often.

His chest vibrated against hers along with his deep chuckle. "Letting you go would definitely not be the right thing to do."

He captured her lips beneath his in a powerful, demanding kiss, like he was staking claim on what was his. No proposition, no request for entry, he stormed the territory and planted his flag. Not that a coherent thought could have formed and been executed from any part of her brain at that moment. The instant his lips touched hers, her resistance melted away. His tongue swept through, touching hers, teasing and playing with her until she fell under his complete command.

And when he finally pulled away, pressing light kisses to her cheek, she betrayed herself with a heavy sigh. He chuckled again, this time against her neck, as he slid his hands beneath her robe.

When had he untied it?

"This is better," he said, letting the robe fall to the floor and pool at her feet, along with her resolve to keep firm against him.

"What is?"

"You, being like this, kissed into silence." He kissed the curve of her shoulder. His beard tickled her skin.

She clung to his arms, not sure if she was gearing up to shove him away or hold him closer.

"I suppose it's better than your belt, too," she breathed as he made his way to her lips.

"Hmmm, when you aren't being so naughty, I'll show you how good my belt can feel." He kissed her chin, cupping her shoulders. "But that mouth of yours needs a lesson."

She sank to her knees before him without any pressure from him to put her there. Her tongue ran along her lip while her eyes took in the bulge of his pants.

He put space between them while he worked his zipper. With his pants open, he pulled his cock free and fisted his hard length.

She swallowed.

She'd seen cocks before. She wasn't completely inexperienced, but she'd never witnessed a man stroking himself. His hand, strong and rough, wrapped around his thick shaft and maneuvered up toward the head and back down. It was mesmerizing.

A small bead of precum formed at the tip, and without thought, without motive, she leaned forward and swiped her tongue across it, gathering up the salty drop.

He hissed as though her touch burned him.

"Again." He shuffled forward a step, planting a hand on the top of her head.

She licked the underside of his cock.

"Give me your hand." He beckoned her obedience. Once she complied, he wrapped it around his shaft. "Hard, Red. Hold me tight." His voice sounded like he'd swallowed a fistful of rocks, scratchy and raw.

She gripped him hard, the slick smooth shaft beneath her fingers as she stroked him then closed her mouth around him and suckled.

He groaned. His fisted her hair, but still he didn't move her, just held her, like he needed something to keep him steady on his feet.

She took him into her mouth, going down, down, down until her nose hit the coarse curls at the base. He intensified his grip, not letting her back off when she tried to move again.

"Hold still." He sounded like his teeth were clenched, but she couldn't look up at him, could only hold the position he held her in.

"Open wide, Red," he ordered.

She sputtered, needing air, but she managed to open her mouth wider, sucking in a bit of oxygen when he slid his cock back. The reprieve was short-lived as he quickly thrust into her mouth, hitting the back of her throat and catching her unaware.

She gagged, but he wasn't deterred, continuing to pump into her throat, cutting off air, choking off her thoughts. Her palms pressed against his thighs, but she would have had more luck moving a steel barge.

"Keep your throat open, Red." He grunted, thrusting harder into her throat. "Your naughty mouth is getting the punishment here, Melinda. Put your hands behind you." He gripped her hair and yanked her off his cock. Drool hung in a thick string between her lip and the tip of his dick.

She folded her arms behind her. Melinda remembered the girl at the Annex, how she'd been merely bent over a table and used. It felt Erik was doing the same—using her to fulfill his primal urge—and yet, she looked up at him with a hunger she'd never felt before.

He slapped her cheek lightly. "Open up," he ordered, and she parted her lips wider, wanting him to do his worst—and his best—to put her back where she felt good again. Where she didn't feel like an annoying brat.

"Good girl." He thrust into her mouth again, holding her down until she started to cough. Only then did he pull back out and slow his movements. He was fucking her throat, using her for his own pleasure.

Her nails dug into her flesh, her mouth tightened around

him, suckling and licking at him best she could while he continued to plow into her. As hard as he fucked her, she matched him with her desire to please. She didn't want to think about the repercussions, or the whys, she only wanted to hear those two words again. *Good Girl.*

Her pussy tightened with need as he forced his cock down her throat. She choked, and he pulled out once more, resting the tip against her lips.

"Stick out your tongue," he ordered. He gripped his shaft. She felt a pull of regret that he was touching himself and not letting her do it, but she obeyed, not wanting whatever consequence would surely come if she didn't.

His fist stayed firm in her hair, while his other one jerked his cock hard and fast. His breathing quickened, and she could see the muscles of his thighs tighten, his balls tucked higher. He was going to explode.

"Fuck!" He groaned just as thick ropes of cum spurted onto her tongue. "Hold it." He continued to stroke himself.

She curled her tongue, not willing to allow any of the warm seed to slip away from her.

After the last bit of cum dropped onto her tongue, he stepped back. "Do not swallow," he ordered, breath harsh and rapid like he'd charged up a mountain. Her heart beat as though she'd followed him.

He yanked his pants up and rebuckled his belt, all casual, as though she weren't there kneeling before him with his cum cooling on her tongue. "Get up." He softened the order by helping her to her feet.

He pulled her arms to her sides.

One finger, one thick, long finger slid up through her sex. She moaned, arching her hips toward him, needing more.

"Your pussy is soaked," he said, licking her juices from his finger. "It's really too bad you were such a naughty girl. Don't swallow yet. You hold that on your tongue."

Her lips trembled, but she held firm.

"Let's go." He led her from the bathroom by her elbow. Her cheeks flashed hot at the image of herself in the mirror. Her hair was a complete mess, her face flushed, and she walked with her tongue still sticking out of her mouth, holding desperately to his cum.

Once near the bed, he turned her to face him.

"Do you think you can talk more respectfully and be more obedient next time you're given a simple command?" he asked in a calm, rational tone. Was anything about that moment rational? Her mind wouldn't stop spinning long enough for her to figure it out.

Unable to talk properly, and not wanting to make a mess, she nodded.

"Okay, swallow." He kept his eyes glued to her mouth as she curled her tongue into her mouth and swallowed down the thick warm fluid. Her lips scrunched, and she swallowed again, the taste of him lingering.

"Now, in bed." He gestured with his head.

She must have seemed as desperate as she felt because he grinned, a wide smile showing his confidence. "Maybe sleeping with the taste of my cum on your tongue and your pussy aching for my touch will teach you better than my belt could."

It was a lesson.

Of course, it was.

She climbed into bed, not sure she could talk to him at the moment even if words would properly form. The burn of humiliation spread through her entire chest and settled in her clit, making it throb and swell more.

"Sleep. Tomorrow's your wedding day." He winked and flipped off the bedside light.

She swallowed again and again, but the taste of him

remained. Her lips were sore from being pulled so tight, and her throat ached from his feverish thrusts.

He'd fucked her throat, used her for his own pleasure then washed out her mouth.

And, in the morning, she would pledge her life to him.

CHAPTER 14

Justice Trenton stood with his binder opened in his hands, looking over his script while Erik stared out the window of his office. The city was quiet first thing in the morning. No loud horns or crowds of people shoving their way down the street. Just a bright sun climbing into the sky.

Peaceful.

When was the last time he'd experienced a peaceful morning? Or any time of day? Since his uncle's death, his world had been topsy turvy with a touch of acid rain.

"Erik." Ian placed his hand on Erik's shoulder. "She's ready."

"Don't want to try and talk me out of this again?" Erik asked while straightening his tie. It was a simple event in his life, this wedding. There wouldn't be anyone besides his brothers to bear witness. Other than a few distant relatives, there wasn't anyone to invite, anyway.

"Would you listen?" Ian asked, his voice gruff. Being the second son, he had the luxury of working with the right and wrong aspects of every decision. He didn't have to make the hard calls.

Erik shook his head. "Not even a little."

"Then get it over with."

The office door opened, and Nico entered with Melinda close behind. A sharp twist went through Erik's neck at the sight of Nico escorting Melinda. It was innocent, but it didn't matter. He didn't like it.

"Well, is this the bride?" Justice Trenton brightened up his smile.

"Yes. Melinda Manaforte." Erik stated her name in hard syllables. "Soon to be Melinda Rawling."

Her gaze snapped up to his; a soft-pink hue swept over her cheeks. This wasn't the way a little girl planned to get married. There was no pomp or circumstance. No father to lead her down the aisle. Fuck, there wasn't even an aisle.

She wore a simple lavender dress, more suitable for spring with the flowing skirt and short sleeves. Her hair had been left down, thick curls cascading over her shoulders and down her back. Only a bare trace of makeup could be seen. She didn't need any of it, but she probably wouldn't listen to him on the subject anyway. And it was her wedding day. Picking a fight would make the awkward situation even worse.

And Melinda didn't deserve that. Hell, she didn't deserve anything that had happened, but that's where they were.

Nico backed away, allowing him to take his place beside Melinda. Erik picked up her hand and laced his fingers between hers, rubbing his thick digits against her thin, cool fingers. She stared up at the justice, her chin high and lips pinched together.

A bride should appear joyful and hopeful, standing ready to make her vows. Melinda looked...resolved.

"Okay, then. Let's begin." Justice Trenton cleared his

throat and read the script laid out for him in his binder. A part of Erik wanted to bark at him to skip all the preamble and get to the vows, but he kept himself under control. Melinda might not have the wedding of her childhood dreams, but she wouldn't have a rushed shotgun ceremony either.

Besides, Ian would probably have a fit if Erik made the situation any worse. Tension rolled off his younger brother from behind him. Nico gave off an agitative energy. Maybe his youngest brother had more of a crush on Melinda than Erik originally thought.

Melinda's fingers twitched when Trenton came to their vows.

"Please face each other," he said, still grinning, though it had slipped in sincerity since Melinda arrived. The justice had worked with high-profile families before. An unenthused bride probably didn't faze him at this part of his long career, but maybe he still hoped he was presiding over a happy couple instead of a manufactured marriage. He would probably have more luck with his goal if he wasn't so quick to take a payment to keep his opinions and judgment to himself.

Melinda squared off with Erik, and he grabbed her other hand. Maybe he was trying to keep her from fleeing, or he was endeavoring to keep himself planted.

"Erik, repeat after me, please," Trenton said.

Erik repeated the vows, word for word. He locked his gaze with Melinda, speaking directly to her. This wasn't a marriage of love, but it would be an honorable union. He wasn't fudging his oaths. He was a man of his word. Always.

Trenton began the vows for Melinda, who repeated them softly.

"And obey…" Trenton said for a second time when she froze. Her lips pressed together in a thin line of defiance. As though she was locking up the words and wouldn't be letting them free.

"Did you have to put that word in there?" she finally broke her silence to whisper. Though she wasn't very good at it, and Nico chuckled from his spot.

"It's an important word," Erik said, keeping his own amusement hidden.

Erik tightened his hold on her hands when she continued to glare up at him in silent protest.

"I promise to love, honor and...obey..."

"Good, girl." Erik rubbed his thumb over her hand.

The pink tint to her cheeks deepened, and she turned her gaze away from him while the justice continued the rest of the ceremony. Once the last vow was spoken, the rings in place, Justice Trenton announced the marriage complete.

Erik didn't wait for the justice to make the suggestion; he simply pulled Melinda to him and kissed her. A fiery, possessive kiss. He didn't break away until he felt her soften in his hands. When he pulled back, he gazed into her eyes, at her dilated pupils, the slight smear of her lipstick, and grinned.

"There are just a few signatures needed, then I can file all of the paperwork with city hall this afternoon." Justice Trenton pulled out several piece of paper from his binder and placed them on the desk.

Erik scribbled his name where he needed and handed the pen to Melinda. She hovered over the line.

"Not signing it won't change anything," he said into her ear.

"I know," she muttered and scrawled her wide looped signature across her line.

"Very good." Trenton snapped up the papers and tucked them away. "Congratulations," he said, but Erik could see the uncertainty lingering.

"Thank you." Melinda graced Trenton with a genuine

light smile. One she had yet to give to him. He rolled his shoulders back, warding off the inevitable stab of annoyance at not being gifted a simple smile. A genuine curve of her lips. It wasn't that much to ask for.

Erik turned to his brothers and let Melinda small talk with the justice while he gathered his coat.

"Nico, go with Trenton here and get copies of everything, then bring them over to Walter Simpson's office. I want those transfers in place by this afternoon." Erik delegated the tasks necessary to finish the estate disbursement. The finish line was coming up fast, and he could finally start working on the property purchases and gambling license. The real work was about to start.

"I'll go with him," Ian announced.

Erik studied him for a long moment. The open hostility toward Erik's activities was missing from his scowl.

When they were children, Ian would often volunteer to run an errand for their mother so he could sneak off to play in the woods or meet a girl he wasn't supposed to be talking with. Erik could always tell he had ulterior motives because of the way he'd gulp after making his offer.

The same way his throat worked now after speaking.

"Okay, fine," Erik said with a narrowed gaze. His younger brother was definitely up to something.

"We should at least go out for dinner tonight," Nico piped up. "Take her out somewhere nice."

Ian nodded. "Yeah. She'd probably like that."

"Fine," Erik agreed. They were married now. She wasn't a prisoner, or a pawn in the twisted game his uncle had forced him to play. A night out would do her some good. Keep her relaxed, and her mind off of what would happen when they got home.

Melinda would become his—permanently.

CHAPTER 15

At eight o'clock, twelve hours after she'd sworn to love, honor, and obey the most arrogant man she'd ever met, Melinda walked by his side into the busiest restaurant in town. Erik's brothers were behind her as they were shown to their table.

They were seated on the raised level, overlooking the main seating area. A week ago, she wouldn't have been able to get a table down there, and now she found herself sitting in the first-class level.

Erik ordered a bottle of wine for the table, and Nico fired off some appetizer requests. Melinda sat with her hands folded in her lap, unsure of where to put her eyes. The three brothers fell into a casual conversation about real estate and commissioner fees, but she wasn't listening. The ring on her third finger felt heavy and out of place.

The silverware clanking and glasses touching faded off into white noise while she continued to finger the ring. Simple in its design, a pink-gold band. No frills or diamonds, just a band linking her life with Erik's.

What a strange evening. She sat sandwiched between

Erik and Ian, with Nico across from her. Like an ordinary family out to dinner. Nico and Ian had never threatened her or been anything but cordial. She'd gotten used to them being her prison guards; now they were just her brothers-in-law.

"I think your phone is dinging," Ian pointed out from beside her.

She took the clutch from the table and pulled out her phone, feeling the heat of Erik's gaze on her. They had barely shared a full conversation since they'd swapped vows that morning. But his attention never went far from where she sat.

Swiping her phone to life, she opened an email and quickly scanned the contents. Her heart, trotting along peacefully with the words, broke into a breakneck gallop.

"What just happened?" Nico asked on a laugh.

She peered up from her phone.

"You're grinning like you've won the lottery."

She practically had. Her cheeks ached from grinning so wide, and even the day's events couldn't pull her smile from her lips.

"What is it, Melinda?" Erik asked, his tone the lightest she'd ever heard it.

She gripped her phone and pressed it to her chest.

"Margaret Edgewater wants my book," she whispered, afraid if the words were given too much weight, they'd fall off the Earth and die in space.

"Who?" Ian leaned toward her. It was the closest he'd gotten to her since he escorted her from Grams' house the first night.

"Margaret Edgewater. She's an editor at the biggest publishing house in town. I hadn't even sent her my manuscript. My professor passed it along to her." She read the email again. "They were friends, or maybe are. I'm not sure." She shook her head and took a deep breath. Her skin lit on fire, tingling with electricity.

"That's great," Nico said with a wide grin.

She nodded and stared down at her phone. Erik still hadn't said anything.

"Yeah, great news," Ian added.

Erik reached over and slid the phone from her hands. Caught up in the bubble of excitement she floated in, she let him read the message. Their fingers touched in a dozen places when he returned the device with an approving smile.

"Definitely cause for celebration." He raised his hand slightly, and a waiter popped out of the bushes or had been walking by. She was too wrapped up in her own thoughts and enjoyment to pay much attention to anything going on around them. But even in her haze, she recognized the power Erik held.

Word had already moved around town about their nuptials. The hostess had congratulated them, as well as their waiter when he first arrived at the table. It seemed, with the requirements of his uncle all met, he was stepping up in the world. She still didn't understand the nature or rules of the world his uncle belonged to, but she could see that, with his claiming his full inheritance, it changed things for him. He had more power behind him now.

Erik ordered champagne and another round of drinks for his brothers.

"So, what's the book about?" Nico asked, shoveling his third brochette into his mouth.

Melinda took a sip of wine. Talking to strangers about her work made her stomach twist into knots.

"It's a murder mystery." She went on to give the short summary she'd memorized from her submission packets.

"So, who did it? Who killed the banker's wife?" Nico asked when she'd finished her spiel.

Melinda laughed. "I'm not telling you."

"Will you tell me?" Erik asked, his dark-silk voice dragged her attention from Nico. His hand covered hers on the table, thumb rubbing circles into her palm. His gaze lit a blue fire inside her chest. He was being playful, sweet. The arrogant man who'd beaten his chest in order to gain her attention instead wore a cocky sideways grin that sent a flood of warmth through her body, straight to her core.

If he'd been this man from the start, a guy having dinner with his brothers and his girl, would things have progressed the way they had? Would she be feeling so overwhelmed and needy in his presence? Or would she have not spared him a second glance. Hot as he was, would he have drawn her to him without all of this arrogance and wolf-pack leadership?

His phone ruined the moment with its blaring ring. Erik muttered a curse and let go of her hand to grab it from his pocket. He cursed again and stood up.

"I have to take this. I'll be right back." Erik dodged the waiter bringing their entrees and stalked off toward the rear of the restaurant.

"He'll have his nose in that project for the next year," Ian mumbled, sipping his drink.

"Project?" Now that she was married to him, she supposed she should know what he did—other than abduct innocent girls.

"He's going to be putting up a casino hotel downtown, on the south side," Nico explained.

"Once he gets an idea in his head, it's like the blinders go on and all he sees is hitting that goal," Ian explained further, cutting into his steak.

"I noticed." She pushed on a smile and picked up her fork. "Have you been able to find out anything about my grandmother?"

"Not much, but we are looking. I promise," Ian said in the

flat tone Erik used when he wanted to impress upon her the importance of his words.

"Thank you." She saw the irony of thanking the two men who had literally taken her from Grams in the first place.

"So, what happens now with your book? This woman, she buys it from you or what?" Nico redirected the subject to something more comfortable. She appreciated the change and ran with it, explaining the next steps and all the inevitable waiting that.

"So, it could take another year or more before the book is out?" Nico leaned back in his chair. "Seems like a long time."

"I can be patient," she said, enjoying her dinner. The flavoring of the pot roast she'd ordered reminded her of Grams' home cooking, and the easy banter between Nico and Ian relaxed her.

"I'll be sure to test that theory." Erik rejoined them and winked at her as he pulled his napkin from the table.

"I think you probably already have," Ian mumbled and shoved a forkful of steak into his mouth.

"Important call?" she asked.

He ran his tongue over his teeth and shook his head. "Nothing to worry about."

She left it at that, not wanting to sour the atmosphere with hostility. This was her life now. Good or bad, this was it, and she needed to find a way to fit into it without feeling like a size-eight foot squeezing into a size-six shoe.

Melinda finished her entree and then the champagne. She sipped the first wine Erik had ordered while Ian and Nico argued over the rules of blackjack. She couldn't help but laugh at the little quips flying between the two, but in the end, Erik won out. He pulled up the rules on his phone and plunked it onto the table.

"There." He pointed at the lit screen. "Ian's right."

Nico picked up the phone and scowled as he read. "Fine. Whatever."

"Whatever, nothing." Ian turned to Erik. "He's not working on the floor."

Erik huffed. "He can manage the waitresses."

"I'm good with that." Nico flashed a wide grin and returned his phone.

Melinda had never felt as though she was missing out on having siblings. Her parents were always attentive, and her grandparents had been the same way. She had friends in school, and she always enjoyed her books. But watching them and listening to their banter, she wished she had a sister. Someone who could help her navigate her future.

"The check's been taken care of already, Mr. Rawling." The waiter stood at his left side with his gloved hands clasped together and a slight bow at his waist.

Erik glanced at Ian and Nico. Both shook their heads.

"Mr. Bertucci called and took care of the bill. He said to pass on his congratulations over your nuptials. He regrets not being able to express them in person this evening."

Melinda watched Erik's expression harden more and more with every word the waiter said.

"Thank you. I'll be sure to convey my appreciation." Erik waved off the waiter.

Nico and Ian's casual smiles faltered. Their expressions slipped into severe masks that matched Erik's. Beneath the table, in the privacy of her lap, Melinda twisted her napkin into a knot.

"We should go." Ian was the first to stand after the messenger left their table.

"I'll take Melinda home. Ash Titon has something for me. The two of you go and pick it up." Erik helped ease her chair from the table and cupped her elbow while giving his instructions.

Ian's jaw tightened, but he didn't argue.

"Do we let on about Bertucci?" Nico asked, buttoning his jacket.

"No. Leave him out of this. We are staying clear of all of that. We don't bring them into the fold unless it's absolutely necessary." Erik helped Melinda into her coat. A gentlemanly action, slipping her sleeves up her arms and fixing her collar for her. While ordering his brothers around, he still made sure she was taken care of.

"Got it." Nico inclined his head toward Melinda. "See you at home. And congratulations on the book. Oh. And marrying this big lug."

Ian grunted.

"I'm sure congratulations aren't want she wants—a divorce is more likely the best wedding gift Erik could give her." Ian downed the last of his drink and shuffled his coat on.

"Brotherly love." Erik narrowed his eyelids, targeting Ian with his disapproval.

Melinda stepped closer to Erik. "I think people are waiting for the table." She motioned to the crowd below.

"They can wait." Erik kept his gaze on Ian.

"What's done is done." Ian inclined his head, conceding the round to his older brother. "It was a joke. In bad taste." He nodded toward Melinda. "Welcome to the family. Dysfunctional but loyal."

Erik gave her a little push toward the stairs. "See you two at home," he said and followed her down the steps.

Erik caught her hand when they reached the first floor and kept her tucked into his side as they moved through the crowd. He didn't shuffle side to side and wiggle through everyone; he had her firm and led her straight through the huddled patrons.

This wasn't a man of great compromise. He wanted what

he wanted, and he would simply take it if necessary. She had already come to know that about him.

But when they arrived at the car, and he opened the door for her, his stare sent a white-hot electric current down her body. He wasn't simply looking at her with desire.

He was the predator.

And she was his prey.

CHAPTER 16

The drive home from the restaurant passed in silence. Melinda replayed the evening, the carefree chatter, the almost sweet looks from Erik. How long would it last before he made demands she wouldn't or couldn't fulfill? Theirs wasn't a marriage rooted in love or even common interests.

"I'd like my attorney to review the documents Margaret sent you." Erik broke the quiet once they were in the house. He took her coat and hung it in the front closet.

"That's probably a good idea," she said. "Although I'm sure it's just standard stuff."

Erik raised his eyebrows. "And what's standard stuff?"

She paused, thinking through what she knew. It was a quick thought process. "I guess I don't know."

He picked up her hand. "Then my attorney will definitely read anything she sends over."

Melinda examined his expression. The tense set of his jaw loosened. Meanwhile, her stomach continued to practice acrobatics. Her gaze drifted to the staircase. It was late.

He brushed her hair away from her face, the light touch

of his fingers contrasting with the roughness of his voice. "We should go upstairs."

The fire of his piercing stare spread through her. He could be so powerful, so intimidating with a simple gesture or look. She wondered if he even had control over it.

"I suppose." She nodded, but her feet remained plastered to the carpeting.

He slid his hand down her arm, igniting a firestorm as he went, down, down, down to her hand. She spread her fingers wide, letting him lace them with his.

"Let's go."

Erik led her up the staircase to their bedroom, her nerves set on edge with each step. The click of the bedroom door closing behind them echoed through her mind.

"You're nervous," he remarked with a hint of amusement.

"No, not really," she lied through her shaking teeth.

He released her hand and walked around her. "You are the worst liar." He chucked her chin with his knuckles. "Are you a virgin?" His head tilted, as though he hadn't thought of it before.

"No." She laughed. Her nerves were out of control.

He narrowed his eyes, inspecting her. Technically, she wasn't. She'd had a boyfriend in college who had wormed his way into her bed. It had been a disaster, but at least it had been quick. He broke up with her a few days later, saying they'd make better friends than lovers.

"Take your clothes off," he ordered quietly.

Her fingers wiggled at her sides.

"Don't make me repeat myself." His warning was soft and clear.

Her heart took a nose dive into her stomach to join the conga party. His bright-blue eyes devoured her. Any resolve she may have pretended to possess shattered beneath his stare. He wasn't just a commander ready to charge up the hill, he wanted to own it, to claim and conquer.

"I can do it for you, but you look so good in that dress. It would be a shame to ruin it." He cocked his head to the side, like he was rolling the idea around his mind.

She shook her head. She could do this; she would do this. They were married now. Hell, with his hungry stare on her, the little nuisance of a wedding didn't enter into the equation.

Her body reacted the only rational way it could beneath such a powerful gaze. She went wet. The heat pooling in her belly spread lower until she could feel her pussy become slick with her arousal.

His prowess, his command, his authority had pulled a sexual need from her before, but tonight, after he was playful and sweet, she needed to touch him. To make sure he was real, that he wasn't going to vanish into a coldhearted monster now that he'd gotten what he wanted.

He made a sound, a growl, deep in his chest, and his hands raised, but she retreated out of his reach.

"No, I will." She grabbed the hem of the dress and yanked it over her head. In her hurry, the collar scraped her nose.

She stood before him, naked, exposed. Not for the first time, but she shuddered as though it was. Before, she'd had anger and hatred to cling to while his eyes moved over her body. Now, she was unsure of the sensations burning through her. She wanted his touch, but she wanted to hide at the same time.

He removed his suit jacket, flinging it onto the armchair in the corner. He removed his shirt without any elaborate dance, but she took in every movement. He was being gentle, soft, and it made her uncomfortable.

The jingle of his belt buckle snapped her attention to the

sound. She swallowed, trying to rid herself of the Sahara Desert having moved into her throat.

He walked to her side of the bed and crooked a finger at her. "Come here."

She obeyed without hesitation. He was holding a belt, after all, and she wasn't trying to ruin the night by igniting his irritation. But it was more than that, it was the slight upturn of his lip when he gave the command, the way his eyes darkened one hue, the way his body—hard and rippling with strength—distracted her from the idea of disobeying.

He put a hand on her hip, sending more shudders of electricity through her. "I'm not a gentle man." His warning came in a low, raw whisper.

She raised her hand, cupping his cheek. His jaw tensed at the touch. "You've never apologized for that before."

"I'm not apologizing." He turned his head and kissed her palm. "I'm giving you fair warning."

She lowered her gaze. He was teasing her.

"Put out your hands." Another order.

Again, she obeyed. She must have had too much wine at the restaurant. Compliance came too easily.

"Hold this." He extended the belt to her. She took it, feeling the weight in her hands. She recalled how hot her ass had been, and how wet her pussy had gotten when he'd spanked her with his hand. Would his belt set her ablaze?

Erik's lips twisted up into a devious grin, and he stepped around her, coming to stand at her back.

"You're not a virgin, hmm? How many men have been between these thighs?" He ran his fingertips over her ass.

She clenched automatically.

"No, sweet girl, don't tighten up on me now." He patted her cheek. "Soften this ass for me."

Her inhibitions were too low; she wasn't blocking him out.

RED

What had he asked?

Too much wine, definitely.

"How many?" he whispered into her ear.

She took her time, blinking slowly and gathering some gumption. Being a virgin might have been less humiliating than the truth.

"Don't make me ask again." His fingers dug into her ass, warning of what would come if she didn't start talking.

"One," she whispered, shame flooding her. She'd acted with such experience when he touched her, fondled her, brought her to the height of pleasure, but in reality, she'd been a fraud.

"You think that's a bad thing?" Erik walked to the dresser and pulled the top drawer out.

"It's not exactly normal."

He paused and looked up at her, his face taking a serious tone. "Normal is an illusion when it comes to this. Most men exaggerate their experience, and women often sugarcoat theirs. But you're telling me the truth."

"Who would lie about such a pathetic number?" She laughed, trying to lighten the thick tension building.

He quirked a brow. "You'd be surprised what people lie about." He shuffled through the drawer. "I prefer you this way. Sweet, honest, nearly untouched."

Melinda's eyes went straight for the black leather riding crop Erik pulled out. Any remnants of his question flew from her mind.

"What's that for?" she asked with a retreating step.

He chuckled and pointed it at her. "It's for whatever I want it for. Back in place and hold the belt up for me. If I want to use it, I don't want to have to ask."

Melinda shifted the belt into her palms and put her hands out, offering him the leather strap. Her eyes fixated on the floor just before his feet. If he looked into her eyes again, he might see the burning arousal getting hotter.

"Obedient tonight." He toed off his shoes and plucked his socks off, dropping them on the dresser. With measured steps, he made his way across the soft carpeting to her. "Hold this." He pressed the handle of the crop against her lips.

She opened her mouth and bit down on the braided leather.

"Don't drool on it," he ordered harshly and delivered a hard slap to her breast. She grunted and stepped away, having not expected it. Her breasts swayed from the impact, giving her a new reason to blush.

Diverting her attention, she took in his body. She hadn't seen a gym in the house anywhere, but he definitely lived in one. There hadn't been any hiding his physique with clothing, but now, seeing the ripples of his stomach and the cut muscles in his arms, she nearly dropped the crop.

He chuckled. "Careful, sweet girl. You don't want to be naughty right now."

If it meant getting his hands on her body, she might take the chance.

He took crop from her mouth and checked the handle. "Good girl," he crooned, lifting one breast with his hand and cradling it like a precious gift. "Drop your hands, but don't let go of the belt."

She put her arms down, gripping the belt to be sure it didn't fall to the floor.

"I'm going to paint these tits red. And you're going to take it for me." Not giving her a moment to hesitate or disagree, he brought the flat of the crop down hard on her breast. She winced but let the sharp pain sink into her body. Again, he brought it down, glancing up at her to gauge her response.

"Such a sweet girl." The swats become harder as he did exactly as he said. He painted her breast with the crop, delivering soft then hard blows until she couldn't guess which was coming. When she hissed, he grinned, and when she moaned, he licked his lips.

"Fuck," she cried out and jumped back out of his grasp.

His eyes darkened.

"I'm sorry!" She stepped forward again, but it was too late. She'd broken the rules; she'd moved.

"Why are you sorry?" He cocked his head to the side, the tip of the crop circling her nipple. Heat spread across her breasts; he'd not missed an inch of them with the crop.

"I moved." She dropped her head. If he was laughing at her, she wouldn't be able to stand the humiliation.

"And you weren't told to move. You were told to stand still." He moved the crop to her pussy. "You're probably soaking my crop right now." He slid the length of the implement between her thighs, through her folds. She squeezed her eyes closed. Just the flick of a touch against her clit had her curling her toes in the carpet. His movements drew her attention, and she opened her eyes to see him.

He pulled the crop back out and leveled it with her eyes. "Yep, look at the mess your little pussy made. Clean it for me." He held the crop horizontally in front of her but moved away when she went to bit down on the handle again. "No, no. Stick your tongue out."

How much more of this could she bear? She needed his touch, her skin was on fire, and she knew one touch from him would put out the flames.

Tears built in her eyes, but she obeyed him and slipped her tongue out.

"See, sweet girl? That wasn't bad." He ran the leather handle over her tongue, wiping her own juices on her.

A tear slipped from her eye, and he caught it with his fingertip, bringing it to his lips. "Such sweet tears. You like this little game, but it embarrasses you at the same time.

Being told to stand naked in front of me, let me beat your tits, play with your pussy. Your body and your mind, they fight." He took the belt from her and pushed her hands to her sides.

"Let go of the fight, Melinda." He tossed the crop to the floor and cupped her face in his palms. "You'll never win anyway. You belong to me, with me, and that will never change."

His lips crushed hers. He didn't need to ask or push, she opened to him, taking his possession and falling into it. Just for the night, she could let him wrap her up in his dominance. She'd fight through it all in the morning.

Right now, she needed him to touch her.

He skated his hands down her arms. "Get on the bed, Melinda."

She scrambled backward and landed on the mattress.

"So eager?" He laughed, climbing on the bed and crawling up the length of it toward her. His eyes, dark and round and full of possession, trapped her.

He gripped her knees and jerked them apart.

"Tell me you want this, Melinda." He leaned over her, brushing his lips across her chin, her cheek before settling his gaze on her. His usual demeanor of control and authority slipped. She wouldn't go so far as to say he seemed insecure—she doubted he ever had a moment when he didn't already know what was coming in the next. But this wasn't a command. He wasn't pushing her to do what he wanted. He was asking for her honesty, for her to be genuine with him.

She lowered her lashes but continued watching him. Of course, she wanted his touch and all the pleasure that came with it. He'd already swallowed her up. The least he could do was make her feel better about it.

"Yes, Erik." She nodded, unable to get anything else out.

He slid over her body, shoving his pants off with expertise before he framed her face again with his palms. His eyes bored into her. His musky scent surrounded her, digging deep into her mind. She knew this scent. It brought comfort and strength. As much as she wanted to shove him away, to force herself back into a place of hate for him, she was lost in him.

The sense of security didn't make her less apprehensive. He was still a dangerous man, and he could hurt her—he could break her if he wanted. But when he leaned down again, brushing his lips across hers then moving lower to her chin, her neck, she drowned in the sensations.

She skimmed her touch down his chest, feeling the hard ripples of his physique. He arched up, letting her have her way with him for the moment, and she took her time. She moved her fingers over his back, over his ass and his hips then slid between their bodies again.

Her fingers trembled slightly as she closed them around the smooth, hard length of his cock.

"Oh, fuck." His head fell forward into her neck. She held tighter, sliding her grip up and down, stroking his powerful length. A small bead formed at the tip, and she wiped it away with one finger, spreading it down his shaft.

His hand dove into her hair, and he pulled her head back. "Don't. *Fuck*. You have to stop." He used his free hand to yank her touch away.

She smiled at him. His control slipped. A fraction, a micro inch, but she'd seen it. And she wanted more. She glided her hand across his cheek.

"Erik. Please."

He moved his hips, pressing the tip of his cock against her entrance.

"Mine," he growled and thrust into her. She cried out from the invasion and dug her nails into his shoulder, but he wasn't to be stopped.

"Erik!" she yelled as he pulled, almost leaving her entirely. He locked gazes with her and pumped into her, inch by inch until he filled her again.

She threw her head back, moaning with want, with need, with fear he'd stop too soon.

"Harder. Don't stop," she groaned when he gripped her hips and plunged forward. She wrapped her legs around his waist, taking him deeper but still wanting more. She ached with the stretch, but she didn't care. The pain mingled with the pleasure, the arousal, and she wasn't ready for it to end.

"Fuck." He gripped her hair again, sending pins flying. He thrust harder, grinding his hips into her clit, sending her closer to the sun.

"Erik. I have to, please, hell, please…oh fuck." Her hands clenched into fists on his shoulders. "Please make me come!" She planted her feet on the bed and lifted her hips, matching his thrusts with force.

"Come, Melinda." He tugged on her hair again, giving her the burn to send her right over the edge she'd been teetering on.

With a flick of his wrist, she was thrown into the burning embers. Consumed by the waves, the hard crashes taking over, she arched up at him, digging her nails into flesh, and screamed with her release.

Her body would break, but she couldn't think of it. The only thoughts were of the pleasure. Hard, fast-beating pleasure racking her body.

He plowed into her again and again until he cried out with his own release. If she hadn't been in the room, half crazed with pleasure, she would've sworn she heard a wolf howling as he filled her with his seed.

He groaned, his teeth gnashing as he slowed his thrusts. "There's my sweet girl."

His forehead pressed against hers. Large paws roamed

over her face, and warm kisses touched her cheeks. He rolled to the side, yanking her with him.

She felt him leave her, his cum sliding from her body and smearing her thigh. Too exhausted, too exhilarated, too stuck in her own mind to care, she wrapped an arm around his stomach.

Melinda looked up at him to find his attention fully placed on her. Time had stood still from the moment he'd shoved her into the bedroom. But now it needed to move again. She needed to remind herself this was an arrangement. A marriage on paper. Nothing more.

She needed to protect herself.

He frowned. "What has you so worried, sweet girl?"

She closed her eyes and snuggled into his chest. He'd had her body, but he would never have her heart.

CHAPTER 17

*E*rik rinsed his razor. When he looked into the mirror, Melinda stood behind him, wearing only a towel. Steam from the attached shower room followed her.

"You're not shaving off your beard, are you?" she asked with mild alarm.

"Would you disapprove if I did?" He poised the razor at his cheek where the shaving cream waited to be swiped away.

Her eyes darted away, and she tightened her hold on the towel.

"It's your beard." He could sense her confusion. She had a preference but wouldn't share it. To share it might mean letting him get another inch closer to her, and after the night they'd shared, she was definitely on the run.

Most nights sleep fucked with him, making it difficult to find and almost never possible to hold on to for more than a few hours at a time. But last night he'd fallen asleep easily after she'd closed her eyes and drifted off. And, for the first time in as long as he could remember, he didn't wake before dawn.

"So, I'll just shave it all off, then." He pulled his cheek taut and repositioned the razor.

"No. Wait!" She darted forward and plucked shaving tool from his hand.

"Did you take my razor from me?" he asked with mock irritation.

"You weren't going to shave it off, were you?" she asked timidly, cheeks flaming.

Grinning down at her, he took the razor from her. "No." He turned back to the mirror, still watching her expression. "Just trimming." He finished swiping the last bit of unwanted hair away and put the razor in its case.

Melinda took a step toward the door, but he grasped her wrist, tugging her to him. "You sleep okay?" he asked, brushing a curl from her cheek. It was all piled high up on her head in the messiest bun he'd ever seen.

"Yeah." She didn't withdraw him, but he could see the war in her eyes. She wanted to stay, but reasonable, fearful Melinda wanted to run and hide.

No more hiding.

"Good." He tugged at the end of the towel she had tucked in place, shoving her hand away when she tried to block him. "No more of that."

She settled her gaze on his chest. He hadn't dressed yet; other than his boxers, he was as naked as her. Cupping her chin, he drew her attention up to him.

The indecision still fought in her eyes. He didn't like the turmoil. There shouldn't be any.

"You make things more complicated than they have to be," he said, running his thumb over her lower lip.

"How so?" She kept her hands at her side while he dropped the towel to the floor.

Taking a nipple between two fingers, he pinched it, dragging it toward him. Her pupils sprang free of the control she had on her body. Her automatic response his power, to the little bites of pain he gave her thickened his cock. She couldn't hide her arousal from him, and he loved it.

"You think too much when it comes to us. There's nothing to fight about. It's done." He released the pressure on her nipple and shoved his thumb into her mouth, hooking her cheek.

Her eyes flashed to his. She didn't panic, but she was unsure.

"Let's see if you shaved today, too. Do any trimming while you were in the shower?" He reached down between her legs and slid his fingers over her mons. A thin strip of hair, but otherwise clean shaven. "Ah, you did." He laughed when the bright blush appeared on her cheeks.

"You can't hide your reactions, and it's fucking beautiful," he said softly. He removed his thumb from her mouth.

"You're just trying to be an ass," she snapped, bending down to pick up the towel, but he kicked it away from her grasp.

"I don't have to try hard, I'm told. But I think it's what you like—you don't have to guess with me. I tell you the truth, and I don't sugarcoat anything."

"I'm cold." She reached again for the towel.

"Hmm, first you take away my razor, and now you're lying?"

Melinda stood with her toes touching his. "You like seeing me naked? Fine. Have a good look at my ass while I walk away from you." She swayed her hips as she sauntered out of the bathroom.

Oh, she was going to get exactly what she wanted. He'd played with little brats before, and she was definitely itching for a spanking.

He made his way into the bedroom and found her standing at the foot of the bed, her hands on her hips. Her robe lay on the bed only a few inches from her, but she hadn't put it on.

"If you wanted a spanking to warm up, all you had to do was ask."

She laughed. "I'm not— That's not— Why would I—"

He opened the dresser drawer and pulled out a small round paddle and a hairbrush then placed them side by side on the bed.

"Pick."

"What?" She glanced up at him then the implements.

"You wanted to play, so let's play. Pick the one you want." He folded his arms across his chest and dropped his chin. Intimidation wouldn't work with her, he already knew, but he so loved the way she worried at her lip when he glowered at her.

Looking like a kid who'd gotten caught staring at a naughty magazine, she fidgeted in front of him.

"Ten seconds to choose, or I'll use both, and this gets a little less fun."

She didn't have a choice here. She was getting her ass smacked if only because he wanted to do it. Which would be a problem if she didn't love it that way, too.

"Ten, nine, eight..."

"Fine!" She snatched up the hairbrush and thrust it at him.

He took the brush from her and grabbed her hand, spinning her around and bending her over his arm. She struggled to get her footing right, but he wasn't waiting. He brought the brush down hard on her ass again and again.

Melinda cried out, but he continued. She danced from one foot to the other, but she wasn't going anywhere.

"Little brats get their asses tanned," he said as he continued to spank her ass, his cock hardening to point of pain at the sight before him.

"I wasn't—"

"Yes, you were." He smacked her again and again until she stopped struggling. Tossing the brush to the bed, he used his hand to massage and rub her bright-red ass.

"You don't have to pick a fight with me, Melinda. I'll always be willing to see this ass wiggle over my lap, strapped to my bed, or bent over a table." He cupped her ass cheek and squeezed.

She stiffened. Ah, he'd struck the truth. She would never be able to fully hide from him, but she wasn't quite ready to accept it. For now, he'd take what she could give him.

His fingers slipped between her thighs, finding her wet and wanting.

"I want you on your knees." He pushed her to the floor. Bright-green eyes looked up at him. No tears and no more indecision. He'd broken through the wall and found the other side.

He caressed her cheekbone with his thumb. "Sweet girl. When will you stop trying to hide from me?"

She didn't say a word, but she didn't need to. Her hands flattened on his thighs, just below the hem of his boxers.

"If you want something, you ask." He traced the shell of her ear with his finger.

"I just wanted to put my towel on," she whispered.

"Why? Didn't like me seeing you naked, or you didn't like how easily your body reacted to seeing me?" He would have the truth. Pushing her a little each time would eventually break the dam.

Her throat worked when she swallowed, and he could see the fight-or-flight tug-of-war building up again.

"Hmm, if you're not going to answer me, maybe we should put your mouth to better use."

Her eyes darted to his cock pressing against his boxers. Her pretty pink tongue ran along her lips. He was being an asshole, letting her avoid talking to him by getting his own needs met. She grabbed his boxers and pulled them down, springing his cock free.

He was used to women doing as he said in bed. They wanted his cock, and he'd been willing to give them what they were looking for. But it was different with Melinda.

She aimed to keep him from a conversation, but she needed him to take her. She needed to feel his power in order for her to free herself of her worries. Soon, he'd make her tell him everything, make her give over those worrisome thoughts to him. But for now, he'd give what she needed and what he craved.

Her fingers wrapped around his shaft, drawing his cock to her mouth.

"Fuck, baby. Harder, I want to really feel you." He laid his hand on her head but didn't push or pull her.

The moment her tongue touched him, he growled. Fuck she was a sweet thing. Too innocent for the life she'd been raised in, too pure for the life he'd give her, but none of that mattered. She was his, and he wasn't letting go.

"Suck hard, sweet girl. Suck hard." He thrust his hips forward when she took his cock into her mouth. Warm and sweet and sensual. Fuck she felt good. So fucking good.

She ran her mouth down the length of him on one side then the other, getting him soaked before stroking him.

"Ah, fuck, sweet girl." He fisted her hair, but still gave her free motion. He just needed to get closer to her, to have the dynamic wash over both of them.

He thrust forward, hitting her throat. When she tried to move back, he held her firmly. "No, don't fucking move." He began gyrating his hips, pulling out to let her breathe then plowing forward.

She gripped his thighs, bracing herself on him as he began

to face fuck her. A moan escaped her, creating a vibration over his cock.

"Fuck." He withdrew all the way out, saliva still attaching them from her lips to the tip of his cock. "Open again. Wide, sweet girl, open wide."

She swallowed then obeyed without hesitation. Again, he thrust forward, not giving her a moment to adjust. "Swallow, that's a good girl, swallow my cock down." He pushed and as her throat relaxed around him, he inched farther down.

Feeling the end barreling down on him, he yanked free. She gasped for air and wiped the spit from her lips. Tears ran down her cheeks, but when her eyes met his, he saw pure arousal burning bright. She didn't simply like being on her knees sucking his cock, she fucking loved his power, his dominance.

"On the bed," he ordered and released her hair. She scrambled to obey, not throwing a smart-ass remark or giving him a look of disapproval. Fuck, he loved her this way. Sweet submissive. Compliant. Ready to be fucked and cherished.

He kicked off his boxers and climbed onto the bed, shoving her thighs apart. No preamble given or needed, he thrust his cock straight into her pussy up to the hilt. She cried out with the sudden invasion but bucked up at him. Wanting more?

Fuck, she was perfect.

"Erik," she panted, arching her hips.

"I know, sweet girl, I know." He pulled out and flipped her over on her belly. "Stick that ass up for me." He smacked her still-pink cheeks.

She pushed up to her hands and knees, glancing over her shoulder at him, smoldering and needy. He could see her so clearly in moments like this. When her walls fell down, and she let her real self free.

"Push back at me," he ordered, sliding the tip of his dick into her warmth.

She thrust her ass toward him, swallowing him whole in one movement. He grabbed her hips. His mind reeled from the power of her submission.

"Erik, don't stop. Don't stop," she urged and bucked at him again. He reached around her, finding the swollen, slick nub. She moaned, the sweetest fucking sound he'd ever heard, and slapped the pillow.

"What's wrong?" he asked, grinning at her naked form.

"Harder, Erik. Please." She looked so sweet when she begged him. He flicked her clit, and her eyes rolled up behind her lids.

"You want to come for me, sweet girl?" he asked as he plowed into her again and again. Whatever thoughts he had of tormenting her with delay had flown out the window the moment his cock sank into her.

"Yes, yes. Yes." She was animalistic in her moments, matching his energy. "Please."

He rolled her clit beneath the pad of his middle finger, pressing down hard and rubbing fast then slow while he sank his cock into her over and over again.

"Oh fuck!" she screamed, and her pussy clenched around him. His eyes flew open as his own orgasm ripped through him. He fucked harder, another pump then one more, and he stilled, letting the electricity make its way through his body.

Her breathing was ragged and heavy when he slipped from her and rolled onto the bed. Dragging her to his side, he clamped his arm around her. She wasn't going anywhere yet.

Her hand rested on his chest, playing with his medallion. He craned his neck and kissed her head. She was too perfect. He didn't deserve a woman so right for him.

"You wear this all the time." She picked up the silver wolf head. "Why a wolf?"

He covered her hand with his, pressing it flat against him.

"Rawling," he answered.

"Yeah, that's your last name, so?" She snuggled closer to his body.

"Our last name," he corrected with a pinch to her hip. "It means wolf. My mother gave it to me when I graduated high school."

"You've never mentioned your parents."

"Not much to mention. My mother married into the Rawling family to get away from her older brother—my uncle. My father's family controlled the underground gambling rings in the area, but once gambling became legal, he went legitimate." He squeezed her to him, sensing she was going to start backing off any second. "He owned his own casino—until my uncle sabotaged everything"

She tensed. "He didn't like your father?"

"He didn't like things he didn't control, and he couldn't control my parents. The casino my father owned went under, he was forced to sell."

"Did he...did he hurt them?"

"No, not physically. He choked off any hope my father had of rebuilding, but, by that time he'd done that, my father was already ill."

"I'm so sorry," she said, and she meant it. No social-pressured words for her, she truly understood what it had been like for him to watch his father slowly wither away to nothing.

"And your mom?"

He let out a hard breath. There had been no preparations for her death. "If you ask Ian, he'll say she died of a broken heart, but her doctor said it was a heart attack. Six months after my father."

"That's horrible." She tucked herself deeper into his embrace. It had been. And she knew the pain better than anyone else. She'd lost her mother and father to a tragedy. In one split second, her world had crashed down.

And years later, he walked into her life and did it again.

"What about your parents?" he asked, turning the subject. Guilt wouldn't get them anywhere. What was done was done. They needed to find a way to move forward.

"My mother fell in love with my father when they were in high school. When she came home from college, he'd swept in and married her." Melinda dropped her leg over his. "They seemed happy enough, I suppose. My father worked a lot, so sometimes they would argue. But nothing so dangerous as the life your uncle lived. What happened to him, anyway?"

"His son wanted what wasn't his and my uncle wouldn't let it go. They got greedy and broke oaths. They went after Ash and his wife." Erik didn't know exact details, but he'd pieced together enough of the puzzle on his own. Ash wasn't to be touched, and the other families took the breaking of an oath seriously. His uncle and cousin had been found dead days later. No investigation needed or encouraged.

"These are men you want to work with?" she asked with hesitation.

"No. Some I'll have to have to work with, but not like my uncle. We're staying legit. The way my father wanted." Erik trailed his fingers down Melinda's arm.

"What about your grandparents?" he asked, taking the spot light off the rot of his family tree.

She laughed. "They were like two peas in a pod...well... except for Gramps gambling issues. But I never heard them fight, I could tell because Gramps would make breakfast the next morning. His way, I suppose, of apologizing."

Erik rested his chin on her head, taking in the warmth of

her body pressed against his. An easy morning. When was the last time he'd had that?

"Your uncle didn't have a wife?" She surprised him with her question.

"He did. She gave him Marcus, his only son. She killed herself when we were in high school." Kristoff barely took a day off to mourn her. The asshole.

"He wasn't good to her?"

"My uncle and cousin weren't good to anyone but themselves."

"He was very powerful, though, your uncle?" It was refreshing and odd to find someone who didn't know the ins and outs of the world his family lived in.

"He was a coward. Controlling a woman with fear isn't being in control."

She lifted her head up and grinned at him. "Yet, you threaten me with your belt?"

He kissed the tip of her nose. "Are you afraid of me? Or my belt?"

"It's a lot worse than I thought it would be—the belt, not you." She rested her cheek back on his chest. A tidal wave of relief washed through him with her acknowledgment.

"If I thought you wouldn't gain anything by it, I wouldn't have taken my belt to your ass. I wouldn't have even approached the subject." He would have starved the beast within him, but he wouldn't have forced her into doing what was against her will.

Melinda sat up, looking down at him with her hair loose from the bun hanging around her face. Perfectly framing a soft, genuine smile.

The one he'd been waiting for.

The one he'd been ready to kill for.

CHAPTER 18

Melinda stepped onto the pavement outside the public library, her heart light. Erik had kept her in bed for most of the morning, growling at anyone who knocked on the door. She hadn't minded his caveman tactics. Especially since she benefited from them so amazingly. The man knew exactly what buttons to press and in precisely what order.

"You don't have to stay with me, Nico. I'm going to be here a few hours. It will get boring." Melinda stopped short of the door he held open for her. He'd been on babysitting duty for the past several days. Erik claimed it was for safety but wouldn't go into more detail.

"I'll grab a book. I'll be fine. But I don't understand why you don't do your writing at home," Nico said.

"I'm comfortable here." She shrugged and headed inside. The steady peace between Erik and her made the transition a bit easier to swallow, and his brothers were kind—never showing her an ounce of disrespect. But it wasn't her home. How could she ever find full peace in a stranger's home?

Nico followed her in his usual manner. He picked up a book from the shelf and skimmed through the pages. During his stint as her babysitter, he'd seemed to become more interested in reading.

"Here. I think you'll like this one." She handed him a book.

His gaze skimmed over the cover and laughed. "This is a romance."

She grinned. "You could use a little in your life, I think. You spend too much time babysitting me and running errands for Erik."

He frowned. "I'm here to protect you not babysit you. And Erik is family. You're family."

"I didn't mean to imply anything." She hadn't intended to insult the man. "It was silly. A joke." She reached for the book, but he tucked it against his chest.

"I know someone who might like this one."

She grinned. "I didn't realize you were seeing someone."

His brow furrowed, and the dark expression Erik wore at times crossed his features. "I'm not."

She didn't push for any more information from him; he wouldn't give it even if she tried. Melinda found an empty table and unpacked her laptop, getting her station ready to work.

"So, how did you get stuck with me three days in a row? Ian doesn't want to hang out in the library?" she joked, sitting down on the hard chair.

"He's been busy with his own project." Nico said, skimming right over any details that would give her more insight into the Rawling businesses.

Melinda logged into the computer and brought up her current project. One more chapter and the first draft would be complete.

"What is he doing here?" Nico stood up from his spot at the table and positioned himself in front of Melinda.

She peeked around him. "I've seen him before," she said. "At the party Erik took me to. They spoke."

"It's Bertucci."

Melinda pushed her chair back to see him walking straight for them, his gaze locked on Nico as though advancing on an adversary.

"Nico." Bertucci gave a curt nod.

"Mr. Bertucci," Nico responded in kind. Neither of them offered a hand in greeting.

"Mrs. Rawling." Bertucci leaned to the left to give her a smile.

Melinda moved to her feet, sidestepping Nico to present herself. "Hello." She held out her hand, a small gesture meant to cool off the tension rising between them.

Bertucci took it, wrapping his fat fingers around hers. His palm felt cold and sweaty.

"We weren't properly introduced at the Annex party. My name is Michael Bertucci."

"I remember Erik telling me. It's nice to see you again." She forced civility to her tone, but her insides cringed. This man reeked of Old-World power and corruption. His faux pleasantries couldn't hide the dangerous man beneath the false smile.

"I hope you enjoyed your dinner the other evening."

"Oh! Yes. Thank you by the way." Her cheeks heated.

"It was my pleasure. When I heard of your wedding, I was only regretful I was unable to attend. Your husband's uncle was a close friend. It would have been an honor to see his nephew married, and to such a beautiful woman."

Nico stepped closer to her, his shoulder pressed against hers.

"What brings you to the library of all places?" Nico sounded more like Erik with his hard tone. His alarm bells must have been sounding; she'd never heard him use that tone before.

"I'm checking out a book for my daughter," he answered without looking away from Melinda. His gaze left a thin coat of slime behind.

Melinda eyed his hands, empty.

"You have been given a book deal, I understand. More congratulations are in order."

Melinda's spine tingled, sending a loud buzzing alert to her brain. No one outside the family knew about the publishing offer. Erik's lawyers were still reviewing the documents.

"It's in the very early stages," Melinda acknowledged slowly, unsure of how to tread these new waters. She wasn't used to word games or manipulations. A map should have been given to her with her new life. She had no idea how to navigate these roads.

"Congratulations anyway. You're working here?" He gave a pointed look to her computer.

"Surrounded by books. What better way to create?" She forced a light touch to her words, suddenly wishing she'd found a dark corner of Erik's house to work instead.

"Hmm." Bertucci scanned her with his stoic gaze. He hid well behind his all-business appearance, but she sensed the anger in him. It rolled off him like the dense fog of early morning.

"I should probably get to work. It was nice seeing you again, Mr. Bertucci." She kept her hands at her sides.

His gaze flicked to Nico.

"I expected a call from your brother, but he must not have my number." He dug a business card from the inside pocket of his well-tailored suit and held it out to Nico.

"I'll be sure he gets this." Nico plucked the card from between Bertucci's two fingers.

"Good." Bertucci slung his sight onto Melinda. His lips curled inward with his forced grin. "It was a pleasure to see you again. I do hope your husband knows what a great treasure he holds. It would be a grave mistake to underestimate your worth, my dear."

Bertucci inclined his head and walked away, leaving Nico and Melinda standing at the table watching him leave.

Nico shoved the business card into the back pocket of his jeans and turned to the table. He shut her laptop.

"Wait. Nico. What are you doing?" She tried to grab the computer, but he had it in the bag and slung over his shoulder before she could be of much use.

"You're not working here today," he said.

"Why? Because he scared you?" she goaded.

"That was a veiled threat." He jerked a thumb behind him.

"I'm sure it was meant to sound that way. This is a public library, Nico. He can't do anything to me, here. I'm not letting some overgrown ego get in the way of my life." She reached for her bag. "I have enough of that with your brother."

"Erik won't like you staying here after that." Nico held fast to the strap, keeping her from winning the tug-of-war.

"Erik doesn't like anything," she snapped. It wasn't true. Not really. He seemed to enjoy spending the evenings with her. Mostly in silence, playing a game of chess. Once he'd found out she knew how to play, it had become the one thing- outside of the bedroom- they held in common.

"Melinda." Nico tugged harder on the bag.

"Oh hell." She let go and threw her hands in the air. "Fine. If you want to run scared with your tail tucked between your legs, let's go."

"That's not—"

"But you're taking me to Into the Woods first. I want coffee." She shoved the chair beneath the table, disturbing several people sitting nearby. She mouthed an apology as she maneuvered toward the front door.

CHAPTER 19

*E*rik slammed the front door of his car and jogged up the steps into the house.

Bertucci had gotten to Melinda. Spoken to her, looked at her. He would ring Nico's neck for allowing it, and then he'd deal with Bertucci.

"Before you get all—" Nico began.

"Why didn't you haul her ass out of there once you saw him?" Erik pounced the moment he came into view.

"And insult him with the blatant snub?" Nico's jaw tightened. He was right, of course. To have given Bertucci a cold shoulder would have insulted him. And to offend a man like him could be opening up an old wound they were trying to close.

"What did he say? Exactly. Every fucking word, Nico." Erik brushed past him and brought him to his office, kicking the door closed.

Nico relayed the conversation again. He'd already gone over it twice on the phone after getting Melinda home, but Erik wanted to hear it again.

"What the fuck is his obsession with her?" Erik picked up

his phone and tapped hard against the screen. "Ash might have something by now. He was looking into a few things for me."

"You said you wanted to keep him out of this. After what Marcus and Uncle Kristoff did, why would he want to help us?"

"Yes, *they* did. Not us." Erik sent the message. "If anyone understands separating from the evil of the older generation, it's him. He has a contact at the police department. We need that."

"Why?" Nico asked.

"There's something, a connection between Melinda's family and Bertucci. She mentioned he looked familiar to her, but she couldn't place him. It might have been a long time ago." Erik rubbed his temples. He'd thought finishing the fucking list and getting the inheritance from his uncle's estate would be the most difficult hurdle. But every step seemed to bring new trouble to him.

Erik's phone dinged, and he refocused his attention. "That stuff you got from Ash the other night. Is Ian still working on it?"

"Yeah, he's out today handling it. He won't tell me how, though." Nico scratched behind his ear. "He's more secretive than ever."

"Leave him be. He's finding his own way." Erik read the next set of messages. "That's good at least."

"What?" Nico asked. "Did you find out something?"

"Yes. Melinda's grandmother isn't in any danger. She didn't take the flight Ian found, but she did get on a train headed up north."

"Was she with anyone?" Nico pressed.

Erik shook his head. "No. Alone and with a suitcase."

"She just ran out like that?"

"As far as she knew, Melinda wasn't going home." Erik put his phone away. "The plan wasn't to let her, remember?"

"We should find a way to contact her," Nico said with more force. "If she learns the situation has changed, she'll come home. Or we can bring Melinda to her."

Erik shook his head. "Not yet. I want some answers, and I think her grandmother might be the key to figuring out Bertucci's obsession with my wife."

"So, what do you want to do, then?" Nico crossed his arms over his chest, frustration seeping from his stance.

"We're going to continue on like normal. I have a meeting set up with Peter Titon tonight to discuss a real estate deal. He owns the strip of buildings across the street from Tower. It's the perfect location for the casino and hotel."

The muscles in Nico's throat worked into a tight knot. "And what about Melinda's grandmother? And Bertucci? Should we ignore all of that while you keep pushing for your damn casino?"

Erik pressed his thumb against the gold band on his finger. "No. Once I have a few answers, I'll have a better idea of how to proceed." Erik advanced on his brother, keeping his glare locked with his. "You don't go charging in on a man like Bertucci. Do you know how much power he holds?"

"I didn't mean to attack him—"

"Our uncle didn't just get himself killed with his stupidity. He ruined the entire fucking family, Nico. Where is everyone?" Erik held out his arms and glanced around. "Nowhere. They all fucking ran off or joined other crews."

"They'll come back now that you're in charge." Nico's chin thrust forward. "Raul and Joey will for sure."

Erik waved off the comment. "Good. Then they can be first in line for the busboy jobs." Erik would never repay their distant cousins' cowardice with any piece of the business.

"Kristoff had a solid business. As much as we all fucking hated him, there was money to be had."

"You want to start selling women, Nico? Is that it? You want to open up the basement and start collecting some stock?" Erik's neck heated. Nico had never spoken of going back into the shit Kristoff had dealt with.

"No. Of course not. He had other dealings, not the girls—"

Erik inhaled a long breath. "Yeah, and Jansen and Bertucci ate up all of those deals. Most of his men went to work for Jansen. This family isn't going down that path. The casino will be enough."

Nico's tongue ran over his teeth. "For you. It's enough for you."

"What the hell does that mean?"

"It means Ian's right. Everything we've been doing here is so you can get that fucking casino. If we had half the manpower that came with putting our hat in the ring, we'd be able to find Melinda's grandmother faster. We wouldn't be relying on the fucking Titons to get us in contact with someone at the police department who is willing to dig around for us."

"We will find her grandmother, and we will figure out this Bertucci mess. All you have to do is protect her when I can't be there. That's it, Nico."

"Right. I'll play bodyguard while you keep working toward everything you want with no fucking regard for what anyone else wants."

Erik took a step toward him but checked himself. "Why the sudden desire to get your hands dirty?"

Nico blew out a long breath. "You have what you wanted. You have the inheritance, and now you'll get your casino."

"No. We have the casino. It's our venture, not mine alone."

Nico shook his head. "And if I don't want the casino?"

Erik's jaw slacked. Nico never mentioned going off on his own before. He never objected to his elder brother's plans. Something had changed.

"Then you take your money and figure out what you want to do with it." There was enough money in the Komisky estate to be split three ways and keep them all worry-free for the rest of their lives.

Nico wiped his hand across his mouth.

"You decide what you want and let me know." Erik's phone dinged. "Where's Melinda now?"

"Last I saw, in the kitchen."

"I'm going to go talk with her. I'm taking her to Tower tonight for my meeting with Peter. So, you don't have to play bodyguard tonight." Erik brushed past him and opened the door to the office.

Melinda tumbled forward, crashing straight into his chest.

CHAPTER 20

The glint in Erik's eye softened Melinda's apprehension. He wasn't angry with her, but she could feel the tension in him.

His conversation with Nico had left him stressed. But he wasn't going to admit it with words. She straightened, unsure of what he would do, but positive she would enjoy it.

"You were eavesdropping," he said in a low, calculated voice when she got closer to him.

"I was…" No sense in denying it. "Yes. I was. What are you two arguing about?"

"Business opportunities." He surprised her by being open and not dodging the question.

"Business?" she asked, leaning to see Nico staring at her with a half-cocked grin.

"Yes." He trailed a fingertip down the length of her nose. "But I don't want to talk about that right now."

She licked her lips. "What do you want to do, then?"

His eyes narrowed, exaggerating the little wrinkles around them. "Short answer—you."

He cupped her elbow and led her away from his office and upstairs.

She thought about her afternoon. All the questions she wanted answers for, and all the worry that would probably bubble up if she found out the truth. There weren't many situations in her life that left her on edge, but that short conversation with Mr. Bertucci had flipped a switch in her. Her skin felt electrified, like she would burst at the least trigger.

She could spend the rest of the day worrying about her future, about the new danger lurking around every damn corner, or she could follow Erik's lead. His plan held more appeal. She could worry and plot later. Right now, she needed him.

He stopped outside their bedroom.

"In there?" She could see the frustration in his eyes, the exhaustion from the world resting on his shoulders. Getting his inheritance didn't alleviate his burdens, but she wasn't entirely clued in to what they were. She knew enough to know he'd be weighed down with them if he didn't let off some of the pressure.

"Yes. Take off your clothes." He stepped in front of the door, blocking her passage.

She cast a worried glance down the hallway.

"Out here?"

He nodded. "Absolutely."

His lips spread into a wide, suggestive grin. The man was impossible. He enjoyed her discomfort.

"You should hurry. If anyone comes along and sees you, I'll have to punish you for exposing yourself."

"And I'm already in trouble?" she asked, hands slipping to the hem on her sweater.

He nodded with raised eyebrows. "The worst kind." The heavy arousal weighing down his words contradicted the glare he gave her. She had no doubt she was in trouble, but it wasn't the idea of a spanking sending her a tremor of fear up her spine. She was in jeopardy of losing herself to him, to whatever was going to happen in that room.

She pulled her sweater off and quickly shoved her jeans down her legs. Her bra and panties were next, and she bundled everything up and held it out in front of her. She needed work on the art of seduction, but, at the moment, she only thought about getting her naked self inside the room.

Marianne could be coming up to clean at any moment.

Erik stood to the side, letting her pass. Quickly, she stepped inside.

"I thought of chaining you to this bed the first night you were here." He walked past her and lifted one of the iron cuffs attached to the bedposts.

"You didn't, though," she said softly.

"No. I didn't." He dropped the cuff and walked to the wardrobe on his side of the bed and opened it.

It wasn't a wardrobe at all. It was a toy chest. Whips, floggers, paddles, and more hung from hooks on the insides of the doors and inside the cabinet. He fingered the toys, running his hands over the thick falls of the floggers and the flat surfaces of the paddles. Melinda's ass clenched when he paused.

He plucked a thick, heavy flogger from its hook and walked to the end of the bed. Crooking his finger, he beckoned her forward.

She stepped to the post, bundles of nerves dancing in her stomach. The stress of his day had brought him to this point. He needed her as much as she needed him. This dance he was beginning with her, it was their dance.

He kept his dark gaze on her as he grabbed one wrist and then the other and secured them over her head. The loud click of the cuffs echoed between them, but she never lost her focus on him.

"Hold this for me, sweet girl." He draped the flogger over her shoulder. The handle rested on her chest, the thick leather falls cascading over her naked back.

She pressed her forehead to the cool wood of the post, hearing him behind her. His suit jacket fell to the bed, his belt unbuckled, and the familiar, titillating sound of his zipper lowering came next. He was undressing. Matching her vulnerability by baring his body to her.

Melinda was chained to the post, though, and she didn't lose sight of who had the upper hand. She gripped the post and waited.

The flogger glided over her skin when he took it from her.

"Your skin is so pretty, so untouched." He dug his nails between her shoulder blades and dragged them down. "At least it was."

The burn was instant, and she hissed, wiggling from him. But there was nowhere to go. She was bound. Helpless.

His fingers dug into her again, and she braced herself, letting the pain seep into her soul as he marked her again. A rush of pleasure filled her when he lifted his hand. Her pussy wept for wanting him.

"Have you been flogged?" he asked, removing his touch from her. The disconnection from him immediate, a chill covered her.

"Once," she answered, no longer willing to hide from him. Knowing he would find her, he would always find her.

"On your ass or your back?" He swished the flogger against her thighs.

"My ass." Her body clenched, waiting for the first real slash of the flogger, but it didn't come.

"I'm going to mark your back, your ass, and your thighs.

And you're going to be a good wife for me and take every bit of it. And when I'm done, I'm going to fuck you. Exactly like you are, bound and held for me."

Her breath caught. Everything he described should have her screaming, yet she spread her feet and braced herself for the first lick.

"Fuck, you're perfect, Melinda. Absolutely perfect." He ran his fingertips over her sensitized skin, tracing the scratches he'd inflicted. "This is going to hurt, baby. Scream as much as you need."

She grabbed the post harder, ready for him to begin.

Nothing would have prepared her. The pain knocked her breath from her body. Her eyes went wide, her mouth poised in a frozen scream.

Again, he struck her. He moved with precision up and down her ass, to her thighs, across her shoulder blades. Careful not to hit sensitive areas, knowing exactly where to hit, how much force to use, to elicit the sounds he craved.

Her voice returned, and she cried out when the falls wrapped around her hip, delivering a sting to her side.

"Such a sweet sound." He lashed her again.

The worry, the fear, the confusion washed away as he brought the flogger down over and over again. All she felt, all she heard was him. Her nipples hardened, her legs weakened and her need for his touch, for his flesh against hers, grew in leaps and bounds.

"Erik!" she cried out when the flogger lashed across her thighs.

He paused and pressed his naked chest to her back. She arched her spine, trying to lessen the impact, and moved up to her toes.

"There isn't an inch of you that doesn't wear my mark." He bit down on her earlobe.

She blinked, feeling her cheeks wet with tears she didn't

recall forming. He'd brought her out of her own mind, out of her body, and now she was settling in.

The flogger fell to the floor at her feet. His hands moved around her body until he cupped her breasts, kneading and tweaking her hardened nipples. She moaned, rolling her head back.

"It's a good thing you kept your hair up today. But I want it down now." He worked the elastic band out of the messy bun and ran his fingers through her tresses.

"Do you know why?" he asked while playing with her hair.

"No," she whispered. Her mind wasn't ready for coherent thought.

He wrapped her hair around his fist and yanked her head back, kissing her cheek. "Because you cry so pretty when I pull your hair." He licked the tear falling from her eye and yanked tighter. She winced at the burn in her scalp.

His cock slipped between her ass cheeks. "It makes my cock so hard when you cry like that, sweet girl."

"Erik. Don't." She wiggled her ass when he started to pull away.

"Don't leave you? Don't fuck you? Do you think you have a say?" He pushed her head until her forehead was flush with the post again.

"N-no."

"Do you want me to lay you down and make sweet love to you?"

Another tear slipped down her cheek. It would be wrong if he was gentle. It was his strength, his power she craved, she needed.

"No," she said in a hard tone.

His cock thrust into her pussy, catching her off guard.

"Push that ass out for me." He slapped her hip. She arched more, giving him what he wanted—what she needed.

One hand fisting her hair hard, the other grabbing her waist, he plowed into her. She sucked in air, only to lose it somewhere in her chest.

He moved his hand around her, finding her clit and rubbing it in circles.

"Fucking sweet girl. Fucking sweet, sweet pussy," he growled, thrusting harder into her.

She grabbed at the post. The metal cuffs bit into her wrists with the jerky movements, but her body only responded to his thick cock fucking her.

"Should I let you come? You were a naughty girl, eavesdropping, weren't you?" His words were harsh, his breath hot against her ear.

"Yes. Erik. I—oh fuck." One more flick of his fingers, and she came unglued. She bucked her hips back, wanting more pressure, needing his cock to thrust harder. He tugged her scalp giving her the right amount of burn.

All sound stopped other than the sound of her own voice. She screamed the rafters down as she exploded. All nerve endings fired, dragging her from any logical moment and thrusting her in a clouded utopia.

He unraveled from her hair then gripped her hips. She held on to the post, keeping herself up while he continued to buck behind her. Even with the haze of her orgasm fading, she moaned with each thrust of his cock. Full and stretched and wonderfully used, she matched his movements, drawing him to the very edge he'd thrown her over.

He thrust hard and held her steady with a growl.

She collapsed against the post, hugging it to her chest as he trailed kisses along her shoulder.

"My sweet girl," he whispered.

The tension in his body disappeared. He'd worked out his stress and taken hers with it. With ease, he unlatched the cuffs and caught her as she sank. Lifting her in his arms, he carried her across the room and through the adjoining door.

Gently, he placed her on the bed and pulled a blanket over her naked, quivering body. Like everything with him, the afternoon had been intense and left her limp and wrung out.

His footsteps were soft on the carpeting as the drawers opened and closed. The closet door creaked, but she didn't open her eyes, afraid she'd have to see reality again. And she wasn't ready for that yet.

The bed dipped when he sat beside her, running his hands over her arm. "Your back is going to be sore for at least a day. The skin didn't break, but you have some welts."

She nodded but still couldn't bring her eyes to meet his. He might see the truth.

"Rest here, and don't leave this bedroom until I come for you. I have a few more meetings to deal with then I'll be back." He pressed a soft, warm kiss to her cheek. "You are perfect, Melinda, fucking perfect," he whispered.

Without opening her eyes, she touched his hand. Needing to feel him, to sense the calm in him. She'd done that. She'd given him that peace. And he'd done the same for her.

CHAPTER 21

Even with the near zero temperatures, a line formed outside Tower. Erik gripped Melinda's gloved hand tighter as they stepped around the front of the line and into the warmth of the club.

"That was easy," Melinda teased.

"There are perks to being my wife." He smiled. It was hard not to after the afternoon she'd given him. After Nico did his best to blacken his mood, Melinda had been there to brighten it again. She'd seen his frustration, but she didn't run from him or goad him. She'd followed him and let him take her into his darkness with him. And in the end, they were both warmed with her light.

"I suppose so." She stuffed her gloves into the pockets then shed her coat, revealing the sleek black dress she wore. The neckline plunged into a deep vee, but offered only a glimpse of her soft curves. The long sleeves and low hemline covered almost every inch of her body from the eyes of the other men. At first, he'd been happy with the dress. No one would put eyes on what was his, but now, he saw the seductiveness of the outfit. Just enough of her curves were hugged by the dress to draw his eye, and those around him.

He glared down a man whose attention had honed in on Melinda. It didn't take much more than that for him to scuttle off into the crowd.

Melinda smoothed her hands over her arms. Even by the coat check, it was still a bit chilly.

Erik handed her coat to the clerk and led her toward the elevators.

"Erik Rawling. I'm meeting with Peter," Erik explained to the guard at the elevator. Only VIP pass holders and private rentals were allowed above the first floor of the club.

"Are you sure it's okay I'm here?" Melinda asked once they were alone in the elevator.

"Why wouldn't it be?"

"I thought women weren't exactly involved with the business you do." As they rose to the second floor, she watched the dancers below through the glass wall of the elevator.

"I think you've seen too many movies," he said. "Besides, the business I'm doing with Peter is completely legitimate. There's nothing you can't hear or repeat." He slipped his fingers through hers, feeling the softness of her skin in his hand.

The elevator door slid open to reveal Peter Titon with a beautiful woman at his side, waiting to greet them.

"Erik." Peter held out his hand. "Glad you could make it. I know it's a little busy here, but we'll have a private room, so it won't be so loud." He turned to his wife. "My wife, Azalea."

"Nice to meet you." Erik nodded to the beauty standing before him. She hadn't extended her hand. Peter was not so different from Erik. Azalea wasn't just his wife, she was his—period—and no one touched her.

Melinda probably thought it archaic, but she didn't understand the appeal of such possession. Yet.

"Melinda, my wife." Erik wrapped his arm around her, gently pressing her to his side.

Peter gave his nod in greeting, but Azalea stepped forward and placed her hands on Melinda's shoulders. Erik released her. Offending Azalea could fuck up his dealings with Peter. Just because they weren't operating entirely within Old World rules, didn't mean some didn't still apply.

"I love this dress." Azalea hooked her hand through Melinda's elbow and led her away. "The room is this way. It's not as noisy, but we'll still be able to see the stage. Master Clintock is going to be showcased tonight."

Melinda peeked over her shoulder at Erik who fell into step beside Peter.

"Congratulations on your marriage," Peter fished as they passed several roped-off VIP seating.

"Thank you." Erik didn't need to get into the details of his relationship with Melinda. Peter knew what Erik's uncle had done with his will and would infer whatever he wanted when it came to Melinda.

"I ordered a bottle of white wine, but if you'd prefer red, I can call down for another bottle," Azalea was telling Melinda when they joined them in the private room.

The other VIP seating areas were only separated from one another by either a velvet rope or a curtain. This room was walled off from the others. There would be complete privacy.

"White is perfect, thank you." Melinda smiled and took the glass of wine Azalea offered her. She leaned in to listen as the other woman pointed out the stage and began explaining the night's events. Her attention was completely wrapped up in whatever Azalea was telling her, but Erik focused primarily on the ease of Melinda's body. No tension, no fake giggles or forced civility; everything about her warmth and kindness came from a genuinely gracious heart.

"Maybe we shouldn't have had the wives with us." Peter laughed, bringing Erik's attention back to their conversation. Erik had been caught up watching a glimmer of joy in Melinda's expression and hadn't heard a word Peter had been saying.

"It's fine." Erik cleared his throat and took a seat at the table beside Peter. "What is the show tonight?"

"Master Clintock is a sensual sadist. My security officer authorized the scene. I'm not entirely sure what he's up to this evening," Peter replied. "You did explain to your wife what she'd be seeing tonight, right?"

"She won't be shocked," Erik said, dragging his attention back to Peter again. Maybe bringing her had been a mistake. Too big a distraction when he was making such a large deal.

"I read the proposal you sent over. Are you sure you're going to be able to keep the casino clean?" Peter went straight to meat of the issue.

"All of my uncle's business dealings died with him. I have no ties and will have no ties to anything he touched. The Red Hood is going to be a hotel and casino, 100 percent legit," Erik assured him.

"This part of town has been on the decline for over a decade. I'm trying to rebuild it." Peter told Erik what he already knew.

He'd made offers on all the real estate within four square blocks in order to do it, too.

"We have the same goal, then." Erik leaned back in his chair. "My father's family grew up in this area. He would want it rebuilt like it was when he was a kid."

Peter nodded. "I'm glad to hear it. When do you plan to break ground?"

"Once we close on the property, we'll start construction within a month. I have the contracts all lined up."

"And the workers?" Peter's eyebrows rose.

"All local builders from this area. Uncorrupt as far as I know. But I'll be watching the project carefully."

"If my uncle was alive to see what I've built, what you're going to build, he'd probably die of another heart attack." Peter laughed. It was no secret how Peter and his cousin Ash felt about the old man. Samuel Titon had been cruel and vicious. The world was a better place without him.

"My uncle would probably have me killed if he were alive to see his money being put into a legitimate business," Erik agreed, his gaze wandering over to Melinda.

She sipped her wine, but her eyes flicked over to him. A soft blush covered her cheeks before she looked away.

"How is it really going with your new wife?" Peter asked, dragging him back to the conversation.

"It's fine. She's adjusting."

Peter laughed. "I'm not sure they are the ones who do the adjusting."

The lights dimmed over the main floor.

"The show's starting," Azalea said.

Peter stood and checked his watch. "Dinner will be up after the show."

Melinda scooted along the wall to the corner, giving Azalea and Peter room to stand beside each other with space between them. Erik came to stand behind her.

"Enjoying the wine?" he asked, taking the empty glass from her hand.

"It's good."

He placed the glass on the table. "You worked all afternoon. I thought you would have taken a longer nap." He trailed his fingers over her graceful neck. She'd stuffed her hair into a complicated updo, exposing the creamy flesh. He could easily forgive her for not leaving it down. It gave him better access to the tender spot behind her earlobe.

"I wanted to finish it."

"Ah." The spotlights turned on the main stage, and Erik dropped his hand to rest on her hip.

Master Clintock walked on stage, eliciting a hush over the crowd. The loud house music was switched out for a softer melody while a beautiful woman in a purple satin robe joined him. She stood beside the St. Andrew's cross and let the robe slip from her shoulders and pool to the floor.

A stagehand appeared from behind her and snatched the material, while two more men held her wrists up to the restraints. Master Clintock busied himself at a small table, inspecting his toys while the stagehands bound his playmate to the cross.

"He should be doing that, not them," Melinda whispered, though Erik didn't think she meant for him to hear it. He agreed with her, though. Settling her into the binds himself would increase the pleasure for both of them. Rendering her helpless against him set the stage.

Master Clintock brought out a pair of nipple clamps chained together.

"Hmm, I wonder what those would look like on you," he whispered, taking her earlobe between his teeth. A shudder ran through her, but she didn't speak.

He wrapped an arm around her waist, resting it below her breasts, propping them up.

"Have you had your nipples clamped before?" he asked softly, so as not to be overheard by Peter and his wife, although a quick glance in their direction, gave him confidence they were busy in their own conversation and wouldn't be paying them any attention soon.

"No," she whispered. Her hand came up to rest on his arm.

"Hmm, but you want them to be." He kissed the little spot behind her ear. She bent her head, giving him easier access.

Either the wine had taken away some of her apprehension or the scene unfolding on the stage was getting to her.

Clintock placed two weighted balls on the chain, pulling his girl's nipples downward.

"Maybe when we get home, if you ask very sweetly, I'll play with your tits." He gripped her hip. "Play with that sweet pussy of yours, too." He nipped her earlobe again. Her chest rose and fell faster as he spoke, as his fingers massaged beneath her breasts.

The woman cried out, wail carrying through the speakers into the private room. Melinda tensed at the sound.

"He's going to bring her right to the brink of orgasm and stop," Erik predicted.

"That would be cruel," she said softly, her nails biting into his arm. His thumb flicked over her nipple. Even through the material of the dress, he could feel the hardened peak.

Fuck dinner, he needed to get her home.

"Cruel can be fun," Erik promised. "Ah, there you see?" He moved his hand from her hip and pointed to the stage. Clintock had done exactly as Erik predicted, and the bound woman shook her head with frustration. "He's going to do it again." Erik chuckled in her ear. "You would be so fucking beautiful like that. Bound, spread open, and tormented with unfulfilled desire." He pressed his hard cock against her ass. Her hand flattened against the glass, making him chuckle.

Her full lips parted, and he imagined his cock sliding between them.

Another squeal blasted through the overhead speakers as the clamps were ripped off the submissive.

Melinda's fingers curled on the glass; she pressed her ass into his body. Erik gripped her wrist and brought it down from the window, settling it at her side.

"Shh, sweet girl. As soon as we get home. I promise." He kissed her neck again and released her, moving to stand beside her, blocking the other couple from seeing the heated flush of her cheeks and the dilation of her pupils.

His girl enjoyed the scene before her.

But she would fucking love what he planned for her at home.

CHAPTER 22

"Thank you so much for dinner. Everything was wonderful." Melinda hugged Azalea. At least, she assumed dinner was delicious; Erik had cleared his plate in record time. Melinda's nerve endings were firing off signals all over her body too fast for her to taste anything going into her mouth.

Just a few touches from Erik and she'd been ready to shove down his pants and ride him right there in the private room. Onlookers or not. And he'd known it.

"I hope we can get together soon." Azalea squeezed Melinda's hands.

"Of course. That would be fun."

"Do you have your phone?" Azalea asked.

Azalea snatched it before Melinda finished pulling it out of her purse. She tapped away and then handed it back.

"There. Now you have my number, and I sent a text to myself, so I'll have you in my phone, too."

"Perfect." Melinda grinned.

Azalea pulled her into another hug. "I know it's weird

right now, but give him a chance," she whispered then pulled away again.

"I...what?"

"I don't think he's as scary as he appears."

"And how do you know?" Melinda asked, glancing over at Erik who was finishing a conversation with Peter. His brows were down, and he had the same severe expression as usual. How did anyone ever get the nerve to talk to him if they didn't absolutely have to?

"Because I know that look." Azalea took Melinda's coat from the man who brought it up from the coat check. "Peter can glare a man to peeing himself, but when he turns it on me, all it does is...well, I've never wet myself yet." She winked.

"That's because he obviously loves you." Melinda shook her head and pulled her coat free from Azalea's grip. The girl had it bad for her husband. Melinda could envy her if she took enough time to examine it, but she'd accepted she wouldn't have anything like that in her life.

"I don't know Erik personally, but I hear things. He's not the sort of man to fake pleasantries."

"What does that mean?"

"Peter isn't the one who suggested they meet here at Tower or that we be included. That was all Erik." Azalea folded her arms. "Now, why would a man who didn't care at all for his wife insist she accompany him to a business dinner?"

Melinda didn't get a chance to answer the question. Erik came up behind her and took her coat, spreading it open for her. Even if he hadn't, she didn't have a good answer. She had assumed when he told her about the meeting, Peter had requested it.

"Ready?" Erik asked.

"Yeah." Melinda extended her hand to Peter. "Thank you so much for a wonderful evening."

Peter glanced at Erik before grasping her hand. "You did me a favor keeping my wife out of trouble for one night." He grinned and released her, sticking his hands in his pockets.

"Ignore him." Azalea stepped in front of her husband. "You have to let me know when your book is being released. I'm going to come up with some ideas to help market it."

"It's just the beginning stages. It could be a year or more."

Azalea was full of energy and high expectations. But she was living a fairytale; she had no reason not to.

"That's fine. Gives us plenty of time to build you a brand." Azalea nodded. "The more people who know your name before the book launches, the better. If you don't mind my nose sticking in your business, I'd love to help."

Erik wrapped his hand around Melinda, letting her know it was time to go.

"I think that would be great. As soon as I hear from my editor, I'll call you," Melinda said. For a while, Melinda had worried Erik's attorneys were going to scare off the publisher, but, in the end, they won, and her book was put under contract. She only had to finalize the contracts with a few signatures, and it would be done.

"I'll be accepting the offer you made on the property. My attorneys will get together with yours to sort out the other details." Peter shook Erik's hand, ending the night.

"Great. I'll let them know, and I'll get the contractors ready to start breaking ground."

Melinda watched Erik, noticing his jaw relax. He'd been worried. Such a strong man doubtful of his own power? She wondered how long he was going to let whatever his uncle had done color his future?

Though, he had his own sins to contend with; she should never forget that.

Erik walked to the elevator with Melinda's hand firmly grasped.

"Azalea does all the marketing for Peter. Maybe she could help with your casino?" Melinda said, breaking the silence in the elevator.

"She's going to be busy with your book, I think," Erik said as the elevator doors opened on the first floor, flooding them with hard beats from the music.

Melinda followed close behind Erik. He walked with his arm out, warding off the crowd while holding tight to her hand. He seemed to be protecting her, though she doubted there was really any danger.

Once outside, he opened the passenger door and waited for her to be safely seated before shutting it. Everything seemed to happen with precision where he was involved. He didn't need to call for his car; it was just there.

She fiddled with the zipper on her purse while he pulled into traffic.

"Erik. What happened to the other girls?" She poked the elephant sleeping in the back seat of the car.

His knuckles whitened around the steering wheel.

"I know there were more than just me. How many?" she pressed. The last few days had been peaceful, giving her hope of a future that didn't involve constant bickering and anger, but the lingering fear of what happened before still plagued her.

"You're the third," he answered in a clipped tone. He may not want to talk about it, but he wasn't going to shut her out either. Another small step, but she would tread lightly.

"And what happened with them? You sold them?" Her voice caught on the last bit of her question. When she first met him, she could see it, could see the cold calculated way of asking a price and taking the cash. But he wasn't that man now.

"One of them bought out her debts, the other—" He paused. "Yes. She was sold."

"To whom?"

"A powerful man who didn't want to waste time with courtship or marriage." He stopped at a red light and faced her. Guilt twisted his lips. "He's a safe man, Melinda. I made sure he wouldn't hurt her, and she could have rejected him. I gave her the option to keep looking. But it was a step up from the hell she'd been living in, so she agreed. The men who had sold them to my uncle in the first place weren't good men. They weren't like your grandfather."

"You're sure she's still safe? This man didn't trick you?" The questions popped out before she could filter them. Erik wasn't the sort of man who could be tricked.

"Ian's made it his mission to track both of them down and assure himself they are safe—and happy," Erik said.

"How?"

"That's his business." Erik accelerated when the light flipped green.

"Is Nico angry with you because of me?" Why not press for a little more information while he was willing to give it?

"No. He's angry because, now that he has money, he wants to follow our uncle's footsteps."

Melinda's throat clenched. She couldn't imagine Nico in the room in the basement. Doing horrible things to girls? Enjoying it?

"I don't know anything about your uncle or any of the things he was involved with, but I can't picture Nico doing —" She couldn't imagine Erik stalking into Grams' house and taking her away, but he had done it. She shouldn't forget how they ended up where they were.

"He wouldn't. He's young and stupid. He doesn't understand what comes with the power he wants. He never really saw my uncle for what he was. Nico was too young to know. My mother sheltered him more."

Melinda nodded. She didn't understand it all, but she grasped enough to know Erik didn't like the path his brother was taking. But would Erik be able to talk Nico away from it?

Erik parked in the attached garage. She took in the easy way he walked, the gentleness of his touch when he held her hand. This man wasn't as scary as he looked—Azalea was right. No matter how angry he got with her, he would never harm her. She sensed it. The good inside of him would blossom now that he was finished with his uncle's terms.

"I want to show you something." Erik laced his fingers with hers once they were inside the house and had shed their coats.

The house was quiet as they walked down the hall to the sitting room next to his office. Erik glanced over his shoulder before opening the door. She saw a flicker of uncertainty. Whatever he was going to show her was important.

Erik flipped on the light once she stepped inside. An office. The room had been converted to an office. Books lined an entire wall. She stepped in, walking to the leather-bound books. They were her books.

"I don't want you to feel like you need to leave your own home to find a comforting space to work."

"From my apartment?" She traced the gold lettering on her collection of Edgar Allen Poe.

"Yes. I had anything related to your writing or reading brought in here. The last coat of varnish on the desk finally dried, so I brought it in this morning." He ran his hand over the polished finish.

"You, you built this?" She asked, walking around the intricately designed desk. Stained in a dark cherry to match the bookshelves. The drawers were hand carved, with polished brass handles.

"It's beautiful," she whispered, running her hand over the carving. A wolf's head, matching the medallion he wore.

"Will it do?" he asked with a hitch in his voice. Was he uncertain she'd like it? Moreover, did he want her to like it?

"I love it." She grinned.

"I was putting some final touches on it. I thought just a desk and your books would keep you focused." His put his hands on his hips.

She stared at him for a long moment, taking in the sweet severity of his features and the absolute strength of his personality. This man, this man who could crush her with one snap of his fingers, had spent the past week building a desk for her. He'd given her a room solely for her to work.

"Thank you," she said softly, unable to face him any longer. He was breaching the distance between them. He wasn't supposed to do that. He was supposed to stay on his side of the line, and she would live happily ever after on her side. Alone.

His hands slipped from his waist to his belt. "Melinda."

She turned back, not sure what she expected from him anymore.

"Take off your dress."

CHAPTER 23

Melinda's eyes widened and shot straight to Erik's belt buckle. He'd already begun unlatching it.

"I haven't done anything wrong," she protested in a hushed voice.

"You're disobeying me right now," he pointed out while stripping the leather strap from the loops of his slacks. It had been a long night of pleasantries and business talks when all he wanted was to get home with Melinda and have a repeat performance of the afternoon.

He would never get enough of her and decided he wouldn't even try to deny himself. He wanted her, and he would have her, take her, own her.

"Someone could walk in," she said, taking half a step back.

He nodded. "Yes, they could." No one was home, but she probably didn't know that. And who was he to take away the little thrill of danger from her.

"We could go upstairs," she said, still hesitating.

"We could, but I don't want to." He shook his head,

looping the belt in his hand and tucking the buckle into his palm. "It would be a shame to ruin that dress, but I will."

She studied him for a weighted moment, probably trying to read him. If anyone could, it would be her. It seemed his brothers had lost touch with him and there wasn't anyone else who could know him like she did. He was trying to get inside her, to know her, but while he'd been doing that, she'd wiggled her way right into him.

"Okay." She reached behind her neck to unclasp the zipper and worked her way out of the dress, letting it fall into a heap at her feet.

"No bra?" he asked with a raised brow.

"No." She shook her head. "My back..." A blush brightened her face.

"Let me see." He twirled his finger, and she obeyed. Most of the marks from their earlier session had faded from bright-red welts to soft-pink lines, but one still looked angry.

He walked to her and touched the mark lightly. "Does it hurt?"

"Only when you touch it," she admitted.

"Are you sorry I did it?"

"No." Her answer came quick and hard, making him grin.

"Turn around," he ordered.

When she faced him again, he tilted her chin up with his fist holding his belt. Her lips parted, and a short breath escaped just before he mashed his mouth to hers. She made a sound, small and sweet, and he swallowed it, intensifying the kiss. She was his, only his, and forever his.

She started to pull away, but he held her fast, pressing his hands to her hips and keeping her where he wanted her. She brought her hands up to his face, cupping his cheeks and meeting his energy.

She took over the kiss. What he had meant to be a claim

on her had been turned around. Her kiss was starved, and she was taking what she wanted from him. Her fingers slid down his cheeks, touching his jaw, giving herself over to him.

He wasn't taking her; she was giving herself to him.

When he broke the kiss, he pressed his forehead against hers, taking in her shaky breath, the tremble of her arms when he touched her.

"You weren't supposed to be so perfect." He dropped the belt to the floor, forgetting whatever preamble he had planned and walked her backward until she was pushed against the wall.

He claimed her mouth again, crushing his lips against hers. He grasped her shoulders, only losing his grip when she groaned. The welts. He pulled away, but she grabbed his jacket with both hands.

"No. Don't." She shoved his jacket from his shoulders, and he let her. He gave over and let her strip him down. His suit lay in a crumpled heap on the floor by the time she was finished. He'd lost two buttons on his shirt.

"This damn hair." He worked the pins out and tossed them to the floor, tugging his fingers through her red locks. She winced when he got caught in a knot, and he grinned. "That's what you get for not leaving it down in the first place."

She sank into his chest, giving him an easier time of getting the last pin out and unleashing all of her thick red curls. His fingers sank into her hair, fisting at her scalp, and she slid down, pressing wet kisses to his chest, his stomach, until she landed on her knees.

"Melinda, you don't—oh, fuck." She took him in her mouth, deep down until the tip of his cock hit the back of her throat. He pulled her away when she gagged.

She wrapped one hand around his thick shaft and worked his cock, up and down with a twist while she sucked and licked his length. His growl wasn't strong enough to convey the pleasure she thrust upon him.

Each stroke, she tightened her hold, sucked harder, and took him deeper. He was tucked in her throat, and she was running her tongue along the underside of his cock.

"Fuck." He yanked her back, drawing his dick free of her mouth.

She stared up at him with startled eyes.

"Did I tell you to fucking suck me?" he asked, leaving off any hint of anger. Who the fuck could be angry with her at this moment?

Her lips curled into a knowing grin. "No. You didn't."

"Did you ask?" He tugged again on her hair; his cock twitching when she winced.

"No, I didn't."

"Pick up the belt," he ordered and kicked it closer to her hand.

Keeping her eyes on him, she reached down and grabbed it, extended it toward him.

He moved down to his knees and slipped the belt around her throat. He looped the leather through the buckle but left it unsecured then tugged on the leash until her face was pressed to the floor. "Keep that ass up."

She nodded and flattened her hands beside her head.

He ran his hand over her upturned ass. Smooth and cool skin, but it wouldn't be for long.

He raised his hand and brought it down hard, one cheek then the other and returned to the first. He spanked her methodically, watching her eyes glaze over, her lips part, and the little gasps escape when he spanked right over her pussy.

With no preamble, he thrust two fingers into her passage. "So, fucking wet for me."

"Yes." She nodded.

He bent low and kissed the small of her back. "Such a good girl for me," he whispered and moved behind her, still holding the makeshift leash.

If he had any doubts about her desire at that moment, it was dashed when she wiggled her ass and scooted toward him. She wanted him, needed him.

And who was he to deny her?

Erik spread her ass cheeks wide, showing off her puckered asshole and unveiling her glistening pussy lips. He pressed the head of his dick to her opening and pushed just a bit inside. She moaned and started to push back at him.

He let go of her cheek and smacked her with the end of the belt. "Bad girl. Stay still."

"But—"

"Stay still or you'll see what it's like to be brought to the edge of heaven and be yanked away again over and over again." Her reaction to the orgasm denial at the club had been so visceral, he'd pocketed the tool for another time. But if she was going to be naughty, he would have to punish her.

"Okay, okay," she agreed hurriedly.

He pulled her cheeks apart again and pushed his cock in another inch, feeling her pussy clench around him, envelop him in her slick heat.

"Your pussy is so wet, so tight." He slipped farther in, tempting himself to thrust hard and take what was his.

"Please, Erik, don't tease." She looked over her shoulder at him, the desire heavy in her voice.

"Oh, sweet girl, this isn't teasing." He could really lay it on thick for her, but he'd be torturing himself at the same time.

"Please..." Her words stuck in her throat when he thrust hard, not stopping until his balls smacked against her pussy.

She sucked in a long breath and pushed up from the floor.

"Down," he ordered, tugging the belt until she moved

back into position. "You'll take this fucking however I give it to you, do you understand?"

"Yes!" But she wiggled her ass, signaling she wanted more, completely contradicting her statement. If his cock hadn't been so damn happy inside her pussy, he might have taken exception to her slight disobedience.

"Fuck." He held the end of the belt, careful not to pull against her throat, and thrust into her again and again.

Her groans of pleasure mixed with his guttural grunts as his cock continued to plow into her hot cunt. His fingers dug into her hip.

"Oh! Erik!" She slapped the floor with her hand.

"You want your little clit played with," he said between puffs of air. Fucking her mimicked what walking through the gardens of Heaven must feel like. "Go on, touch yourself. Play with your clit while I fuck you."

She lifted one hand and slid it beneath herself. Her fingers found her clit, but only after brushing against his cock as he plowed forward.

Her pussy clenched harder around his cock, sucking him closer to the edge. The very place he'd threatened to take her and yank her away from.

"Harder, Red. Harder." He let go of the belt to use both hands to hold her ass, dragging her toward him as he plowed forward.

Her ass tensed a split moment before she unleashed a howling scream. She bucked back at him, riding him as much as much as he was her.

"Fuck, fuck, fuck." He yanked her ass harder and thrust once more, fully embedding his cock in her pussy as his orgasm ripped through him, shredding every ounce of control he held.

Her body shuddered beneath him. He undid the belt from

her neck, and rolled to the floor beside her, pulling her closer to him.

"Fuck, Melinda," he whispered as she flipped to her other side and buried her face in his chest. He held her fast to him, pressing soft kisses to her head.

"You weren't supposed to be so damn perfect," he whispered into the air.

CHAPTER 24

Melinda zipped up her bag and slung it over her shoulder while popping the last bite of a croissant into her mouth.

"Sure, you don't want some eggs, hon? I don't mind making a batch," Marianne said for the third time since Melinda had breezed into the kitchen. She'd slept like the dead and straight through her alarm.

"No time. Sorry. I have to meet with Erik's attorney in twenty minutes, and I'm already going to be late."

"He's your attorney now, too," Erik said, entering the kitchen with an empty coffee cup in hand.

He had gotten up before Melinda, leaving his side of the bed cool and empty. Though, his tousled hair and his usual suit, having been traded for a pair of well-fitting jeans and a black T-shirt, gave her the impression he'd slept through his own alarm as well.

He waved Marianne away and poured himself a cup of coffee. A thick lock of hair fell over his forehead, nearly covering his right eye. It gave him a boyish look, definitely less scary, but not any less dangerous if the flip-flops of her stomach could be trusted.

"I suppose he is." Melinda cleared her throat. "I noticed my car is in the garage."

He stirred his coffee. "It's been at the mechanic. Ian brought it back yesterday." He took a sip and leveled his stare on her. "You don't take great care of your car. The engine light was on, and two of the tires were low on air."

She shrugged a shoulder. "It just needed an oil change, and it's winter."

He laughed, a throaty sound sending a tingle to all of the right spots of her body.

"It needed more than an oil change, and I'm not sure what winter has to do with your tires being low, but it's all been fixed." He turned, leaning against the counter and crossing an ankle over the other. The dark swirls of his tattoo ran down the length of his arm. She hadn't taken the time to really look at it until that moment. Maybe him being so casual, so non-threatening meant she could let down some of her guard.

Unable to make out the whole design she, stepped over to him and pushed up the rest of his sleeve. She traced the intricate design of a wolf standing over a pack. Other smaller designs and symbols rained down his arm, but the pack leader captured her attention.

"You?" She moved her fingers to the other wolves gazing up at their leader. "Your family."

When she brought her eyes up to his, her breath caught. His mesmerizing stare pierced her. She'd gotten used to his dominant glares, but this was different. There was care, interest, genuine warmth dancing with his usual dominant exterior.

"I had it done after my parents died." He broke the spell. She dropped her touch from his arm.

"I'm going to be making shepherd's pie for dinner, so I

need to run to the market." Marianne walked out of the pantry and whirled through the kitchen, her coat already bundled up.

"I can drive you," Melinda piped up. "Since my car's here," she hedged.

The right side of Erik's lips curved upward, and he gave another low chest-rumbling, panty-wetting laugh. "You're not taking it out yet." He set his coffee cup on the counter.

"Melinda, you ready?" Nico stepped into the kitchen, tugging on a pair of leather gloves.

Erik tilted his head, probably waiting to see if she would argue with him. The little fire brewing in her wanted to, she wanted to assert her independence, but with Nico and Marianne bearing witness, she decided to take it up with him later.

"When do you think I'll be able to drive myself places?" she asked, doing her best to keep her tone even.

"Once we figure out Bertucci's angle," Erik said. She couldn't dispute the oddity of Bertucci's interest, and his aggression at the library had left her standing on shaky legs.

"Fine." She breathed out. "Nico, can you take Marianne to the grocery while I'm at the attorney's office? You can swing back around to grab me after?"

Nico's gaze flicked to Marianne then Erik. "I'm not dropping you off. I'm gonna stick around," he said. "Just in case."

"I'll drive myself, like I always do." Marianne jingled her keys and walked off toward the garage.

"She's stubborn," Melinda commented, eliciting another laugh from Erik.

"Yes. *She's* the stubborn one around here."

"You're in a good mood." Nico frowned.

Erik straightened his stance. "Nothing wrong with that." He wrapped his arm around Melinda's waist and pulled her to him, pressing a quick kiss to her temple. "Be a good girl today," he whispered in her ear.

She would have melted into a puddle of arousal at his feet if Nico hadn't broken the moment with his presence.

"I'm not sure how much trouble I can actually get into while talking with a lawyer, but I'll try." She tried to sound casual, but even she could hear the little wisp in her voice.

"No other stops, Nico. Straight there and back." Erik returned to drinking his coffee.

Melinda didn't have a chance to argue the point of being talked about because Erik gave her hip a squeeze and abandoned her to the hands of his youngest brother. Nico shook his head with a grin playing on his lips.

"He's awfully relaxed today," Nico reiterated.

Melinda followed him to the front door in silence. Telling Nico what a powerful exchange she'd experienced with his oldest brother wasn't exactly the conversation she wanted to have.

In the car, Nico checked his phone, swiping through screens and typing quickly. His brows clumped together as he continued tapping away.

"Everything okay?" she asked, noticing the time on the radio. They would need to hurry, or they'd be stuck in morning traffic.

His fingers tightened around his phone as he looked up at her. The fierce expression faded into a blank slate within a blink of an eye.

"Yeah. Fine." He dropped the phone into the middle console and pulled out into traffic.

"I'm sorry you have to play babysitter so often. I'm sure you have much more important things to do." she tried to fill the silent air between them.

Nico cleared his throat. "It's fine. Once Erik's sure you're safe, you won't need someone hanging over you all the time."

His knuckles whitened with his grip on the steering wheel. The lighthearted dance of his humor was missing.

"You sure you're okay?" After having had him acting as her warden since the beginning, she'd gotten used to his easy smile and calm demeanor. The lit firecracker driving the sedan seemed out of place.

"Yeah." he nodded but kept his focus in front of him. His phone dinged, and he grabbed it, swiping the screen alive. Melinda looked away, not wanting to encroach on his privacy.

"Nico!" she yelled as he drove straight through a red light.

"Fuck!" He dropped his phone and swerved to the left, missing the oncoming car by a breath.

She pressed her hand to her chest, easing her breath back into working order while Nico shoved his phone into his jeans pocket.

"Sorry about that," he mumbled and made a left turn.

With her heart still lodged in her throat, she nodded.

"Nico." She turned read the street signs they were passing. "This isn't the way to the attorney's office."

They were outside the business section of town already. The shops transformed into apartment buildings, and the houses because more elaborate, more spaced out.

"Nico. You're going the wrong way." She clutched the arm rest of her door.

"It's fine, Melinda," he said in a detached voice.

"Nico. What's going on? Where are we going?" She twisted around in the seat, trying to gauge where they were. The surroundings were unfamiliar. Whoever lived in the large houses they were passing had money. Lots of money.

"Nico!" She pulled out her phone and started to dial Erik, but he reached over and snatched it from her hand.

"Just be quiet and please…." He blew out a long breath. "Please do what you're told."

"Why? What's going on?"

The car pulled up to a gate, and he rolled down his window. He spoke into the intercom, announcing their arrival.

"I'm not going in there." She announced as the gate started to creak open. Running on pure instinct, she yanked the door handle. Nico's hand fisted in her hair, and he pulled her back to him before she could get the door open.

A loud *click* resounded as he engaged the lock. "I *just* said to do what your told. Melinda, please, don't make this worse."

Panic clawed its way up her throat, burning her with the severity of it. He released her hair and gave her a gentle shove.

"Be smart here, Melinda."

Nico pulled through the open gates and drove up the winding driveway to the house. Fear blinded her to the scenery around her. When he parked, she made another attempt to open the door, but it wouldn't budge.

"Nico." Melinda's eyes widened as two men in black slacks and black button-down shirts climbed down the expansive steps of the house toward the car. No smiles, no casual walk. These men were coming for her.

"Do what they say, and don't fight them." He opened his door and stepped out.

Behind the ogres walked Mr. Bertucci. Smug in his tailored suit, he slid his hands into his pockets and stopped on the third step from the top. Nico walked up to him, hand extended.

Her view became obstructed when the men stood in front her, one hand on the handle. Another *click* sounded, and the door opened.

"No!" She tried to shove her way to the driver's side to find an escape, but one large hand wrapped around her arm and yanked her forward. Another grabbed her, and she was hauled to her feet on the driveway.

"Easy boys." Bertucci said from his stair. "No harm comes to her. Take her down below."

"No! Wait!" Melinda tugged and kicked, fighting with everything she could muster up. Fear fueled her actions, and she wouldn't stop fighting to get out of their grips.

"If she doesn't calm down, administer a sedative," Bertucci called as she was dragged up the steps. She tried to twist around in their hands to see Nico, to implore him to help. This had to be a mistake.

"Nico! Don't do this!" She jerked to the side and twisted enough to sink her teeth into the hand on her arm.

The man cursed but didn't let go. She tried again, but she'd been yanked to the other man.

"Don't!" she cried out. A sharp prick in her neck stopped any further protest, and her vision faded to black.

CHAPTER 25

"Erik." Ian walked into Erik's office with Ash Titon directly behind him.

Erik stood from his desk, interpreting Ash's scowl to mean he wasn't there for pleasantries or a social call. Ian stepped to the side while Ash moved forward.

"I got word this morning from my connection at the precinct," Ash started. "I thought it better to bring this to you myself." Ash handed over a manila envelope.

Erik peeled open the flap and retrieved the papers from within. His gaze swept over the report and then the next and the next.

"How'd you get this?" Erik passed the reports to Ian.

"When he dug into Melinda's family history, he found the original arrest warrants. The track wasn't hard to follow after that. He wasn't cooperative at first, but after the accident, he took the deal." Ash pulled out a chair from the desk and took a seat.

"And your man, he found the location?" Ian asked dropping the papers on the desk. His skepticism leaked through his question.

"Wasn't hard once they found his mother."

"The train she took up north? That was to meet with him," Ian said.

"Yes." Ash nodded.

"Do you think Melinda knows?" Ian asked.

Erik shook his head. She couldn't keep something like that from him; he would have seen it on her face. "She doesn't."

"If I was able to get ahold of this information, anyone else with the same pull could, too." Ash noted.

"Is Nico home with Melinda?" Erik asked, checking the time on his phone. Her appointment with the attorney should have been over by lunch, and it was already two in the afternoon.

"I didn't see him," Ian said.

Erik dialed Melinda's phone and tapped his fingers on the desk while the rings piled up unanswered. When the voicemail picked up, he disconnected and dialed a second time. Again voicemail.

He moved on to Nico's phone. Straight to voicemail.

"Ian, call Nico." He dropped the phone on the desk. "He's not answering me."

Ian also tried. "Nothing."

"Montgomery," Erik's attorney answered his cell.

"Is my wife still with you?" Erik asked, getting straight to it.

"She never came," Montgomery said.

Erik's fingers tightened around the phone, the pit of his stomach opened up and swallowed his lungs.

"Why didn't you phone me?" Erik growled.

"Nico called and said she was busy. She'd reschedule."

A sharp pain ripped through his chest, sending a chilled shiver down his spine.

"Everything okay?" Montgomery asked when Erik kept

silent.

"Did Nico say anything else?"

"No." Montgomery said. A car horn blared in the background.

"If he contacts you, you call me next."

"Yeah, sure, of course."

"Thanks." Erik ended the call and focused his attention on Ian. "We need to find Nico now."

"What about Melinda?" The same accusatory tone lifted his question.

"If we find Nico, we'll find Melinda."

"What do you need from me?" Ash asked.

"I'm going to need men," Erik said. "And you have no reason to help, after what my uncle did."

"His sins were his own." Ash pulled his own phone out and quickly tapped away on the screen. "You'll have the muscle you need."

"And where exactly are we going with these men?" Ian asked. "You wanna clue me in here?"

"Our little brother made a decision today," Erik said in a hard tone.

"What the fuck are you talking about? Nico wouldn't go against you. He wouldn't betray us." Ian's hands cramped into fists at his sides.

"Melinda never showed for her appointment today with Montgomery. Nico called him and said she'd reschedule. Nico hasn't come home with Melinda, and neither of them are answering their phones.

"That doesn't mean he did something to her."

"Ian, I know you've had your head wrapped up in undoing the mess Uncle Kristoff's will caused, but you have to see clearly here. Nico came to me saying he wanted to pick up some of Kristoff's business dealings." He turned to Ash. "Not trafficking, he's not that far gone, but he wants his own contracts, and he wants to rebuild what our uncle destroyed."

"What? Why?" Ian said.

"Maybe Clarissa Bertucci has something to do with it." Ash aimed his screen at them to show a picture of Nico walking across a street. A woman followed him, her hand enclosed by his.

"Did you know he was seeing her?" Erik asked Ian with as much control as he could muster.

"No. I knew he'd started seeing someone, but he didn't say who. And we were otherwise occupied with all the women trafficking." Ian's words shot straight through him. He hadn't allowed himself to use that particular word to describe his actions, but there was no other word for it.

"If Bertucci is using Melinda as bait, you'll only have a short window here, Erik. Taking her today could mean the time's right," Ash spoke up.

Bertucci had Eric's wife in his clutches. Cold ran up his neck.

"What if she's not there?" Ian asked. "What if Nico didn't take her to the attorney because she wanted to go somewhere else? Isn't it possible she's not with Bertucci at all? Maybe she wanted to get away, and Nico helped her." Ian's words mashed together in the desperate tone of a man trying to make sense of his brother's betrayal.

"Melinda's manuscript getting published means everything to her. She wouldn't have missed that meeting for anything," Erik stated flatly. Melinda's passion for her writing matched his own desire to reach his dreams. She wouldn't delay it.

"Not even to get away from you?" Ian's eyes narrowed as he squared off with Erik.

Melinda had seemed content, happy even at times. When she didn't realize he was watching her, she seemed peaceful.

He didn't have to coerce her into sharing time with him or warming his bed. Could it all have been a cover to find an opening?

"Where would she go if she did run away from me, Ian? As far as she knows, her grandmother went off on a vacation. She has no other family in the area, and all of her things have been moved out of her apartment."

"Nico's involvement with Clarissa Bertucci doesn't suggest he was playing hero to Melinda," Ash interjected, stepping forward. "Clarissa Bertucci is his only child. She'll inherit everything once he goes."

"Has he named a successor?" Erik asked. Ian would have to come to terms with Nico's betrayal in his own way. And so would Erik, but he didn't have the luxury at the present. He needed to find Melinda.

"Not as far as I know. He only had one nephew, and he was killed in prison last month," Ash said.

"The man Melinda's father put away with his testimony," Erik stated firmly. "Bertucci has every reason to want Melinda. He's using her to drag her father out of hiding."

Ian's jaw clenched. "And Nico is fucking helping him because if he does, he could get the girl and possibly take over his family businesses."

"It would be a slap in the face to his men who've been with him forever, but seeing as Nico comes from old family ties, they'd accept him," Ash agreed.

"And having him hand deliver Melinda will only work to gain favor with the rest of his crew." Erik's muscles balled into tight fists throughout his body. They weren't moving fast enough. He needed to get to Melinda.

"Peter will meet us at Bertucci's." Ash looked up from his phone.

"Then let's get moving." He had a man to kill and his woman to save. And a brother to deal with.

CHAPTER 26

The scent of lilacs dominated the room. Melinda sat on the narrow bed in the corner, staring at the bowl of potpourri perched on the end table. Other than the bed and the table, the dank room was devoid of furniture. No lamps, only one bulb hanging from the ceiling in the middle.

It reminded her of the secret basement at home. Cinderblock walls, concrete floor, and a steel toilet in the corner. It was a prison cell, not a room.

The drugs pumped into her to sedate her were still working their way out of her system, leaving her limp and drowsy. It had taken most of her strength to prop herself up against the wall when she first woke. Time ticked along as it normally did, she was sure, but she couldn't tell. Nothing moved or changed in her cell. No windows to let in sunlight. It could have been one day or three since she left home with Nico.

Tears stung her eyes. Nico had betrayed her and his family. He'd brought her straight to Bertucci and handed her over with a virtual bow attached. She vaguely remembered him asking about her when she was dragged away, and again later she heard his voice. Maybe he was the one who'd put the sweet-smelling flower petals in the room to cover up the stench of dried blood and death.

Metal scraped against metal, echoing in the small space. She shoved herself farther into the corner of the bed, pulling her knees up to her chest and hugging them. Her initial response was to bolt, but her legs wouldn't hold her—they were too heavy, her mind too foggy. The door swung open, and Nico walked in carrying a tray.

Food.

He'd brought her food, not salvation.

Bertucci followed him, his hands in his pockets and his lips pinched together in a deep frown. The door was pulled shut from outside. Her guard, maybe.

She kept her eyes trained on Bertucci while Nico moved the bowl of potpourri and slid the tray onto the table.

"Just a sandwich and some water, but you should eat," he said in his usual calm manner. Like they were at home, having lunch in the kitchen, and Marianne was nearby making him a batch of sweet tea.

"Why am I here?" she questioned.

Nico turned away from her and moved behind Bertucci. The perfect lap dog hiding behind his master. Betrayal nauseated her. Seeing it on his face, a shred of remorse, of uncertainty made the rolling waves in her stomach sharper.

"Because you're useful here." Bertucci shrugged.

"Useful how?"

"I'm expecting a visitor soon," he answered.

"What does that have to do with me? With Nico?" She raised her voice, regaining some of her strength.

"Melinda, be patient," Nico warned. "Do what you're told. Don't fight. It will be over soon enough."

Melinda scooted to the edge of the bed and pressed her

feet to the floor, testing the power of her legs before standing. She wobbled and stumbled back until she could hold the wall to keep herself upright.

"What will be over soon enough?" she asked, her patience cracking under the pressure.

"Your—"

"No." Bertucci sliced his hand in the air, cutting off Nico's words. "She'll find out when I'm ready."

"You're an idiot. Both of you!" Her temper shoved the last of the drug induced fog from her mind. "Erik will find me. He's not going to just let me walk away. He's going to look for me."

"I'm sure he will, but he won't find you." Bertucci slipped one hand from his pocket and ran it across his face. "I'll send someone when it's time for you to make your appearance. Until then, get comfortable. This may be the last few days you have."

Nico's head snapped toward Bertucci with his words, but he didn't question him.

"I'll give you a minute, but I expect you to keep your word," Bertucci said.

"Of course." Nico's forehead wrinkled.

Bertucci gave him a narrowed look before leaving them alone in the room.

"Nico." Melinda sighed. "What's wrong with you? Why would you do this?"

"You're going to be fine. You have to go along with him," Nico said, but his tone twisted with worry. He was in over his head.

"You think he's going to just let me walk home after he does whatever he's planning? Erik will come for him. You know that! He's your brother!" Her fists had tightened so much, her fingers tingled.

Nico dragged both hands through his hair and settled a glare on her. His nostrils flared, and his jaw tensed. "I'm aware of who Erik is. And I'm also aware that being the youngest brother, I'll get nothing without his fucking permission or charity."

"Erik said you and Ian both inherited from your uncle. It wasn't only him." She tried to understand where all Nico's anger came from.

"We did. Not like he did, of course, but enough I guess." Nico nodded.

"Then what the hell is going on?"

"There's room for more. More money, more power. All we had to do was take back what was rightfully ours, but Erik and his damn need for that fucking casino. He didn't want to get his hands any dirtier than they already were."

Melinda blinked several times. His words stacked on top of themselves in her brain.

"The girls you mean?"

Nico laughed. "Yeah, the girls. I have to be honest, I didn't think he really had it in him. And Ian was giving him so much shit about it, I thought he'd cave. But he did it. Three girls, all collected, and all debts paid." Nico rubbed the back of his neck. Maybe the tension of his own betrayal had finally worked its way into him.

"He's never going to let Bertucci do anything to me." As true as the statement was, she wasn't sure if she was telling him or herself. Erik wouldn't suspect Nico's betrayal; he'd be looking in all the wrong places.

"Bertucci isn't going to do anything to you," Nico stated flatly. "You're only the bait. Once he has what he wants, you'll be free."

Melinda sank onto the narrow bed, her fingers grasping the edge. "You have to know that's not true. He can't just let me go, Nico."

Nico's throat worked as he swallowed hard, his gaze flicking to the door.

"He gave me his word."

"And how do you think this ends? If he lets me go, Erik will come at him. You get all of that, right? I'm a loose end." Her stomach dropped several inches as the true desperation of the situation settled inside. If Erik didn't find her in time, Bertucci would have to get rid of her.

Nico stared at her.

Moments passed in a haze of fear and understanding. There would be no going home for her if Erik didn't find her.

"I'll figure this out. Don't do anything to piss Bertucci off. Don't give him a reason to hurt you, Melinda." Nico jerked the door open and slammed it once he was gone.

Melinda ran to the door, tugging on the handle. Of course, it was locked.

She rested her forehead on the chilled surface.

Erik would find her.

He would.

She repeated the words over and over until she sank to the floor, trying her best to believe herself.

CHAPTER 27

*E*rik flung open his front door to find Melinda's grandmother standing on his stoop. Her eyes widened when she took him in. His immediate presence seemed to startle her nearly as much as hers did him. His gaze swept past her to the man standing behind her on the stairs. Even with the graying hair along the man's temples and the deep wrinkles around his eyes, Erik could see the mirrored resemblance.

"Where is my daughter?" Christopher Manaforte said from behind his mother.

"Please. Where is Melinda?" Grams said, her hands folded together. "Is she still here, or did you—" She bit down on her bottom lip. "Is she still here?"

"Erik what are you doing? We need to—" Ian stopped directly behind him. "Manaforte."

"Come inside." Erik stepped back and made a sweeping motion with his hand. "I'm not talking about this on the front stoop. Come in," he pressed when they remained motionless.

Erik shut the door once they were in the front hall. "We

can go into my office, Ash. I think we may have a different approach now."

"Agreed."

Ian led them into the office and offered seats to their new guests.

"What's going on? My mother said you took Melinda. You have intentions of selling her off? Is that true?" Manaforte met Erik's gaze.

Erik took in the sight of Manaforte. Old enough to be his own father, but more worn out from the pressures of hiding, the weighted guilt of his previous actions colored his tired features. A man who left his child behind while he turned state's evidence and went into hiding.

"What are you doing here?" Erik questioned in a hard tone.

"Looking for my daughter." Manaforte stood from his chair. "You took her."

Erik nodded. "I did." He owed him nothing more than that. It was because of this man Melinda had fallen into Bertucci's crosshairs. Her father abandoned her, her grandfather sold her—had any man in her life been loyal to her? Had anyone actually taken care of her?

"Where is she?" Manaforte demanded, though he had no right to claim Melinda. Not after leaving her behind and letting her believe both her parents had died in that car accident. The anguish she must have felt, standing at their funeral, wanting nothing more than the loving embrace of her mother and father.

Erik stepped forward, his temper pounding in his ears. "Bertucci has her."

Manaforte's eyes widened, his jaw slacked at the news.

"Your testimony put her at risk, but you didn't make sure she was safe. You left her behind, unprotected."

Manaforte's lips thinned. "I didn't have a choice."

"Really? Tell me how that went, then?" Erik tilted his head.

They were wasting time, but Bertucci wanted Manaforte. Melinda was the bait to bring her father out of his court-appointed security. She would be relatively safe for the very short future.

"I don't owe you anything." Manaforte advanced, his jaw set.

"Christopher," Grams intervened "we need to find Melinda. If she's with Mr. Bertucci, we will need Erik to help us."

"You can help, too." Erik stepped closer to Manaforte until the toes of his shoes touched his. "You can turn yourself over to him. You're why he took her. He was drawing you out. Mario was killed last month."

Manaforte paled. "I know. I heard. I didn't think they'd go after my daughter. I thought she'd be safe with my parents."

"Why wouldn't they? Did you really not know the sort of people you were working for?" Erik asked. "Even as a kid, I understood the men my uncle worked with were dangerous. You can't have been that naive as an adult."

"He left her behind because I begged him to. I was scared they'd find him, and she'd be hurt. I had already lost my son. I didn't want to lose my granddaughter, too," Grams said.

Manaforte grabbed his mother's hand and squeezed. "It's not your fault, Ma."

"At this point, the blame can be spread around to pretty much everyone in this room. It doesn't change anything. We need to get to her before Bertucci loses his patience." Ian spoke the truth. Erik's desire to have his own casino had led him to fulfill his uncle's requirements. If he'd given up on it, he would have left Melinda alone. She might have still been safely tucked away at her grandmother's home.

"We can't just walk into Bertucci's house. He'll have all

the power. We need to meet somewhere neutral. I'll give myself over to him in exchange for Melinda," Manaforte said.

"There has to be a better option." Grams clawed at his shoulder. Erik noted her panic. Sending Manaforte to Bertucci was a death sentence, and she knew it.

"No, Ma. I have to do this. I've already lost my wife and my daughter over the stupid choices I made. I won't let Melinda lose anything else because of me."

So much of her life had been mapped out because of the people around her, because of their choices, their wants.

"I'll call him. We'll set up a meet outside his house." Erik pulled his phone out and dialed, walking to the windows of his office to look at the city bustling outside. Strangers strolled along the streets, hand in hand, oblivious to the turmoil boiling inside him. He couldn't recall a time of such innocence anymore.

"Rawling." Bertucci's hard voice came through clear.

"Bertucci. You have my wife." Erik kept his temper in check. Going off the rails would only succeed in getting the entire situation derailed.

A rough laugh. "I do. Yes."

"I have her father." Erik fisted his hand in his pocket. "That's what you want, right? You want Manaforte?"

A short pause. "Thirty minutes. Meet outside the old toy factory on the South Side."

"My brother."

"He'll be there."

"If you hurt her—" Erik pinched the bridge of his nose, willing the anger to simmer down enough for him to control his voice.

"Not a scratch, I assure you." Bertucci could be lying.

"Thirty minutes." Erik clicked off the call and turned to the audience staring at him.

"So, what's the plan?" Ian asked.

Erik caught Ash's gaze and shook his head. "We make the switch."

"You're sending my son off to be killed." Grams turned her fury on him.

"No. I'm protecting my wife. I'm doing whatever is needed to be sure she is safe and comes home. She will not pay for the sins of her father." Erik pointed finger at her.

"Your wife?" Manaforte whispered. "You said that to Bertucci, too. You married her?"

Erik stood straight. "Yes."

"Promise you'll keep them both safe," Grams said.

"Your son and your husband both failed Melinda," Erik said. "I won't."

It wasn't the promise she wanted, but it was the only one he could give with honesty. Melinda was his priority.

Her safety above all else.

Even his own.

CHAPTER 28

Melinda's stomach hurt. Not the little butterfly dance you get when waiting to get on a roller coaster, but a true pain that lurched with every turn the car made. She'd be lucky not to vomit all over the back seat. Though Nico would deserve it, to have her puke in his lap.

When he'd come down to her cell, he'd given her a dress. *You need to look good, Melinda. You can't let Erik think you've been mistreated,* he'd said. Mistreated? She'd been locked in a moldy, stinky cell in the pits of Bertucci's estate. She'd been given food, and even some privacy to use the steel toilet in her room. At least she thought she had privacy. For all she knew there were hidden cameras in her prison.

The sun had already gone down, leaving the car dark and the street lamps the only illumination she could use to make out their positioning. Bertucci sat in the front passenger seat, his pimp hat perched on his overly fat head, and his suit freshly pressed. He could easily be mistaken for a wedding guest and not the incurable monster he truly was.

They weren't in the heart of the city anymore. The buildings shortened then spaced out, until she could only make out factories and broken-down housing. They were on the south side of the river. There wouldn't be anyone around at this time of day. Maybe a few factory workers, but they would know to mind their own business.

"Where are we going?" she asked again.

Nico sighed. "Don't worry about it. This will be over soon. I promise." He sounded tired. It probably took a lot more energy to betray your family than he had anticipated.

"Don't worry? You won't even tell me where we're going." She caught Bertucci's glare in the mirror as she swung her gaze back out the window. Revulsion. The only way she could describe the way he looked at her, with complete revulsion.

What could she have done to earn such emotion from him?

The car jerked as it passed over old train tracks and led them into an open lot. The aged sign still hung over the factory. Tony's Toys. A small banner, torn and ratted from the winds and weather of the winter, flew from the top of the sign. *Going out of business.*

She took an uneasy breath. Her lungs couldn't get enough air; her stomach refused to chill the fuck out. She wouldn't make it through this evening without getting sick. She saw no hope for it.

The car pulled to a stop in the lot, near the front doors of the factory. Two more sedans were parked a hundred or so feet away. She recognized them.

Erik.

Nico's fixed jaw and pinched lips didn't offer any comfort to her.

"He's your brother, Nico," she whispered. "He'll forgive you, but you have to help me here."

Bertucci's driver got out of the car and went to his side to open the door for him.

"You stay here." He pointed a sausage-like finger at her and climbed out of the car, making it sway from the redistribution of weight.

"You don't know him like I do. He won't ever forget," Nico said. She could hear the fear, sense his apprehension. He was going up against his oldest brother, and he'd taken Melinda. He'd taken what Erik had claimed as his.

"He will never forgive you if something happens to me," she said firmly. It was a gamble, playing on Nico's emotions. Erik may not really give a rat's ass if she survived the night. It could be his pride, his possessive claim that brought him to the toy factory, but she had few options.

Nico faced her, his brow line wrinkled. He tilted his head one way then the other. The tension in his muscles obvious. "He'd get over it," he announced and popped open her door. "Get out."

"Nico." She tried once more, but he shoved her toward the door. She scrambled to get her feet out of the car to keep from falling to the concrete. The winter wind smacked her in the face when she righted herself, blowing straight through the cotton dress she'd been forced into. Nico hadn't given her a coat to wear, and the wind blew the flowing skirt up around her legs, sending chills running through her.

She wrapped her arms around herself, rubbing her arms to ward off some of the chill while searching the lot for Bertucci.

"Let's go." Nico grabbed her upper arm and propelled her forward. She kept up with his strides while trying to shield her eyes from the headlights aimed at her. The more steps they took, the clearer the scene became.

Erik stood among three other men. She recognized Ian's frame, too similar to Erik to be mistaken for someone else, and she also saw Ash Titon from the Annex. Squinting, she tried to make out the third person, recognition dancing on the far edge of her memory.

"Daddy?" she whispered. Her mind had finally snapped. She was seeing what she wanted, what she'd longed for since the night she'd found out her parents had been killed. Her father stood beside Erik.

She tried to yank free of Nico. It had to be him. He was there, right there.

"Daddy!" she yelled out, catching the attention of the men. Erik stiffened.

"Melinda, wait." Nico yanked her hard back a step. "You stay here." He intensified his grip, biting into the tender flesh beneath her arm.

"Melinda!" Her father took a step in her direction, but Erik stilled him with an arm across his chest.

"How is this possible?" She asked, stumbling forward when Nico dragged her toward Bertucci's side.

"Easy to explain," Bertucci said with a satisfied joviality. "Your precious daddy ran off all those years ago. He went into hiding like the coward he was and left you behind."

Melinda shook her head.

"Melinda. Are you all right?" Erik asked, but he didn't look at her. He kept his focus on Bertucci.

"I'm fine—"

"She's unhurt. Like I promised." Bertucci splayed out his hands.

"Let her go," Erik demanded.

Bertucci shook his finger in the air. "Not yet. I want Manaforte first."

"Let my wife go, and you can have him." Erik remained stubborn. Always trying to have things his way.

Bertucci paused, looking over his right shoulder at the two men standing at his side, ready to protect his life if needed, then his left shoulder at Nico. "He's going to let you go, but you stay over here. If you take one step toward your husband, I'll kill him…and your father."

Melinda nodded, trying to read Erik's expression. He was back to a blank slate, keeping her from getting a sense of his thoughts. What exactly was the plan here?

"Let her go, Nico," Bertucci ordered, and Nico's fingers fell away from her arm. She took a step to the side but not forward. The instinct to run to Erik had to be quenched. She wouldn't risk her father's life or Erik's, but she needed space from Nico.

Nico made his way behind Manaforte.

"Manaforte comes forward." Bertucci produced a gun from his coat and aimed it at Melinda's father. The pain in her stomach intensified, gripping her hard and sucking the breath from her.

She watched her father take three steps forward. Each time his shoe touched the ground, her heart rammed against her ribs.

"My nephew is dead because of you." Bertucci's fingers tightened around the butt of the gun.

"You killed my wife." Melinda's father's rage shook his voice as he took another step.

"You should have both died in that accident," Bertucci said, cocking the gun. The sound, the little click of the hammer echoed in Melinda's head.

"You can have me, but let Melinda go to her husband." Her father jerked his head in Erik's direction.

Erik's gaze locked on Bertucci. She recognized the tic in his jaw, the little movement of his muscles as he concentrated on his prey. How had she not been more fearful of this man? He looked ready to rip Bertucci's head from his shoulders.

"Melinda." Bertucci shook his head. "I keep hearing about fucking Melinda."

"I'm losing my patience," Erik said in a low tenor.

Bertucci pointed at her father. "Killing you would give you an easy escape." Bertucci turned slightly toward her. "Killing her would no doubt leave a better mark." He raised the gun, pointing the barrel at her. Her breath caught, and fear gripped her body, freezing her to the concrete.

"No!" someone yelled.

A gunshot fired then a second. The third sound came just before she was tackled, her head hitting the ground.

"Melinda!" Erik's voice, raspy and angry. "Melinda!"

"Don't." Another voice. One she didn't recognize.

She opened her eyes, rolling to her back. Nico scrambled off of her, getting to his feet. A man she'd seen briefly at Bertucci's house when she'd arrived stood with his gun drawn. He hadn't been with them when they left, why was he here?

"Dad!" She pushed up to her knees. Her father lay motionless only feet away from her. Blood pooled beneath him, covered his chest.

"Don't fucking move," the new voice demanded. She turned. Another of Bertucci's men stepped forward, his gun turned on Nico. Bertucci laid on the ground, his arm outstretched and his gun still in his hand. A clean shot to his head had stopped him from hurting her.

"Justin, he was going to kill her," Nico said, waving a hand at Melinda. His other one held a gun.

"What did you think was going to happen? She was just going to go home with hubby?" The sneer in Justin's voice sent a chill through her. "Do you really think you were just going to waltz in and take a seat at the table?"

"Justin." Erik's gun was trained on him. Erik didn't close the distance between himself and where Melinda knelt, taking in the horror before her.

She watched her father's blood seep through his shirt, down his chest. He needed help. She needed to get to him.

Ash stepped forward, carrying no weapon. "Justin. This is over. Bertucci was going to kill the girl, and you know that couldn't happen. Isn't that why you showed up?"

Justin swung his gaze over to Melinda. Her breath hurt as it passed through her throat. Had she screamed? She didn't remember it, but her throat burned like she had.

"Bertucci's revenge for Mario would have brought more shit down on the family," Justin said plainly. "Going after Manaforte was fine, but once she had connections to the Rawlings, he should have backed off." Justin's voice remained calm, collected as he spoke. He wasn't being ruled by emotions like Bertucci. It wasn't revenge he sought, it was control.

"That's true. I can't let Jansen be the only powerhouse in town. He'll run everyone out. Too much territory for one family," Ash continued, stepping closer to Justin.

Panic ran through Melinda. They were discussing power and territories, while her father lay bleeding onto the cold pavement. She'd just found him; he couldn't leave her, not so soon, not yet.

Justin turned an angry expression on Nico. "You forget about Clarissa. You get out and you never come back."

Nico started to argue.

"Nico's gone," Erik stated, his tone flat and distant. He might as well have been talking about a stranger.

"Erik—"

"He's gone." Ian stood beside Erik, his eyes trained on Justin.

Nico took a step back, his gaze searching franticly around the lot.

"Go," Justin said, pointing his gun at him. Nico swiveled on his heels and ran across the parking lot into the darkness.

"He needs a hospital." Melinda's voice cracked, and she shuffled on her knees toward her father.

"Get him there," Justin said.

"You don't make another move toward my wife or her father." Erik kept his gun trained on Justin.

"You stay out of my business, and I stay out of yours. I have no quarrel with you, but Jansen will need some help accepting me as head of this family."

"That's your problem to deal with. I'm out of that shit," Ash said firmly.

"You'll get no help from us, either," Ian added.

"That's fine. Just stay make sure you stay out."

"Erik. Please." Melinda picked up her father's head and laid it in her lap. She pressed her fingers to his neck, searching out a pulse. "Please. Help me!"

Sirens blared in the distance. Justin and the other men scrambled into their cars and peeled out of the lot, leaving them.

"Go." Erik nodded to Ash and Ian.

"I'm not leaving you," Ian stated with force.

"Ian, I'll take you to the hospital. That's where they'll be." Ash smacked him on his shoulder.

Lights flashed, and Melinda looked up at Erik. His eyes were finally on her, finally locked with hers.

"Please. Don't let him die," she begged. Tears ran down her cheeks, blurring her vision, blocking out the sounds around her.

CHAPTER 29

Melinda stood at the window in Erik's office, watching the cars roll past the house. People walked past, buses still ran; no one seemed to understand the darkness that had descended around her.

"Melinda." Erik's voice penetrated the thick bubble of seclusion she'd immersed herself in.

"Yeah?" she asked without turning around. Outside, everything remained the same as the day before and the day before that. The world hadn't crumbled outside.

"Your grandmother called." Erik's voice was tender, cautious. He tiptoed around her like she would explode at the smallest spark.

"What did Grams want?" Melinda asked.

"To talk to you," he said. She felt him behind her. The warmth emanating from his body, the strength of him wrapping around her.

Melinda huffed. "Did you see the newspaper?" She motioned to the folded-up paper on his desk.

"You don't need to look at that," he said, but it was too late.

She'd already spent a solid hour reading the article about her father and his murder. She read about how he'd turned state witness after his wife was killed in a tragic automobile accident that was believed to be orchestrated by Bertucci himself.

"Why not? It seems the journalists knew my father better than me." She wrapped her arms around her middle, but not to ward off the cold. No, she welcomed the chill now. It reminded her she hadn't gone completely numb. There was still life inside her.

During the course of her reading, she'd learned her father's work had all been a front. He was a cleaner for the Bertucci family. Washed the money to keep the cash legit for spending. But something happened, something that made her father vulnerable to investigation, also a risk to Bertucci. If he talked, members of his family could be taken down. In the end, the "accident" hadn't killed both parents. It worked to scare her father right into the protective arms of the police.

"Melinda, your father was protecting you," Erik said.

She huffed. "Protecting me?" She spun around to face him. "And did that work out? I grew up without my parents, and, in the end, I was sold off like some little bauble anyway." Her chest clamped tight. "And then he walked right back in, he was there, only feet away from me." Tears rushed to her eyes while her throat shut down air traffic. "I didn't even get to talk to him. To feel him." She lowered her head, and the tears rolled off her chin and onto the plush carpet below.

"He came home to save you."

She sniffed. The pain burst through her chest, still too large for her to contain. It seemed to leak from her pores, but still the pressure of it didn't relent.

"Save me from you," she whispered. "And he failed at that, too."

"I didn't know your father was still alive. Your grandmother didn't tell me." Erik sounded defensive. For the first time since she'd met him, he sounded unsure of his actions.

"Would it have made a difference?" she asked, raising her chin to see him. Puffy bags hung beneath his eyes. They'd shared a bed the night before but hadn't touched. Sleep had ignored her, and she wondered if he'd had the same night.

"I don't know." His jaw went firm.

"Because your uncle required you to collect all the debts owed to him in order for you to inherit." She nodded. "I remember. What I don't get? Your uncle had to have known who I was, that my father was the one who put Bertucci's nephew in jail."

"Everyone believed your father died in that accident. He never gave public testimony. After his death, the judge allowed his written testimony said to have been taken before his death," Erik explained.

Memories of standing beside two gravesites as a teenager, watching two caskets lowered into the cold earth while her heart burst into shards at her loss flooded her. She'd have to relive it again in a few short hours.

This time, there would be no fanfare. No line of friends and neighbors to mourn with her. Grams would be there, but Melinda wasn't sure she could face her. So many things had happened, so much pain and treachery she didn't know where to put the blame anymore.

"So, since they thought they'd killed him, no sense in beating the dead rat by hurting his daughter." Melinda took a shaky breath.

"None of this is your fault." Erik blew through the space between them and cradled her face between his hands. "You didn't do any of this, you don't deserve this."

A tear ran down her cheek and then another. "That doesn't change anything, though. Does it?" She wrapped her hands around his wrists. His touch brought warmth to her cold interior, and she wasn't ready for it. She couldn't face his empathy. She wanted the raw hatred back. She wanted to be angry and throw things. Not have this gaping hole inside of her chest that filled with pain as though playing on a never-ending loop.

"I should get dressed." She pulled out of his hands, already missing the warmth of his touch.

"You should call your grandmother before we leave," he said, not moving to stop her from walking away.

"I'll see her at the cemetery." Melinda pushed her hair behind her ear and stepped around him.

"Melinda." Erik's commanding tone stilled her step for a brief moment, but she didn't let it keep her in the office. She'd had enough of everyone around her controlling every step of her life.

* * *

"Melinda," Grams called to her from the drive. She climbed out of the passenger side of Ian's car, waving a hand at Melinda.

"Hold on." Erik pulled Melinda's elbow to stop her from walking away.

Turning into the crisp afternoon wind, Melinda watched Ian escort her grandmother up the gentle incline of the hill toward them. Her father's grave, the one holding an empty casket, had already been re-dug. The mound of dirt lay behind Melinda. With winter slowing down, the ground wasn't frozen. They didn't have to wait for spring to get the show over with. Small favors.

"Grams." Melinda didn't move to hug her grandmother, but rather took a step back from the older woman when she made her way up the hill.

"Melinda. Please. Give me a chance—"

"To explain?" Melinda finished. "To explain how you lied to me about my father? About how you let Gramps sell me like a whore? Or did you want to explain that, instead of coming to me at Erik's estate to tell me about my father, you ran off to get him yourself?"

Erik's hand tightened around Melinda's arm. A warning to keep her temper down.

"Yes. I knew your father was alive. I shouldn't have known, but he came to me and Gramps before he left. We knew." Grams reached out and touched Melinda's arm with her fingertips. "I swear I didn't know about the idiotic deal Gramps made. He was a fool, an idiot. I was scared. I didn't know what to do, so I left. I went to find your father to bring him home to help. I didn't think…we didn't know Mario Bertucci had been killed."

Tears lingered in Grams' eyes, and her bottom lip quivered. To her, this was fresh, a new death. Melinda had already mourned, and, as shocking the last few days were, she had never believed her father alive. Grams faced her son's death for the first time.

Melinda pulled Grams close and hugged her, letting the bubble burst and sobs rack her. Although this was not a new grief to her, it was a new sort. She'd lost so much without even knowing it. Grams clung to her, crying into Melinda's coat for the loss of her son, for the betrayal of her husband. Grams had been hurt in all of this betrayal as well. Her only goal had ever been to protect Melinda.

"I'm sorry," Melinda said, sniffling and pulling away.

"You have nothing to be sorry for," Grams said with a pointed finger. She wiped the tears from her eyes then grasped Melinda by the shoulders.

"He came back for me." Melinda's voice cracked beneath the weight of her guilt. If she hadn't been in Bertucci's clutches, her father would have been safe. He would have shown up at Erik's house, and they'd have had a bit of drama before dinner. But he'd be alive. He wouldn't have been gunned down like a common thug.

"I'm sorry, ladies, but the priest is waiting," Ian interrupted softly.

Melinda nodded. "Right. Yeah." She wiped the tears from her face.

Erik's arm slinked around her waist, and he led her to the gravesite. Two empty chairs were positioned there, and Erik helped her into one while Ian sat Grams in the other. The men took their places behind them. Erik's hands rested on Melinda's shoulders.

She took another long breath and grabbed Grams' hand as the priest opened his booklet and began his prayers. Melinda didn't need the dog-and-pony show, but she knew Grams would rest easier with it. Having to bury her son without the comfort of her prayers would cause more pain. And there'd been enough of that to add to it.

Erik's fingers tightened and relaxed during the ceremony, easing the tension from her body. He had such an easy way with her, like he knew exactly what she needed and when. With all that had happened, her father dying in her lap, the police pretending to investigate, and Nico going into hiding, she hadn't taken time to evaluate the situation with Erik.

What would happen now?

How was the next chapter supposed to go?

CHAPTER 30

"Here's your breakfast." Marianne slid a plate of scrambled eggs and toast onto the kitchen table and plunked down a fork.

"Thank you." Erik picked up the utensil. "Has Melinda been down yet?" he asked, digging into the eggs. He'd woken up before the sun rose as usual and left her sleeping in bed. It was the first time in days he'd seen her sleep soundly through the night, and he wouldn't be responsible for waking her. But that had been hours ago.

"No," Marianna answered, pouring coffee into his cup. "She's up, though. I heard the door to her office close about an hour ago." She patted his shoulder. "I'll bring her some coffee."

"Here you are." Ian sauntered into the kitchen. "I checked your office."

Erik wiped his mouth and crumpled his napkin in his hand. "How'd it go?" Erik's chair scraped against the tiles as he stood up.

"About as good as I expected." Ian picked up a mug from the counter and reached for the coffee.

"I'll bring this to Melinda." Marianne picked up the tray she'd been getting ready.

"He's safe?" Erik asked, walking to the fridge and leaning against it.

"He is." Ian nodded.

Erik's jaw clicked. The sting of his brother's treachery was still fresh. "He knows he can't come back here, right? If Justin gets even a whiff of him in town, it will start a war."

"He knows," Ian said with more force. "He knows how badly he fucked up."

"You think it's my fault," Erik accused. "The oldest always bears the responsibly of watching out for the younger ones, so it's obvious I drove him to what he did."

"No." Ian shook his head, cradling his cup in his hands. "Nico's his own man. He made his own decisions."

"He wanted more, and I wasn't paying attention." Erik balled his hands into fists. He should have seen it. He should have been watching for the greed and hunger for power. They may be Rawlings by name, but the Komisky blood still ran through their veins.

"You had other things going on." Ian said, his words missing the usual accusations and contempt.

Erik glanced at the kitchen doorway. Melinda was in her office, tucked into her sorrow and anger. His youngest brother was in hiding. The land for the casino had been purchased, and he'd have his dream fulfilled within months. And all it cost him was his brother and the innocence of a woman.

He'd put his wants in front of everything of everyone around him. And now they were all paying the price.

"Why didn't he fucking say something? To you if not me?" Erik knew he could be overwhelming when he had his mind set on a goal, but Nico had Ian.

"I don't know, but, for now, he's at least safe."

"Do I want to know where he is?"

"Just leave him be. I know you're still pissed—"

"Pissed? Ian, he took my wife and handed her over to a fucking lunatic! Do you think he wasn't going to kill her? If we hadn't been there. If her father hadn't shown up—" Erik bit down on his lip. His voice rose with each word, and Melinda would hear. "I could have lost her."

Ian put his cup down, the hard clank testimony to his own aggravation. "But you didn't. She's here. Right in the other fucking room, but you've avoided her as much as she avoids you. Since when do you allow that?"

"I'm not allowing anything. She needs time to heal. Her fucking father died, Ian. Killed right in front of her. Because of me."

"No. Because of her father! It was his past that caught up to him and her." Ian jabbed his finger at Erik.

"She's never had a chance. Every fucking turn she's made, there's been someone there fucking everything up for her. I'm not doing that anymore." Erik shoved away from the table, his decision made and the course set. He wouldn't be the reason Melinda withered away in despair.

* * *

MELINDA SAT at her desk when Erik entered the office. She didn't look up from her computer; her fingers continued to fly over the keys. He'd watched her before while she was typing. It was like she had no idea the real world continued to move around her while she was lost in her mind.

"Melinda." He stood at her desk, his fingers pressed into the well-varnished wood. If he'd put as much thought into what the right thing was when his uncle's attorney explained the requirements for his inheritance as he had into crafting the perfect desk for her, she wouldn't be hurting now.

Her fingers paused over the keys.

"We need to talk," he stated.

Her chin snapped up, bringing her gaze in line with his.

"About what?" she asked softly. Apprehension played in her features. How could it not? Nothing had been fully in her power in her entire life, and even less so in the last months.

"I've made a decision." He rolled his shoulders, straightening his spine. "Since my inheritance has been fully transferred and all the strings my uncle had me tied with aren't an issue anymore, there's no point in continuing on with"—he paused a beat—"us."

Her eyes widened a fraction. "What does that mean?" She sat back in her chair, her story forgotten. "You're just letting me go? After all your insistence?"

"Now that I have the land for the casino and the business plans settled, I've realized there's no need to hold you to our vows. So, yes, you're free to go." His tongue thickened on the words. If his uncle's lawyer wanted to enforce the divorce clause, he'd find a way to deal with it. It wasn't worth her pain. Not anymore.

"Just like that?" She stood from her chair, studying him. The feathery quiver in her voice gave her away, but he wouldn't point it out. He'd let her wear her mask.

"Yes. Just like that." He dragged in a long, heated breath. "Ian will take you to your grandmother's house. I have your bags being packed right now. Of course, you may take the desk, but it will have to be delivered to you later. For now, take what will fit in the car, and I'll have the rest packed up."

She flinched, as though his words had smacked her. "You want me to leave now?"

"Yes. Now." He nodded. "I'll have the papers drawn up for your signature. I figure we can be done with all of this within a week."

Her bottom lip trembled, but she hid it quickly behind

her fingertips. The muscles of her throat clenched, and he noticed the tension building in her shoulders. She would hold herself back. She wouldn't make herself vulnerable to him, not after what he'd already said.

"So, that's it? You got your casino, and now I'm useless to you?" The anguish leaked into her words, though he knew she'd tried to cover it up.

The icy hand gripping his heart squeezed harder. "Yes. This was never really a marriage, we both know that. It was fun, but…well, it's not now."

Red covered her cheeks, in fury or despair he wasn't sure, but it didn't matter. He was getting his point across.

"Not fun," she whispered, lowering her gaze from his.

"That's right." He nodded, moving his stare to the bookshelves behind her. He could feel the pain he was causing, but he couldn't stop it. She wouldn't go if she knew what this was doing to him. If she could sense the enormity of his concern for her, the intensity of his want for her, she would stay. And it was better for her to be away from him.

"There will be reparations set up for you, of course." Erik stopped to clear his throat, a hitch in his voice wouldn't convey the finality he was trying to get across.

"Of course." She slammed her laptop closed and jerked it from the power cord. "And the other girls? What about them?"

"You don't need to concern yourself with all that." He lifted his chin. "You should get your coat and your laptop bag. Ian will be ready to drive you soon."

"That's it? That's all you have to say to me?" she called to him when he turned his back on her.

His hands fisted, but he did not turn around. To see the tears in her eyes, or to so much as sense them might break him, and he was doing the right thing this time. He was putting her needs, her future ahead of what he wanted.

Because if he did what he wanted, he'd have her in his arms. He'd lift her off her feet and carry her to bed and love her until all the pain, all the grief was nothing but a faded memory.

"There's nothing left to say, Red. I needed you, and now I don't." The last sound he heard before the door closed behind him was her sharp intake of breath. The bubble of pain he'd been easing himself around exploded, but he didn't allow himself to be ruled by it.

"Erik, I don't think—" Ian protested, but it was too late.

"Take her to Grams. I don't want her here anymore, Ian. Take her." Erik stalked into his office and slammed the door behind him. Leaning back against the wood, he closed his eyes, letting the rumbling sensation of anguish roll through his body. He deserved it. He'd caused enough, and now it visited him.

He'd taken from everyone in order to get what he wanted.

Now, he ripped out his own heart in order to give some of her back to herself.

She'd be okay in a few weeks, he told himself.

But he would never heal from the hole he'd just punctured in his own soul.

And he deserved that, too.

CHAPTER 31

"You have to eat something." Grams pushed the plate of pizza closer to Melinda.

"I did, Grams. I had some salad." Melinda unscrewed the cap from her soda and took a sip.

"When?" Grams pushed.

Melinda concentrated on getting the cap back on the bottle. Even small things seemed to need her full concentration.

"This afternoon," Melinda finally answered when she noticed Grams glaring at her over her reading glasses.

"Melinda." Grams leaned forward and grabbed her hand. "You can't lock yourself away and wallow."

"I'm not wallowing. I'm working." Melinda pointed at the stack of papers beside the pizza box. "I've been editing all day. My eyes are tired. I'm tired." She forced a smile.

It had been two weeks since she'd been dropped off in front of Grams' house with a few suitcases at her feet. Ian had tried to help her up the walkway, but she'd told him to leave it. Every day she woke up thinking she'd feel better than the day before. Time was supposed to heal everything, right?

Except, every morning, she woke up to the memory of her father dying and then Erik's words would hit her in the chest, knocking the wind from her. He didn't need her or want her. It wasn't fun anymore.

"Okay, well, I'll put the pizza in the fridge, then. Eat something before you go to bed tonight, promise me," Grams said in her typical grandmother voice.

"I promise," Melinda said. "Did the plumber come by yet about the bathroom sink?"

"Yes. All fixed." Grams grinned and shoved the pizza box into the fridge. "You know you didn't have to run off and find an apartment so fast. You could have stayed home longer."

"I know, but I needed to get to work, back to my life, you know?" Melinda hoped Grams could understand because she couldn't.

Erik had tossed her out. It should have been easy to grasp, but she found herself lying in the dark at night going over conversations in her head. She'd been so fierce at the beginning, fighting off any inkling of a feeling toward him. But he'd maneuvered himself right beneath her defenses, when he wasn't barreling through them with his intolerable domination.

"I know." Grams sighed. "Have you talked with him?"

"Who?" Melinda busied herself with the dishwasher.

"Don't go doing that. You know who." Grams chastised, while handing over her empty wine glass.

Melinda slid the glass into the slot. "No. And I'm not going to. I don't want to. It's better not to." She pushed the settings and closed the door, starting the cycle.

"Which one of us are you trying to convince?" Grams asked with her lips pinched together.

"Shouldn't you hate him?" Melinda asked.

Grams shrugged. "I should, yes. If he hadn't taken you, then your father"—" She dragged in a harsh breath. "Your father would still be in hiding. But all of that's not entirely Erik's fault." She held onto Melinda's shoulders. "Or yours."

"It doesn't matter," Melinda said, reaching along the counter and picking up the envelope that had arrived that afternoon. "It's over." She handed the thick package to Grams and wiped down the dinner table.

Grams opened the envelope and began browsing the papers. Melinda had spent all afternoon reading the documents. Divorce papers and compensation agreements. Erik was willing to pay her a small fortune to stay the hell away from him.

"You haven't signed it yet," Grams noted.

"Don't make anything out of that," Melinda warned. "We need to go back to how things were before. Pretend he never showed up that day."

Grams slid the packet of papers onto the countertop. "And you think it will be that easy?"

Melinda grabbed a bottle of wine from the rack in the corner. "It has to be."

"Melinda—" Grams had that sound, the one where Melinda knew to settle in for a long lecture, but she wasn't in the mood for it.

"Grams." Melinda cut her off. "He doesn't want me, and really...something had to be severely wrong with me to think we'd actually make something out of the mess. Who marries the man who basically kidnapped her?" She took a wine glass from the cupboard. "I mean, seriously, I should have my head examined."

And her heart. There was definitely something wrong with her heart. It ached, and her lungs weren't doing much better. Every breath since she'd stepped out of that house burned.

"Tell me again what he said." Grams grabbed the bottle of wine from Melinda and poured herself a glass.

Melinda laughed. "I'm not reliving that conversation." The humiliation had been outweighed only by the tormented internal scream suffocating her. "He got what he wanted, and now I'm free. It's a win-win, really, Grams," she rambled. "I have to finish some revisions for the book launch, and then it's a waiting game until it goes live. But I have another story in submission, so hopefully, the publisher will pick that one up, too. I have a lot going on. I don't need the drama that comes with Erik Rawling."

Grams sipped her wine. "Then sign the papers." Grams pushed the envelope down the counter.

Melinda stared at the manila envelope. She should. No good came from delaying it, and Erik was making a generous offer. He'd set up a fund for her, enough to keep her comfortable for decades if she was smart. She should scribble her name and move on.

Nothing but trouble came with being Melinda Rawling. Even if Erik wanted nothing to do with Justin or the Jansen family, there would always be a link. There would always be someone lurking in the shadows to find a way into his casino, or to watch for Nico.

And he was a great reason to sign away the name. Nico, his own brother, had snatched her up and delivered her to a man who would have killed her. Not exactly the makings of a warm family Thanksgiving dinner.

Reasons to be done with him stacked high. Yet, when she glanced at the papers, another twinge in her chest snatched her breath.

"Grams. I'm tired." Melinda put her wine glass down.

"I know it," Grams said quietly. "I'll leave you to your

work. But promise me, you'll come up for air and you'll think —really think about what your next steps are. I didn't like him for obvious reasons, but I saw him with you at the funeral. I saw the tenderness. The care he exhibited. That's not a man who saw you as nothing more than a means to an end." Grams brushed the hair from Melinda's face with the gentleness Melinda remembered as a child. If only the same calm could come to her now as it had then.

"I will, Grams. Promise." Melinda hugged her grandmother.

Sometimes, even the arms cradling a person, so full of love and understanding, weren't enough to mend a broken heart.

CHAPTER 32

"Construction should be completed by the end of March." Erik sat across from Peter Titon at his offices in Tower. The casino plans were moving along as planned, and they would open their doors before summer took hold of the city.

"Perfect. I know Azalea's excited about the marketing plan she's been working on with your team. I think she had gotten bored working so much on Tower." Peter grinned.

"She's been a great asset I'm told." Erik folded his hands in his lap. It hadn't been part of the deal to buy the land, but he'd seen how well Tower was doing due to her marketing skills. He would have been a fool not to take advantage.

Peter's smile twitched at the corner, and he readjusted his seating. "She wanted me to ask about your wife. She hadn't seen Melinda around lately."

Erik's spine straightened at the mention of his wife.

"Things didn't work out the way we'd hoped." Erik's fingers dug into his knees. Six weeks of not hearing from Melinda had left him on edge. Long days turned into impossible weeks.

Peter studied Erik quietly. "Hmm. I heard about her father and Bertucci…and your brother." He tapped the table with his fingertips. "It's a lot for anyone to take in when family betrays family. And I'm sure it's even harder for her to grasp everything given the situations."

Erik's jaw clenched. He didn't want to talk about Melinda. He wanted to get this meeting over with and get on with his day, so he could dive into a bottle of bourbon.

"That's true," Erik said when Peter seemed to be waiting for a response. Discussing Nico's betrayal never eased the burning anger inside.

"She's moved out, then?" Peter pressed. Why was he pushing this?

"Yes." Erik had tracked her down to an apartment on the north side of town. Despite her desire to be left alone, he'd had a man stationed outside the building, making sure she was safe. Every day he watched the mail, waiting for those fucking papers to show up with her delicate signature affixed.

"And it's not fixable?"

"If it were, I would have fixed it," Erik ground out. The meeting was finished. He had things to do.

Peter nodded. "You don't strike me as the sort of man who stands by while what he wants sails away."

"What the hell does that mean?" The pleasantries were over. He'd already been blocking Ian from talking about Melinda and trying to force his hand at seeing her. He didn't need it from a business associate as well.

Peter cocked an eyebrow. "Men like us don't choose our lives. They were charted out by our fathers and grandfathers before we were even born. That doesn't mean we can't change the course. And it doesn't mean you have to give up the love of a good woman out of misguided guilt."

Erik's shoulders tensed. "She wasn't given an option in any of this. She was forced."

Peter shrugged. "So?"

"What do you mean, so?" Since when did making a woman marry against her will become acceptable?

Peter grabbed his drink and took a sip. "I'm not suggesting you take away her choice. I'm saying, give her a reason to choose correctly." Peter finished his drink and plunked the glass down on the desk.

"And if her leaving was the right choice?" Nothing good had come of their marriage. It had been forced, it had been fake, and everything had been orchestrated. Just because she softened toward him near the end didn't mean it was anything more than her trying to survive. He'd put her in an awful situation, and she'd made the best out of it. He'd done what he always did. He'd set himself a goal, and he strived for it, no matter who he had to take out to get to it. And in their case, she'd suffered for it.

This was the right course. This way, she could live her life exactly as she wanted. No more orchestrated moves by anyone on the outside.

"I saw the way Melinda looked at you—how you eyed her every few seconds. Her leaving wasn't the right choice. For either of you." Peter patted Erik's shoulder and opened the door.

Erik made his way out of the building to where Ian waited for him against the car, fiddling with his phone.

"Let's go." Erik opened the door and climbed inside. Ian finished typing and walked around the front of the car and got into the driver's side.

"Home?" Ian asked, flipping the turn signal on and pulling out into the midafternoon traffic.

"Melinda," Erik stated, keeping his eyes on the road. He needed to see with his own eyes she was all right.

His attorney wouldn't give him many details about her, no matter the threats he made. His integrity had been his selling point, but it was getting on Erik's last nerve. He needed to be sure she was being taken care of. She hadn't touched any money in the account he'd set up for her. How had she been paying her bills?

How was she sleeping?

Before he'd made the final decision, she hadn't been sleeping well at all. She'd cried in her sleep, snuggling into him while he held her through the nightmares, through the horror her mind relived. But she hadn't known. And he hadn't told her. He'd given her space, and he'd drowned them with it.

"Here it is." Ian pulled the car into a spot across the street from the building. "She's the third apartment up on the left."

"It's a fucking dump," Erik snapped. More than a coat of paint would be needed to fix the place.

"It looks like shit, but everything inside works fine. I checked the maintenance of the building, and everything's up to code. It's safe."

"It's a rat hole. You let her stay here?"

"Let her?" Ian huffed a laugh. "You said to leave her be, just watch to be sure none of the old Bertucci crew harassed her."

Turned out Bertucci wasn't missed by anyone in the city, but members of his crew might be looking for payback if they weren't happy with their new boss. And with Melinda out of Erik's reach at the moment, she could still be targeted.

"Why isn't she using the money I put in her account to get a better place?" Erik asked, knowing Ian wouldn't have the answers. Once her things had been delivered to the apartment, she had cut all communication off.

"Aren't you going to go up there?" Ian asked when Erik leaned over the console to peer up at the building.

"No." Erik eased back in his seat and slid his sunglasses on. "Let's go."

"Erik." Ian paused a beat. "Get up there and talk to her."

"You know, you're getting a mouth on you I'm not sure I like." Erik tapped the gear shift. "Let's go."

Ian shook his head with a heavy sigh but threw the car into drive. "Between the two of you, I'm not sure who is more stubborn or willful."

"Ian..." Erik warned.

"Seriously. She hasn't left that apartment since she moved in except to go to the market down the street. She hasn't been to her grandmother's. Grams has gone to her a few times, but that's it." A few men were contracted under Erik's new business. Ian was in charge of putting them to work on security, mostly watching Melinda for the time being.

"She's better off this way." Erik said, more for his one benefit. He wouldn't force her.

"Better off? Erik, that girl hated you—despised you—and somehow you managed to worm your ass into her heart, and then what do you do? You toss her ass out. Better off?" Ian shook his head, apparently deciding not to back off just yet. "She should run from you. She should sign those fucking papers and never see you again. But she hasn't, and why do you think that is?"

"When you stop this car, I'm going to kill you," Erik threatened, but it was empty—and they both knew it.

"She didn't fucking sign them because she doesn't want to. You gave her a choice. And she didn't sign them," Ian pointed out, jerking the car around the corner. At least he was heading home where Erik could get a stiff drink.

After several heated moments passed, Erik readjusted his seat again. The car was too small. He couldn't get comfortable with all the tension taking up the space.

"Are you done?" Erik asked, breaking through the silence.

Ian gave him an annoyed glance. "Yeah."

"Good." Erik rolled his shoulders. "When we get home, I want Grams brought to the house."

CHAPTER 33

The car sprang to life with the twist of the key. Melinda sat back against her seat and looked out at the road. Her car had been dropped off weeks ago, but she hadn't had any use for it.

Until today.

Her grandmother had called, telling her to come to dinner.

Quit hiding and come to dinner! It hadn't been an invitation, but an order.

She hadn't been hiding. She'd been working. The excuse had worked for the first few weeks after moving out of Grams' house and into her apartment, but even Melinda could see the holes growing in the excuse. Leaving the apartment meant seeing the outside world. Everyone out there was alive. They breathed, and their hearts beat, and they were happy. Melinda couldn't face them yet. Not even after so many weeks had passed. Every day her thoughts traveled to Erik. To the fluttering of her heart his touch could cause, the way her breath caught when she found him staring at her.

It was twisted. She knew that, but for the brief time she'd had it, she'd held his attention, his care, at times, she'd even convinced herself it could have been love. But all of that was gone now.

With cleansing breaths, Melinda made her way through town and pulled into her grandmother's drive. The same way that had led her to meeting Erik. She parked outside the garage and made her way to the door.

The doorbell rang inside the house, but there were no footsteps.

Melinda tried the door. It was open, so she let herself in.

"Grams?" she called, walking down the hall. The light in the kitchen was on, and the warm smells of dinner simmering lured her forward. "I hope you aren't going to a lot of trouble." Melinda hadn't eaten a full meal in weeks, but she didn't have the energy to dive into a full Grams meal either.

When she entered the kitchen, Erik stood at the stove, stirring a pot with a wooden spoon. She blinked a few times, sure her mind was fucking with her. Glancing around the kitchen, she saw no sign of her grandmother.

She'd been tricked.

Again.

"Why, Grams, you've grown since I've last seen you," she muttered, pressing herself against the wall. He gave her a rueful smile.

"What better way to protect you," he played along.

Melinda eyed him silently. He wasn't making a move toward her; he just kept stirring the sauce. Pasta boiled in another pot.

"Such big hands, too," she commented when he lifted the pot from the stove and drained the noodles in the sink.

He finished draining them and put the pot on the stove, casting her a stern grin. "The best to spank you with."

Melinda swallowed hard. Tears sprang to her eyes. He was there. Standing two steps away.

"W-where's Grams?" she asked, unsure of the motive behind his presence but not sure she really cared. The immediate response from her body at seeing him threw her off guard. For weeks, she'd expected him to show up at her apartment, pounding down the door to drag her home. But he'd never shown up.

"She'll join us later. Right now, you and I have talking to do." He pointed to the table set for two. A glass was already filled with red wine, and she grabbed it. She needed the courage, liquid or otherwise.

"Sit," he ordered when she remained standing beside the table. She sank onto the wooden chair, watching him as he finished plating her dinner.

"I didn't know you could cook," she said softly when he placed the plate in front of her.

"It's pasta. I can manage that much at least." He pointed to her fork. "Eat every bite. Don't think I don't know how little you've been taking care of yourself." His eyes wandered over her form. With spring approaching, she'd forgone the winter coat and only worn a light long-sleeved blouse.

"If you wanted to see me, you didn't need to trick me," she said as he dished out his own dinner. He'd worn a black T-shirt that tightened across his back as he moved.

"Didn't I?" he asked, taking his seat across from her. "Ian told me you kicked him out of your apartment building when he tried to talk to you last time."

She had. Ian wasn't who she wanted to see.

"Eat." He pointed to her dinner again when she hadn't picked up her utensils.

"You can't make me—"

"I think you've forgotten who makes the rules around here." He stuffed a forkful of spaghetti into his mouth, keeping his stern gaze locked on her. His steely blues locked her into the moment. He was there, glaring at her, feeding her pasta.

"I don't think that really applies anymore," she said softly, but scooped up some noodles.

"Really?" he asked, leaning back in his chair. "So, you signed the divorce papers?"

Of course, he would bring that up. She had found them in one of the boxes he'd sent over to her new apartment. A shoebox compared to the suite at Erik's house, but it was hers. Paid for with the advance from the sale of her manuscript.

"No." She shoved the pasta around her plate. "I didn't."

"Then it still applies." He shoved more pasta into his mouth. A noodle smacked against his beard before he slurped it up into his mouth.

"You tricked Grams into letting you lure me here under false pretenses again."

"I did." He nodded, still chewing his last bite. "If I had shown up at that awful fucking place you live, I wouldn't have been able to stand it. I would have dragged from there. You wouldn't have liked that." He raised his eyebrows. "Besides, I wanted to be sure you'd show. If I'd asked you, I didn't think you would. I wouldn't blame you, but I wanted to be certain."

"Why did you want me here?"

"We need to talk." He pushed his noodles around.

"Okay. Let's talk." Melinda put her fork down.

"After you eat," he said and took another bite.

She had to admit it smelled delicious, and, for the first time in weeks, her appetite had made an appearance. A few bites wouldn't hurt.

She cleared the plate, even swiping the sauce up with a

chunk of warm bread. Erik hadn't spoken a word while she'd dug in. Feeling his presence had been enough to set her nerves at ease.

It shouldn't have, though, right? She should have been nervous having him so close, but his being there calmed her.

"Melinda." He grabbed her hand.

Tears sprang to her eyes again. Just feeling the warmth of his skin against hers was enough to make the longing, the desire flood her in full force.

"You have to decide."

She lifted her gaze to meet his, sure she'd find a hard, unrelenting glare. But instead, she saw uncertainty, vulnerability. "You want me to sign away everything, like it didn't happen. Like you didn't matter, I didn't matter."

His eyebrow arched, and he placed his fork beside his plate.

"Melinda." There was a warning in his tone. "That's not it at all. I wanted you to have a choice. You had none going in. You've had people arranging things for you your whole life, and you didn't even know it. This time, I wanted it to be your choice."

"I wanted to sign them. To be done with you and get rid of everything that happened. But signing a piece of paper doesn't change things."

His thumb ran along her knuckles when she stopped talking.

"When I saw him turn the gun on you, when I saw his finger—" He sucked in a breath. "I knew he was going to shoot. And all I could imagine was you lying on the ground dying." His voice was ragged, raw. There was a pain in him that matched hers, both in strength and depth.

Tears fell easily down her cheeks, but she didn't wipe them away.

Erik yanked on her hand, pulling her out of her chair, and quickly maneuvered her into his lap. He flicked the tears from her cheeks with his thumbs. "I was a fucking idiot. I couldn't let you go. I never did," he said softly, tucking his fist under her chin to force her gaze to meet his.

Pain laced his glare. Was he waiting for her to let him loose or hold him tight?

She was tired. So tired of trying to figure out what the next move should be. How would he react, how would she? The calculating was too hard.

"I loved you. Your arrogance and your overprotectiveness and your annoying hulking presence somehow got to me, but you…you didn't feel the same way."

"Of course, I did. Why the hell do you think I sent you away? I was scared…more scared than I ever had been in my life. And I wish I could wipe those words away from your memory. I wish I could take that pain I gave you onto myself. I'd bear it all to save you from a moment of anguish. I wish I could go back and do everything fucking different. Not be so damn selfish." He slid his hand behind her, cradling her before him.

"Because I loved you, too," he whispered. "I just didn't open my fucking eyes wide enough to see it."

She sniffled. She was making a mess of herself with all the tears and sobs, but he didn't seem to care. He drew her to him, pressing his warm lips against hers briefly.

"And now?" she whispered when he withdrew.

He maneuvered in his chair and pulled out a small, black satin box. A shiver ran down her spine when he opened it, and a silver band with a pink diamond in the center was presented to her.

"Now, you have to decide. Do you wear my ring, or do we sign those papers?"

She picked up the ring and started to slip it on her finger, but he caught her hand and took it from her. He slid it up her finger and held it tight against her skin.

"You're mine, Melinda. Forever."

"And you're mine."

EPILOGUE

"Say it again," he barked, walking behind a naked and bound Melinda.

"I'm yours," she cried out as the belt lashed across her round, red ass.

"That's right." He grabbed her ass, red and welted from the flogger and the belt he'd used on his wife. She hissed at the fierceness of his hands, but he would not relent.

A month had passed since she came home to him. A month he'd spent making up for the time he'd lost after his fear drove her from him.

He'd bound her to the whipping post in the play room, and she'd begged him to use his belt.

"Should I let you down?" A rhetorical question, but he enjoyed seeing her toy with the idea of control. He licked her shoulder. She loved this almost as much as he did, but it was in the moments of her indecision that he loved it best.

"I need you, Erik," she said, unbalancing him for a moment. It wasn't the words but the softness with which she'd said them.

She'd come back into his life with roar of the wolf.

Settling into a normal life had taken time. She still battled her nightmares, her insecurities. So, when she went soft, when she begged for his arms around her, he would stop at nothing to give her what she needed.

He unhooked the cuffs and had her on the bed in moments, lying beside her. She peered up at him, her eyelids heavy with arousal, her lips swollen from the face fucking he'd given her before trussing her up on the whipping post.

"Anything you need. It's yours," he promised and pulled her thighs apart, settling between them.

"Just you. I need you." She cradled his hand in hers. "Don't be gentle. Please."

He grinned.

"I wouldn't even if I could."

In one thrust, he was inside her, his balls slapping against her ass as he fucked her the way she loved. Hard and fast and without apology.

Her nails dug into his flesh, dragging down his back. He'd have marks in the morning, but he didn't fucking care. They would match the ones he'd given her.

She arched up at him, and he knew she was close. So easily read, so easily played. He toyed with her, but only until he couldn't hold back any longer.

He bit down on her shoulder, sending a ripple of pain through her body and into his own.

She screamed, but he barely heard it as his body exploded along with her. He held her close, riding her until they were both a heaped mess in the bed, clinging to each other.

"I fucking love you, Red." He breathed out and pinched her hip.

"I love you, too." She laughed, playing with the medallion he still wore around his neck. "My wolf."

Thank you so much for reading Red! I hope you loved meeting Erik and Melinda. They'd love to meet all the people. So please spread the word, and tell a friend about these books!

Want exclusive content, giveaways, and special news? This isn't the end of the Ever After Series, so make sure you join my email list to hear when the next book is due for release. Join Measha's Email List! You'll also get a free ebook!

Still craving more romance in the Ever After world? You're in luck. Turn the page to get a glimpse into Daddy Ever After, a Girls of the Annex Novella.

DADDY EVER AFTER

Candles burned in their sconces along the outer walls of the ball room. Jaelynn stood in the far corner, watching everyone. Her stomach had finally stopped twisting into intricate knots, but that probably had more to do with the two shots of amaretto she'd taken before leaving her room and coming down for the party.

Drinking was forbidden for the girls of the Annex right before a party, but amaretto wasn't really liquor, was it? Sure, it had some alcohol content, but it wasn't tequila. Not that she would ever make an attempt at a shot of tequila. In fact, she was pretty sure amaretto wasn't really a shot type liquor, but it had done the job, so she wouldn't dwell on it.

Ashland Titon, owner of the Annex, had already given his speech laying out the ground rules for the evening. Most of them were put in place to keep the girls safe. But she still wasn't all that sure any woman would be safe around Ash, or any of the men milling around the room.

Power flowed through the air. Then again, it could have just been her imagination. She had a way of doing that. Seeing things that weren't there, feeling things that weren't

DADDY EVER AFTER

realistic. And she'd made a fool of herself one too many times. Some called it anxiety, she called it life.

But it was the power she sought out at the moment. From one man in particular. If she could just find him, get close enough to him, she could get the job done and be rid of the Annex. But for the time being, until she could make her move, she'd have to keep playing submissive to the alpha assholes who came looking for a good time. At least they paid well.

"Jaelynn, let's go. You have to socialize." Jeffrey, the man assigned to escort her through the room, jerked a thumb at the room.

"Right." She nodded and smoothed out the skirt of her dress, taking a deep breath. "Let's do this." With a nod she pushed herself to start mingling among the rich and powerful.

Though catching the glance of a man looking more terrified than she felt, she wondered how powerful some of them might be.

"You're going to do fine. Just remember, anyone makes an offer, you direct them to me. Peter will have final say since this is your first party." Jeffrey rambled on while she made her way across the room. What was she supposed to do exactly? She couldn't just pace the room like a piece of pie in a rotating case at a diner.

An older man, old enough to be her grandfather, licked his lips as she passed him. She lowered her gaze and picked up her pace. Hopefully he saw the gesture as her being a skittish submissive. If she were to insult one of the guests unprovoked she'd be meeting with Peter again. And she would rather not meet up with the disciplinarian again any time soon.

Once she reached the opposite end of the room, she turned on her heel and started walking back to her original position. She'd make a round after that, she promised herself. Eventually, she would need to actually try to meet up with one of the men in the room, while searching out her prey.

Taking on a man for the night or weekend wouldn't be the worst thing. She had every confidence that Ashland wouldn't allow anyone access to one of his parties without being thoroughly vetted and deemed safe. And she had been assured she had final say on what went into her contracts. If she said no sex, there wouldn't be sex. Which worked well, since she wasn't sure how easily she could fuck a stranger. Playing a little slap and tickle was one thing, and she even enjoyed it to a point, but having some man she didn't even know huffing and puffing over her didn't make the cut. She'd be checking no in that box.

But if she was lucky, she'd find the man she was doing all this for. If she could get him to buy her for the night, she would be able to get close enough to sink her knife into his throat.

If he showed up. It was a hit or miss situation with him and the catalogue parties. Being older now, he didn't partake as often, but she knew he'd come. Eventually, he would, and she could get to him.

Until then, she'd continue working in the Annex, biding her time.

"Jaelynn, I need to get to the front door. There's a problem. You are to stay right over here." Jeffrey grabbed her arm and pulled her to the corner near the bar. "Stephan, I have to step out. Keep an eye out for her, okay?"

The man behind the bar pouring a glass of wine nodded. "Sure thing. Jae, just hang here, okay? I can't leave the bar right now."

"No problem, Stephan." She leaned against the bar and let out a relaxing breath. Who knew putting yourself on a display rack would be so intense. It was like eyes were on her every time she moved.

Specifically, at the moment, she could feel it, the warm stare of a man. Sweeping her gaze around the room, she didn't see anyone ogling her from a distance. Most of the men were already mingling with the girls or engrossed in conversation with each other. Some of the girls had warned her that the guys usually just hang out for a while at first and don't start picking any of them out until toward the end of the night.

The sensation didn't go away once she looked around. If anything, it grew more intense. A heat washed over her. She wasn't just being watched, she was being hunted.

Standing in the corner only made the feeling more intense. She had nowhere to go, nowhere to hide. Not that she should.

Justice—her mantra, but it wasn't working in that moment. Whoever had her locked in his sights was giving her a chill.

"Stephan, I'm just going to walk over there," she tried to tell him. But he was busy pouring drinks.

"Jaelynn, no. Stay," he said when she started to walk away. *Stay.* Like she was just going to obey him on command. He could still see her if he looked up from pouring, and if she was approached she'd bring the gentleman back toward the bar so Stephan would be in hearing range.

Once she was in the open area again, her breathing came more naturally. The heated sensation of being stalked eased away.

She checked the time on the delicate gold chain watch on her left wrist and sighed. Only another four hours before Ash would call the evening to a close. It wouldn't be enough to entertain a few men with conversation throughout the night; she had to eventually find someone to play with. She couldn't let Ash or Peter get the idea she wasn't there for the work.

Being distracted in her own thoughts, she didn't notice a man step up beside her. Her body tensed when she got a whiff of his aftershave. Musk, a woodsy leathery scent. It was almost calming, until she brought her eyes up to meet his.

Dark. Everything about this man screamed run. The severity of his stare, the tightness of his chiseled jaw. The black swirling tattoos that crept up from under his shirt collar and spread over his throat. Around his neck. He rubbed his chin while she continued to gawk at him; more tats. All over his hands. Did any inch of him not have ink?

"I don't think you're supposed to be over here." His deep voice cut through her mental observations.

"What?" She blinked. Her mind had blanked out on her. "Oh. Yes. No. It's okay," she assured him, taking a small step to the left. She couldn't see Stephan with the way this stranger positioned himself between her and the bar.

"Ash made it clear none of the women were to be unescorted. I don't see your escort." His dark eyes never left hers.

"He had to see to something. It's okay."

"Not a rule follower?" he asked with an arched brow. What was the right answer, what did he want to hear? If she said she was, maybe he would find her boring, but if she said she wasn't, maybe he wouldn't find her submissive enough.

"I, I'm Jaelynn." She threw her hand out toward him. Maybe if she drew the conversation back to the beginning she could get him to stop glowering at her.

"Yes, I know." He grabbed her hand, but not to shake it. Instead he cradled it, running the rough tips of his fingers across her palm. "We get a catalogue when we respond to the invitation for the party," he explained when she kept silent.

Yes. That's right. Catalogue. Party. She was supposed to

be finding him. Justice. Yes. It was all coming back to her now.

"This is your first party," he added. "You know, Ashland does a good job of vetting all of these men, but it doesn't mean they are all safe. They won't hurt you anymore than whatever terms they agree to, but they aren't nice men."

If he was trying to warn her away from being at the party, it wouldn't work. She was already there, and she already had her goal.

"And you? Are you a nice man?" She threw on a soft smile, tilting her head a little. Maybe some playfulness would smooth out his edges.

"No," he answered bluntly.

Her smile dropped. The chill that went up and down her spine earlier at the feeling of being watched returned with fervor. He'd been the one. He'd been watching her.

"What's your name?" she asked, still trying to see around him to Stephan. Why hadn't he come to look for her? And where the hell was Jeffrey? He shouldn't be away for this long. If Peter was going to take his belt to her ass for talking to this man without her handler, then Jeffrey better be right beside her.

"Hunter," he said, still not giving her any room to move. "I think we'll stay here until Peter or your handler bothers to find you," he said, his voice full of promise and danger.

Her heart started to patter away. She needed to get around him, back to the open area. She couldn't be blocked like this.

"Why?" she asked softly.

"Because I'm taking you home and I believe Peter will have the final signature since it's your first party."

"You're taking me home? I haven't agreed." She clenched her hands at her sides. How arrogant. Hot, maybe, but fucking arrogant as hell.

"You will."

"Jaelynn." Peter's hard voice crawled over Hunter's back to get to her. Hunter's lips twisted up into a smile and he finally stepped aside to give her room to move.

Peter's fierce expression landed on her as soon as Hunter cleared the way. It might be better if Hunter went back to blocking her. Peter was pissed.

"Peter, I—"

He waved a hand for her to keep her mouth shut. "You were doing exactly what you aren't supposed to be doing. Stephan called me, saying you disappeared into the party and he couldn't see you."

"Jeffrey left—"

"Jeffrey left you with Stephan and you were told to stay put." Peter pressed forward. Giving her one harder glare, he turned to Hunter. "Hunter," he said with some surprise to his tone. "I didn't realize that was you."

Peter extended a hand as did Hunter, and they shook, exchanging greetings.

"I saw her over here, and figured she was probably not supposed to be," Hunter said, no longer looking at her at all. "But I was just starting to negotiate terms with her, so it's probably better you're here."

Peter glanced quickly down at Jaelynn, and she held his stare for a brief moment. What did that mean? Was he approving or not?

"What terms?" Peter asked.

"Whole weekend. Full time. Complete submission. Discipline when needed," Hunter stated and Peter nodded along. Were they going to include her in any way?

"Sex?" Peter asked.

"Yes," Hunter nodded.

"No," Jae said at the same time.

Peter raised an eyebrow. "She does still have final say, even if she's been disobedient this evening."

"Define sex." Hunter posed the question to Jaelynn.

"Excuse me?" If he didn't know, maybe he was in the wrong place.

"Define what sex means to you." Hunter pushed again, his intense stare still winding up her body.

"Sex. Penetration." She started to say more but Hunter already turned back to Peter.

"Okay, I'll agree to no vaginal penetration unless she changes her mind." She wasn't sure the way he said that made it better. Unless she changed her mind? Not likely. Sex wasn't something she was willing to give away to just anyone. Just because she was contracting her body out for other play didn't mean she would open her legs for anyone.

"Anal?" Peter asked Jae the question.

"No," she said, hard.

"That's fine. A weekend doesn't really give me time to train her properly for it anyway," Hunter agreed.

Train her properly? Heat rose up her neck. She'd played this moment out before in her mind. A man negotiating what he could and couldn't do to her body, but this wasn't playing out right. They barely let her into the conversation.

Once they had finished, Peter turned to her. "Anything you want to add? I have your hard lists already and he's agreed to them."

"No. I guess not. What about pay?" she asked, getting to the heart of the matter. She should at least pretend the money was what brought her there.

"Twenty-five hundred for the weekend," Peter said.

"Five thousand," she countered. Twenty percent went to the Annex for a booking fee; no way she'd be low-balling herself. Not when she was giving up her chance to be there when her prey finally showed.

Hunter sighed. "Fine."

"Okay, I'll have this drawn up, and you can meet her for the signatures. I need to take her for a few minutes before you leave." Peter waved over Jeffrey, who finally showed back up. "Here's the details for the paperwork. Please escort Mr. Bianucci to have this drawn up and signed. I'm taking Jae to my office for a few minutes."

Jeffrey glanced at Jae and shook his head. Peter's office meant she would be getting a few licks of his belt before she was sent off.

"I'd rather not be delayed," Hunter interjected.

"She was unescorted when you spoke with her. It's against the rules and she knew it. She was told to stay at the bar with Stephan while her handler was busy. If she isn't dealt with, it sets a bad example," Peter explained.

"Like I said, I'd rather not be delayed. I am more than happy to see to her discipline when we get home."

A new tingling drove through her spine with the smooth and hard way he said those words.

"Peter." Jae stepped forward. "I only walked away for a minute. I just couldn't stand over there, there was too many people. I did tell Stephan," she explained.

"And he told you to wait," Peter countered.

"I don't want her marked," Hunter stated bluntly.

After a long pause, Peter relented. "Mr. Bianucci will see to your punishment." Peter leaned closer to her, his dark smile increasing as he spoke. "But if you think you're getting off lightly, you're wrong. I've seen him punish his girls before. You'll wish you'd let me handle it."

She swallowed.

"Let's get the papers done," Peter said and dismissed Jeffrey.

Hunter flattened his hand against her back and firmly led

her to where she would sign away her freedom for the weekend.

Two full days of being completely Hunter's.

Why wasn't she terrified?

See the rest of Hunter and Jaelynn's adventure in Daddy Ever After!

ALSO BY MEASHA STONE

EVER AFTER

Beast

Tower

GIRLS OF THE ANNEX

Daddy Ever After

OWNED AND PROTECTED

Protecting His Pet

Protecting His Runaway

His Captive Pet

His Captive Kitten

Becoming His Pet

BLACK LIGHT SERIES

Black Light Valentine Roulette

Black Light Cuffed

Black Light Roulette Redux

Black Light Suspicion

Black Light Celebrity Roulette

UNTIL SERIES

Until You a novella

Until Daddy

WINDY CITY

Hidden Heart

Secured Heart

Indebted Heart

Liberated Heart

Made in the USA
Coppell, TX
01 July 2022